Praise for the novels of Lee Tobin McClain

"Lee Tobin McClain dazzles with unforgettable characters, fabulous small-town settings and a big dose of heart. Her complex and satisfying stories never disappoint."
—Susan Mallery, *New York Times* bestselling author

"Fans of Debbie Macomber will appreciate this start to a new series by McClain that blends sweet, small-town romance with such serious issues as domestic abuse.... Readers craving a feel-good romance with a bit of suspense will be satisfied." —*Booklist* on *Low Country Hero*

"[An] enthralling tale of learning to trust.... This enjoyable contemporary romance will appeal to readers looking for twinges of suspense before happily ever after."
—*Publishers Weekly* on *Low Country Hero*

"*Low Country Hero* has everything I look for in a book—it's emotional, tender, and an all-around wonderful story."
—RaeAnne Thayne, *New York Times* bestselling author

Also by Lee Tobin McClain

The Off Season

Cottage at the Beach
Reunion at the Shore
Christmas on the Coast
Home to the Harbor
First Kiss at Christmas
Forever on the Bay

Safe Haven

Low Country Hero
Low Country Dreams
Low Country Christmas

Look for Lee Tobin McClain's next novel
The Bluebird Bakery
available soon from HQN.

For additional books by Lee Tobin McClain,
visit her website, www.leetobinmcclain.com.

LEE TOBIN McCLAIN

the forever farmhouse

HQN

ISBN-13: 978-1-335-42742-7

The Forever Farmhouse

HQN
22 Adelaide St. West, 41st Floor
Toronto, Ontario M5H 4E3, Canada
www.Harlequin.com

Printed and bound in Barcelona, Spain by CPI Black Print

Recycling programs
for this product may
not exist in your area.

To all who work to preserve the islands of the Chesapeake

the forever farmhouse

CHAPTER ONE

THE FERRYBOAT REACHED Teaberry Island just as the last bit of sun sank behind it, turning the bay into a glossy golden mirror.

Ryan Hastings considered himself a serious scientist, not given to surges of emotion. Nonetheless, as he stepped onto the small, isolated island, happiness washed over him like a gentle Chesapeake wave.

"Traveling light, are you?" The ferryman handed Ryan his single suitcase and accepted the substantial bonus Ryan had offered for the late-evening ride. "Got a place to stay?"

Ryan nodded, even though he wasn't sure of his welcome. "With Betty Raines."

"Oh, uh-huh. Shame about Wayne." Then he squinted at Ryan. "You're one of their foster kids. The genius, right?"

Ryan's face heated. "I lived here with them as a teenager, yeah."

The man shook his head. "Never thought the three of you would amount to anything. Shows what I know."

"You weren't alone." None of their social workers had expected much from the foster placement.

It had been a last-ditch effort to isolate three near-hopeless teens so that at least they didn't influence or harm anyone else.

Ryan, Cody and Luis weren't related by blood. They had never met one another before they'd arrived, separately but within a month of each other, broken, hurting, in trouble with the law. Wayne and Betty Raines had welcomed them into their rambling farmhouse on the shoreline, had provided them with good meals and warm beds and rules.

But most of all, there had been the bay, stretching all around them, a protective moat against their different but equally ugly pasts. There'd been a canoe and a rowboat and the freedom to spend endless hours exploring the marshes and wetlands, the sun baking their pain away, the lap of water against the dock's pilings soothing whatever nightmares each of them had faced in childhood.

Four years of that, and they'd all healed enough to make something of themselves. They'd also become brothers in every way that mattered.

As the ferryboat chugged away, Ryan turned and lifted his head to sniff the salty, beachy fragrance of the small fishing port. He *was* traveling light. Was hoping this would be a short trip.

Get here, check on Mama Betty, get out. Hopefully within twenty-four hours.

Silvery moonlight lit his path as he walked the half mile from the docks to Betty's home. He glanced to his right, toward the island's tiny downtown, but saw few lights. That was the reason the stars shone brighter here, a welcome contrast from his home in Baltimore.

Betty's two-story clapboard house rose in front of him, circled on two sides by a wide porch where Ryan had spent plenty of time staring at the cottage— actually, the girl—next door.

He didn't look in that direction now. Mama Betty was the focus, not himself and his childish, romantic dreams.

After ascertaining that there were a couple of lights on upstairs, Ryan climbed the steps and tapped on the front door. Arriving at 9:00 p.m.—especially as a surprise visitor—could be considered rude, but Betty wasn't an early-to-bed type.

And if he'd warned her he was coming, he was afraid she'd have declined the visit.

There was the Forever sign that had always hung beside the front door. It had meant the world to him when Betty had told him that, foster or not, she'd act as his mom forever. That he'd always have a place here. But that went both ways; he needed to be here for her, too.

He tapped again, louder, and rang the doorbell, anticipating Betty's face when she saw him. No matter what dirt he and his brothers had acquired on their traipses through the marshland back in their teenage years, no matter what trouble they'd gotten into, she'd always welcomed them with open arms.

He owed her everything: his career, his sanity, his life.

Ryan knocked and rang the bell once more, uneasy. Could Betty be away, visiting a friend? But no, she never left more than a tiny light on when she went out. Like most of the islanders, she was frugal, had to be. Likely she was caught up in a book from the tiny island library.

Ryan had always felt the most responsibility for Betty. They'd been close, sharing an interest in books and learning, while Cody and Luis had connected more with their foster father. Since Wayne had died nearly three months ago, they'd all tried to call Betty often, but Ryan was the one who'd been in the most regular phone contact.

Not so regular lately. She'd stopped answering her phone most days. Just when he would start worrying, though, she'd send him a late-night text. I'm fine. Just not in a talking mood.

Even the succinct late-night texts had gotten less frequent recently, and he'd made the decision to come see her himself.

Where was she? She couldn't be *that* involved in the latest thriller or fantasy novel, could she? He sidestepped to the window, cupping his hands around his eyes to peer in. There were signs of habitation—a stack of recent magazines, an open crossword puzzle book by a chair—but no Betty.

Tension knotted his stomach but he tried to ignore it. No point giving in to emotions, regrets that he should have come sooner. She was probably fine.

He'd spoken to his brothers about it yesterday. They'd agreed her silence was concerning, but they'd

LEE TOBIN MCCLAIN
13

come to the same conclusion: Ryan was the one who should come check it out.

"You have to," Cody Cunningham, just six months younger than Ryan, had insisted. "My unit won't be stateside anytime soon, and I used up my leave for Wayne's funeral."

"And I'm in the middle of a deal that could be huge." Luis Dominguez, a year younger, was already wealthy, but still driven and intensely ambitious. Neither Ryan nor Cody questioned his dedication to work. If Luis wanted to change, to open up to friends and love and a family, he'd have to make that decision himself. They'd be here for him.

Ryan had quickly agreed to come. He'd wanted to. But now, his throat constricted. What if something was wrong, really wrong?

Ryan glanced over at Mellie's house. Lights on there, too, but no movement. If only he and Mellie hadn't parted on such bad terms, he could have called her to get her take on how Betty was doing.

Could Betty be hurt, or sick? He tried the doorknob. Locked, but easily picked. He pulled out his pocketknife and knelt, studying the lock.

"Stop it right there. I have a weapon."

The female voice was pitched low, but Ryan would have known it anywhere. Static sparking up and down his spine, he dropped the knife, lifted his hands and turned to face his would-be assailant. "Mellie. It's Ryan."

She went still, her features hidden by moon shadows. "Ryan...Hastings?"

"It's me." Slowly, he lowered his hands and stood, but didn't move toward her even though longing tugged at him, strong as an ocean's riptide.

It was something he shouldn't feel.

A whole, healthy man would have moved on from his first love. Met other women, gotten married, started a family. But Ryan wasn't healthy or whole, not in his heart where it mattered.

For the first time her weapon registered: a baseball bat. His lips twitched, even on top of his deeper feelings. Mellie had always been a great hitter, driving balls way into the marshland when it was her turn at bat.

She could have packed a wallop if he had been a real intruder, even though—from what he could see in the dark—she still looked as slender as she'd been in high school.

A dark figure moved behind her. "Mom? What's going on?"

"Everything's fine, hon." She reached out and put an arm around a young boy, maybe ten. "Go back to bed."

"Who's he?" The boy pointed at Ryan, yawning, leaning against Mellie.

"This is...Mr. Ryan." It was the island's respectful, slightly Southern way kids were taught to address adults. "Ryan, this is my son, Alfie."

Ryan's image of Mellie reconfigured to include this new information. She had a son?

He can't find out the truth about Alfie.

Mellie Anderson stared at Ryan, her body going from hot to cold and back again. Of all the people breaking into her neighbor's house, Ryan Hastings was the last one she'd expected. He hadn't been back to the island for several years, and before that, his rare visits had been planned and spoken of in advance. She'd been able to make sure she and Alfie were away.

Even in the dim moonlight, she could see his brown hair, square jaw and muscular build. He'd filled out since his teenage years. Grown up. Gotten sophisticated.

A light flicked on upstairs. A window opened. "Somebody out there?" Betty called, her voice nighttime-scratchy.

"It's me, Mellie." Her own voice came out shaky and she consciously relaxed her shoulders. "Thought I heard something. Everything's fine."

"Hi, Miss Betty," Alfie sang out. "There's a—"

"You okay?" Mellie called up to the window, silencing Alfie with a firm hand on his shoulder. Her son was sweet-natured and adored their older neighbor, but he tended to be a blurter.

"Fine. *Trying* to sleep."

"Sorry. See you tomorrow."

"Good night." The window creaked down and banged shut.

And then Mellie beckoned Ryan away from the porch, playacting calm. "Come on, she hasn't been sleeping well. Show up unexpected, and she'll be up all night. You can talk to her tomorrow if it's not an emergency."

"It's not." He picked up his small suitcase. "This was a bad idea. I'll walk into town and stay at the inn."

"Is it open this late?" Alfie, who'd inherited Mellie's caretaker gene, looked worried.

"Not likely." She double-checked the time. No way was Ryan getting a room this late. The inn's office closed down once the last ferry had come and gone. Nobody showed up after that, anyway.

Well, unless they had the funds to pay for a private charter and a reason to arrive at night.

Mellie should just go back inside and let him and Betty deal with it. She didn't have to shoulder every burden, take everything on.

Except where would Ryan stay if she didn't help out?

Concern for him outweighed her worries that he'd learn the truth. "Too late for the inn. And you weren't wrong to check on Betty." She sucked in a breath and said what she did *not* want to say. "Come on over. You can sleep on my couch."

AFTER SHE'D GOTTEN Alfie back into bed, Mellie took deep breaths and wrapped her arms around herself, standing outside the door of her son's room.

Ryan was *here*. In her house. Spending the night.

Why, oh, why had she let her impulse to help and protect Betty send her out into the night, there to encounter the man who'd broken her heart and kicked it aside on his way off the island?

And given how much he'd hurt her, why had she invited him to sleep on her couch?

Every minute he stayed made it more likely he'd find out the truth about Alfie. The possible consequences of that tried to push their way into her mind, clamoring for attention, but she firmly shoved them back into the dark cellar where they usually lived.

Then she straightened her shoulders and walked down the stairs to face Ryan.

He'd remained standing and was looking at the pictures on her mantel. He'd always been intense and focused, even when, as now, he was doing something mundane like looking at family pictures. "Em had a baby?"

Mellie forced a smile, nodded. "Not a baby anymore. John Junior's three."

"They live off-island?"

She nodded. "Both Em and Angela. Em's in Annapolis, so I see them some. Angela's in Sedona finding herself." She smiled to make him think she didn't worry about her youngest sister, although she did.

The normal thing. She needed to do the normal thing so he wouldn't see her agitation and start to wonder about the cause of it. "What can I get you to drink? Coffee? Tea?"

"A cup of tea would be good. Thanks, Mellie. I really appreciate this."

She fixed the tea and put slices of leftover pound

cake on a plate. A plain snack, but the best she could do for unexpected company.

Especially when her hands were shaking.

How could Ryan be here? Wasn't he supposed to be doing research in the Galápagos Islands? He'd missed his foster father's funeral for that reason. And it was important research, too. He'd gotten grants and made discoveries; Betty had framed a magazine cover with him on it, when he'd won a Young Scientist of the Year award.

He was brilliant, she'd always known that. And, unencumbered, he'd gone from the island and made something of himself. A lot.

Now this famous scientist whom she'd once thought she loved was in her living room. And she had a big secret to keep from him.

She carried in the plate and set it and the tea on a table beside the big, comfortable recliner. She cuddled up in her rocker herself. *Act normal, act normal.*

He studied her in that precise, scientific way he had. Precise, and scientific, and intense. "You look good, Mellie."

She looked down at her T-shirt and sleep shorts. "I didn't exactly dress for visitors."

"You didn't know you'd have one." He took a bite of the pound cake and smiled. "This is good. Thank you. You always did like to feed people, just like Betty." Then his cheeks flushed a little.

Was he remembering the picnic when they'd fed each other strawberries?

He cleared his throat. "Tell me about Betty," he said. "She didn't sound like herself. Is she all right?"

"Not exactly." She was glad of the change of subject. "I was thinking of calling you guys. I'm in touch with Luis occasionally, but I didn't want to bother him. And Cody's back with his unit overseas."

"And you didn't call me? You know I'd have come." His brow wrinkled.

"Well," she hedged, "I thought you were still away for your research. Besides, Betty says she talks to you, so I figured you were aware."

"I'm back in the States for good. And I knew something was wrong, but not what. That's why I'm here." He leaned forward. "What's going on with her, Mellie?"

Mellie sipped tea. "She's depressed. Which of course you'd expect, since she just lost her husband three months ago. Not even. But it seems more than normal. Like, she often won't leave her house for days."

He propped his chin on his hand, frowning. "Is she able to run the market?"

"No. She won't go to work. I'm doing it for her. Which is okay for now, but there are decisions only the owner can make. She needs to get involved again." As she described Betty's issues, her overactive mind hummed with worry.

If she portrayed to Ryan how badly Betty was coping, he wouldn't feel okay about leaving. Knowing him, he might even stay and try to help her get out of her funk.

Whereas if she downplayed it, he'd probably leave tomorrow, to get back to his important work.

"Thank you for doing that for her. She's lucky to have you as an employee and friend."

"I'm happy to help her. She's helped me plenty." Betty had always been her go-to babysitter for Alfie and her supportive friend when she was struggling with motherhood. She'd tried to give Mellie the daytime shifts at the market, so she could work mostly when Alfie was at school.

In fact, Betty had been a wonderful neighbor ever since Mellie had been a child, growing up in this very house. How could she even think of hiding the extent of the older woman's problems from Ryan, who might be able to figure out how to help her? "The depression seems like it might be serious," she said reluctantly. "And another thing. Her house is bad."

He must have heard the concern in her voice, because he looked at her with a penetrating gaze. "How so?"

"It's a mess. Really, really cluttered. I wouldn't call it a hoarding situation, but Wayne didn't like to throw anything away. She needs major help cleaning it out."

He frowned. "Would a cleaning service be useful? Because I would be glad to pay…" As Mellie shook her head, he trailed off.

"That's a nice idea, but I don't think she'd let strangers into her house. And the truth is, she needs more than a cleaning service. She needs counseling, most likely, but I'm almost positive she won't accept it." She hesitated. "I don't want to overstep. You brothers are her family."

Ryan's quick nod showed her he appreciated that. "So, no strangers, and no counseling. That doesn't leave a lot of options."

"Maybe one of your brothers could come stay with her for a while. I know Cody's overseas, but maybe Luis—"

Ryan shook his head. "He's in the middle of a big business deal." He frowned, looking at the floor, then nodded decisively. "Since I'm not teaching this semester, there's no reason I have to stay in Baltimore. I have a grant to write and getting more data from fieldwork here would only improve my application. I can come work on the island for a little while."

"Oh, I'm sure she won't want you to stall out your career." Ryan couldn't stay here. She couldn't keep the agitation she felt from showing on her face.

He misunderstood the cause of her upset. "Don't worry. If I did come, I'd stay at Betty's. Not here."

"Right," she said faintly. Even having him next door would be way more than she could handle.

Because if he stayed close by, how could she keep him from finding out that he was Alfie's father?

CHAPTER TWO

One week later

"WE HAVE TO walk a little faster." Mellie reached out a hand to Betty Raines and urged her forward. "I don't want to miss Alfie's boat."

It was 4:00 p.m. on the Tuesday after Labor Day, and her anticipation was high, as was her anxiety. She was praying that school had gone well for Alfie.

The first day of school was always stressful, even for Alfie, who loved to learn. But the first day at an off-island middle school with kids two years older than him and more...that pushed the stress level off the charts, especially for a high-strung kid.

The Chesapeake was flat today, and the air was clear. Out on the horizon, she could see the school boat coming as well as a couple of other boats, a fishing boat and a powerboat she didn't recognize.

"Sorry." Betty slowed back down. "This is the most I've walked in a month. You go on ahead."

Mellie felt bad then. "I'm sorry. There's time. I'm just nervous for him."

At least Ryan's two-day visit last week had gotten Betty to leave the house a couple of times. She'd seen them going out for a slow walk down to the bay, and then that evening to dinner at the Dockside Diner.

And then, after two anxiety-filled days of keeping Alfie busy in town and on a boat ride and anywhere but at home, next door to the man he had no idea was his father, Ryan had left.

Ryan's visit had helped a little, and, not wanting to give him cause to return, Mellie had tried to follow up. She'd asked Betty to come sit on her porch, and then had suggested the older woman might want to come in to the market for just an hour or two, ease back in.

Not ready, had been Betty's response.

Mellie of all people understood that grief was a process. It had taken her, what, eight months, to leave the house for anything other than the necessities, after her husband, Georgie, had died.

The difference was that she'd had a kid, so there had been a lot of necessities. She'd been forced out into the community from the beginning, and it had been a healthy thing.

At least Betty had agreed to come with Mellie to meet the school boat. It was a step in the right direction.

As they reached the dock, she squeezed Betty's hand and helped the older lady sit down.

"You're always so sweet," Betty said. "You've loved helping others since you were a little girl. A little mother, everyone used to call you. My boys included."

Of course she'd been a little mother; she'd had two younger sisters and there'd been no one else to do it.

But it was true, she loved caring for people. That was how she connected with them, by helping them.

She didn't do it for anything in return. It was just who she was, she couldn't help it. Even, as her friends jokingly reminded her, when someone didn't especially want to be cared for.

The boat's whistle blew, and as the vessel motored toward the dock, she searched the front for Alfie's face. When she saw it, her heart sank. The lines across his forehead, his paleness, meant that he hadn't had a perfect, exciting day. Her chest tightened. "I'm thinking it didn't go well," she said to Betty.

"Give it time."

Another boat was pulling into the dock, too, loaded with boxes and equipment, but Mellie was focused on the school boat.

Alfie got off the boat and ran to her, hugged her tight. At ten, he rarely did that anymore. Uh-oh.

She hugged him close and glanced over at the other kids departing the boat. Were they making fun of Alfie for being a mama's boy?

But they weren't, and Mellie let out a sigh of relief. They were just going about their business. They were island kids. They knew Alfie.

"How was day one, buddy?"

"Awful. I don't want to do it anymore, Mom."

Not good. Her stomach tightened with worry, but she kept her face fixed in a smile. "No decisions until after a snack and some decompressing." Alfie needed both, maybe more than other kids.

"Oh, I have a note from Dr. Martinez." He fumbled in his backpack and handed it to her.

Double uh-oh. Dr. Martinez was the principal and hadn't been keen on Alfie skipping two grades to go to her school. "Go say hi to Miss Betty," she told Alfie as she ripped open the note and scanned it.

Day one was rough. I have concerns. Let's give it a couple more days and have a phone call.

So it wasn't just Alfie's perception that things had gone badly; the principal thought so, too.

Betty reached out and patted Alfie's arm, then tugged him into a quick side-hug. "It's not easy being the youngest kid in a school," she said. "Tell you what, I made a lemon cake today. Stop over before you go home and I'll cut you a slice of it."

Alfie nodded, frowning, clearly torn. Most likely he couldn't wait to get home, home to be alone with her and tell her his story, home to relax and be himself. He didn't have serious social anxiety, at least Mellie didn't think so, but he'd been raised on Teaberry Island where he knew everyone and everyone knew him. He definitely felt the strain of being with a bunch of new people.

On the other hand, he did love Betty's lemon cake.

An island dog, named Spotty for its black, brown and golden spots, trotted over and pushed its way between Betty and Alfie. Automatically, Alfie knelt down and rubbed the dog's chest and sides, and it nosed him joyously, giving more comfort than it received.

Mellie knelt beside her son. Betty, a few feet away, petted Princess, another of the island's many dogs.

As usual, the dogs were a solace. With the help of Betty and the dogs and her community of supportive friends here on the island, she and Alfie would get through this rough stretch.

The school boat chugged away, and Betty stood. She headed over toward the powerboat instead of turning toward the island and home. More stuff was being unloaded, buckets and pumps and a clear case holding some kind of water meter and PVC equipment tubes. A couple of fishermen stood by, watching. Not much happened on the island, and this was something new.

"Can we watch?" Alfie asked.

"Of course." Anything to make him feel better. She'd gotten the afternoon off from the store so that he could be her focus.

A few more boxes came off the boat, and then a man emerged with luggage. A tall, muscular man. Betty hurried over and hugged him, and he set down his suitcase and hugged her back.

Mellie's heart pounded and her throat tightened.

Ryan. He was back, this time with lots of bags and scientific gear.

She looked at Alfie standing next to Ryan and her heart rate accelerated more.

They looked alike. Way too much alike.

Which made sense, given that they were father and son. But who else was noticing?

RYAN GAVE INSTRUCTIONS to the lab assistants he'd paid to help him move. He'd have to put his equipment into Betty's shed for now, but he hoped to get set up just as soon as he'd figured out the situation and the house. He'd find a couple of locations to sample water and sand, for starters, hopefully by an existing breakwater. He'd have to work with the little island post office to send his samples back to the university lab for analysis.

Even though he'd only be here a short time, he couldn't afford to get behind on his research.

He turned and there were Betty, Mellie and the little boy. His heart rate jumped up a notch. Had Mellie come to meet him? And if so, what did that mean?

She looked…good. Better than good. Red hair, gone messy in the breeze. Jeans that hugged her slender legs. A bright green sweater that made it so you couldn't help but notice her big, green eyes.

When he realized he was staring, he forced himself to look away.

He put an arm around Betty and she leaned into him, and that in itself made him glad he'd come back. She needed help, needed him, which was rare enough in his world.

They turned toward the others. "You know Mellie real well," Betty said, "but I don't know if you've met her son, Alfie. Alfie, this is *my* son, Ryan."

Those words made him feel warm inside. He'd

spent most of his childhood not having anyone call him "son," at least not with pride.

Betty had filled that hole in his life. He'd never stop being grateful for all she'd done for him.

The little boy held out a hand for shaking. "Nice to see you again," he said. Rote, but polite.

Of course Mellie would teach her son good manners. "Likewise," Ryan said, smiling at the boy, who really was a cute kid. And then he turned toward Mellie, trying to school the emotions that rose in him. "Hello, Mellie."

"Hi, Ryan. We're going to head back home so Alfie can chill. First day at a new school."

So she'd come to meet her son at the school boat. Of course, and he'd been foolish to think she'd come to welcome Ryan to the island. She was probably as glad to see him here as she'd be to see a harmful red or mahogany tide overtaking the bay.

He needed to tame his own emotions, cool them off the way hers had undoubtedly cooled. He shouldn't have let himself wonder how she'd react to him as he'd planned this longer visit.

Of course, unlike her, he hadn't moved on with his love life. He was stuck in the past, but that needed to change. He needed to use her attitude as a model, make excuses to keep a distance. Just like now.

She repeated her claim that her son needed to get home quickly, urging him to walk ahead with her.

Ryan saw through the excuse and tried to be glad they wouldn't all have to walk together. It was better that way.

The boy threw a wrench in that plan. "But, Mom, Miss Betty said I could have some lemon cake."

Mellie's smile looked forced. "So she did."

Betty rubbed her hands together. "Come on over, you two, and sit down for cake with Ryan. He's not been here in an age, and he may stay awhile. Needs to meet people, see people, aside from his old mom."

Mellie smiled at her with genuine kindness. "Of course we'll come sit."

That was Mellie. She'd only come to meet Alfie's boat, not to welcome Ryan. And clearly she didn't want to spend extra time in his company; no surprise, considering how he'd treated her years ago.

But she was a giver. Always did what was best for others: her sisters, her father, her neighbors.

So they walked together to Mom's house. *His* house.

The big rambling farmhouse wasn't fancy, but it was the best place Ryan had lived throughout a chaotic childhood. Situated at the end of a residential street—one of only a few on the island—it overlooked the bay and adjoined a marshland that had been the key to Ryan's love of the area, the beginning of his interest in the bay's ecosystems.

Next door, with plenty of yard in between, was Mellie's much smaller house, where she'd grown up with her father and two sisters. It was surrounded by flowers, a rainbow of them, pretty enough for a garden magazine. Even as a teenager, Mellie had liked growing flowers and plants, and it looked like the hobby had become a passion.

Mellie and her sisters had been in and out of Mom's house constantly; Ryan had seen her with skinned knees and covered with mosquito bites and mud far more often than he'd seen her dressed up.

In fact, there was a streak of mud on her leg now. He quelled a very inappropriate urge to wipe it off with his finger.

Betty's kitchen smelled of lemon cake and a mustiness that was new. It looked the same as last week, cluttered but livable. Nothing that couldn't be fixed in a day or two.

Good, he wouldn't have to stay long. Last week, Betty hadn't been keen to show him the whole house, but he'd peeked into a few rooms, had stayed in a messy guest bedroom after that first night with Mellie.

He could see why she needed help with the house. Even more, he could feel her sadness. That was why he'd returned and was planning to stay a few weeks at least.

It had been overkill to bring his equipment, but Ryan was self-aware enough to know it was a security blanket. And part of the academic game, too; he couldn't let his rivals for the grant know that he was tending to a family matter instead of working. The psychological edge was everything.

The grant was competitive, but he'd won competitive funding before.

It had never felt this important, though. The Chesapeake, his beloved Chesapeake, was ailing; everyone knew that and there were multiple teams of scientists and policymakers working on it. But he wanted to do his part. If he got the grant, he could help solve the problems facing the island and maybe the bay, too.

Mama Betty turned on the kettle for tea and sliced lemon cake, and they all sat down at the old wooden table where Ryan had fought with his foster brothers so many times, squabbling over the last pork chop or chicken leg, even though they'd really all had plenty. Matter of principle.

"So, tell us about your work, Ryan," Betty said as they munched.

He automatically scaled his words to the layman's terms he used in school visits. "Marine ecologists study living things in the water and on the shoreline. Mostly in the ocean, which is what I've done in the past, but now I'm starting to research the Chesapeake. It's unique in the world, and there's so much to learn about man's influence on natural marine environments. And the bay's influence on the land, too."

"People pollute the bay," Alfie piped up. "That makes me mad."

Ryan smiled. "Me, too, buddy. That's why I went into science, so I could try to help solve the problem."

"And you're after a big grant, your brothers tell me," Mama Betty said.

Ryan nodded. "If I get it, I can set up my own good-size lab and focus entirely on the bay."

"Mellie, here, worked hard to get us a grant to restore the park downtown."

Mellie waved a hand, her face reddening. "A few

hundred dollars for playground equipment," she said. "Nothing like what you do."

"But important." He watched Mellie as she pushed her slice of cake around her plate. She was nervous, he could tell. Why? She couldn't still have feelings for him, could she?

Ryan was nervous around her, too, but it hadn't stopped him from devouring two slices. "Thanks for making my favorite cake," he said to Betty.

"Of course. I'm happy you're here." She grimaced. "Not thrilled about cleaning out the house, but it's got to be done."

"It doesn't look bad at all," Ryan said.

Mellie and Betty looked at each other. "You haven't had the tour," Betty said. "Want to see it now, see what you're getting into? I figure you might go running back on the next boat once you do." Her tone was light but there was something serious underneath it. She really did fear he'd leave.

As they walked from the kitchen to the front room, Mellie didn't follow, and they both turned back. "Are you coming?" Betty asked.

"I don't think we'll stay. We need to get home."

"Come back over later if you want." Betty made the offer offhandedly. Clearly she and Mellie were in and out of each other's houses often.

"Okay, we'll see." Mellie waved, and she and Alfie headed out.

"Mellie has been a wonderful blessing to me." Betty opened the door to the TV room.

Or what had been the TV room. Stacks of papers

and books lined the walls and the top of the TV, which looked like it hadn't been used in ages.

"Hmm," he said.

"I know. We just let it go. You know how Dad was—he didn't like to throw anything away that he might need for one of his sermons."

"Let's see the rest."

They walked upstairs to the room that had served as Wayne's study. As a pastor, he'd done a lot of his paperwork and sermon preparations at home.

Ryan tried the door, but it wouldn't open. "Is it locked?"

"No, you have to shove." She turned the handle and demonstrated.

Inside, the stacks went from floor to ceiling. Folders and magazines and pamphlets.

"Wow. I guess that's from preinternet days?"

"He always printed everything out, even after the internet. Which is spotty here, if you remember."

"How are the other rooms up here?"

"Aside from your bedroom and mine, more of the same."

So maybe this would take longer than he'd thought.

He was committed to helping Mama Betty, and he'd do it. But how long could he afford to stay? How long could he bear being this close to Mellie and acting like they were just cordial neighbors, like his emotions didn't rise to a chaotic, uncomfortable level every minute he spent around her?

Any amount of time felt like too long.

CHAPTER THREE

PUTTING ALFIE ON the boat for his second day of mainland school hadn't been easy. In fact, it had almost killed Mellie to see his set jaw, strained face and scared eyes as he'd marched, straight-backed, onto the boat, smaller than all the other kids, backpack over his scrawny shoulder.

She walked down High Street, waving at Tammy Granger, who was headed for the clinic, inhaling the fragrance of fresh muffins from the Bluebird Bakery. She lifted her face to the soft breeze and said a prayer: *Let him be okay, Lord. Let this be the opportunity he needs.*

Even if he had a rough start at the new school, Alfie had had a different, more insidious problem attending the island's elementary school: boredom. He'd started acting out, causing trouble, which wasn't the way she'd raised him. He simply needed more stimulation, she and his teachers had all surmised, and this was the solution that was available.

The alternative was moving away from Teaberry Island. And that, she just didn't think she could do.

Her family had lived here for generations. While her parents were gone, her grandmother ran the post office and two uncles were local watermen. At church, she couldn't look in any direction without seeing a cousin.

That was what had saved her when things with her parents had gone south, when she'd been a kid, and that was what would save Alfie.

Look at her sisters. They'd left, and both were struggling with life on the mainland. She was in the process of trying to convince her youngest sister to come on home where she belonged.

They all belonged here.

Last night and this morning, she'd done everything she could to smooth out Alfie's adjustment to the new school. She'd removed the superhero patches from his backpack, called a couple of the high school kids and asked them to watch out for him and coached him about how to respond to bullies.

She walked into the market, inhaled the smells of produce and deli meat and dust, and felt her shoulders relax.

There was nothing she could do about Alfie's day now. She'd stay busy today at work, and the hours would fly by, and she'd go pick him up on the boat and bring him back here to do his homework at one of the tables in the tiny lunch area by the deli counter. The second day had to go better than the first. Didn't it?

"Thank heavens you're here," Delores, one of the part-timers, said. "My Ellie's sick and I need to take her over to the clinic. I'll try to be back by noon... is that okay?"

"Of course. I can manage. Hope Ellie's okay." So she'd be extra busy at work today. All the better. She could push her worries about her son to the back of her mind.

Unfortunately, her other worry came rushing in to fill the gap: the fact that her son's father was temporarily living next door.

Ryan. With him staying at Betty's, there wasn't a chance she could avoid him.

Would she even have wanted to if not for the secret?

The market was mostly empty now, aside from Ezra and Deacon Wells, two sixty-something brothers who'd lived together all their lives, having their morning coffee while reading the paper. So Mellie pulled a load of boxes out to restock shelves.

First, that meant dusting off the old cans and taking note of what wasn't selling. She pulled out her clipboard and noted every item that had four or more cans that hadn't sold. Lima beans and beets didn't seem popular anymore so she listed them and continued methodically through the shelves, the mechanical activity soothing, allowing her to think.

She'd been right to keep her pregnancy a secret from Ryan; she'd never questioned that. It hadn't been just her own hurt feelings. His freak-out after the one time they'd made love—the first for both of them—and his assertion that he didn't want a relationship or a family, those had hurt, sure.

A lot, if the truth be told.

But she'd known him well enough, cared for him

enough, to realize that he had a promising career in front of him, one that would be derailed by having a baby so young.

She'd still have told him, most likely, but Ryan's foster father had known about the relationship and had discovered she was pregnant. He'd taken her on a long walk by the bay and put a huge dose of fear in her. Told her statistics about how often kids who'd been abused became abusers themselves, warned her that Ryan's childhood had been horrific. "You'll have to put your baby first now," he'd said, "and that means protecting him, or her, from a father who probably can't help repeating bad patterns."

She'd gotten scared, but she was also worried about how to support a baby, herself, at eighteen. "Look," he'd said, "I'll help support the baby with Ryan's college fund, since he didn't need it." It was support she'd accepted for a couple of years before getting on her feet enough that she didn't need it anymore.

When Georgie had come around wanting to get back together, soon after she'd learned she was pregnant, she'd been honest with him about the situation. She'd always been grateful that he'd agreed to marry her, move into her family home and claim Alfie as his own. That had protected her from her father's wrath and allowed her to continue raising her sisters.

It had been a cobbled-together solution to the age-old problem of unintended pregnancy. The best an eighteen-year-old could do.

She'd always intended to tell Alfie when the time

was right, and that hadn't changed. But now certainly wasn't the time, not with all the stress he was facing with his new school.

"Mellie?"

Ryan's deep, rich voice above her, just when she'd been thinking about him, made her drop her clipboard. Papers flew everywhere. "You startled me, sorry," she said, eyes down, cheeks warming as she scrambled over the floor to pick them up.

"I'm sorry." He knelt, too, and gathered papers, and then they were too close together, there on the floor of the market.

He handed her the papers and stood, and she kept her eyes down, shuffling them into order and putting them back into the clipboard.

"I'm sorry to bother you," he said, in that radio announcer voice of his that was surely some part of why he'd risen so rapidly in the scientific ranks. What student, what professional audience, wouldn't sit rapt, listening to him talk, even if it were about algae?

"It's no bother." She scooted away and stood, pushed back her hair and tried to regain her composure. "Can I help you find something? Is Betty okay?"

"She's fine," he said. "Or as fine as she can be. But I wanted to get a few supplies, so I stopped in." He was standing, too, now, wiping his hands down the sides of his jeans. "Scratch that. I do need a few things, but mostly, I wanted to talk to you. Do you have a minute?"

"Um, sure." Her heart was pounding. "I'm the only one working, but it's quiet now. What can I do for you?"

"Can we sit down?" He gestured toward the seating area, now empty.

"O-o-okay." She followed him over there. "Coffee? It's fresh."

"Sure." He waited while she poured them both cups, turned down cream and sugar. She sat across from him, nearly choked on a too-hot sip and waited.

"Listen, Mellie," he said. "I've always felt bad about how I left things between us. How I left *you*, after..." He broke off, two high red spots appearing on his cheeks. "I was rude, and I acted uncaring, and I'm sorry."

"It's fine," she said. Whatever she'd thought he would say, it hadn't been *that*. "We were both young, too young. I understood."

"You did?" He still looked troubled.

"Well, no. Not at the time, I didn't, but I do now. I was hurt, but I got over it and I'm fine now."

And she *was* fine. She didn't need the coddling attention so many women seemed to effortlessly evoke and enjoy. Her marriage had been a practical arrangement on both sides, and although love had grown, she'd never been cherished like some woman in a Hallmark movie.

She was good with that.

He watched her closely, thoughtfully, as she spoke and then went silent. He really listened, she remembered that now. No one could pay attention like Ryan

Hastings. Maybe it was a result of his difficult childhood, maybe he'd *had* to pay that kind of attention to stay safe, but it had resulted in an unusual man who listened more than he spoke. Ryan had every reason to brag about himself, but knowing him as she did, Mellie would lay odds on the fact that he never did it.

"You're doing okay now?" he asked, and seemed to really want to know. "It can't be easy to raise a son alone."

He doesn't suspect. That's a normal thing to say.

He was waiting for her response. "You're right, it's not easy," she said. And then, for whatever reason, she ended up telling him about Alfie, how he was too bright for elementary school, especially the island school that was too small to have a real gifted program. How she herself couldn't keep up with him, having never been the academic type. "But he's emotionally just a little kid, and I hate to think of him at the junior-senior high school with all those bigger kids."

He nodded, not discounting her concerns. "That's a tough situation," he said. "I know, because I was like that, too, although nobody noticed I needed enrichment until I moved here." He didn't say it with self-pity; he recounted it as if it was just a fact of his life. "I don't have any great advice for you," he said, "but if you want me to, I can spend a little time with him while I'm here. Maybe if he hears about how somebody else handled being gifted, he'll get a little more comfortable in his own skin." Then he flushed. "Sorry. I don't mean to sound like I think I'm a big deal."

She laughed. "Ryan, no one would call you egotistical. And no one would deny you're gifted, Mr. Young Scientist of the Year."

His face got redder and he looked down, laughing a little. "That was just silly. Do you know I had to wear *makeup* for the TV appearances?"

He sounded so horrified that she laughed. "I bet you looked good in lipstick."

"Hey, now. My manliness is offended." They were smiling at each other, and Mellie felt that old connection being restored.

It was a connection forged of four adolescent years of being next-door neighbors, of understanding a lifestyle foreign to most North Americans, here on an isolated island. A connection that had grown, slowly, and then at breakneck speed, into a passion scary in its intensity.

And that had dissipated like a soap bubble bursting, she reminded herself. She scooted back in her chair. "If you get the chance to talk to Alfie, that would be nice, but don't go out of your way." She stood and looked around the store, anywhere but at Ryan. "I'd better get back to work."

And she'd better quit thinking about this man, before her old feelings got reawakened. He still had a superpromising career he needed to focus on. And he still wasn't interested in her.

So keeping his relationship with Alfie that of a friendly-but-distant mentor was paramount.

"See, I was right." Ryan smiled at Mama Betty as they walked together down her grassy lawn toward the bay.

It was late afternoon on Thursday. A hot, sunny day, but already tapering off to the cooler evenings of September.

Ryan was here to help clean out the house, of course, but more important, he was here to assess and help improve Betty's state of mind. Which wasn't the best. She hadn't wanted to help with the house decluttering, so after being here two days, his progress had stalled. There was just too much she needed to weigh in on, but she mostly sat at her kitchen table doing crossword puzzles and playing games on her phone.

Her low-energy, low-emotion demeanor was completely different from the foster mother he remembered. Was there something in particular that was wrong, bothering her, or was this just what it was like to be a new widow?

He didn't have a whole lot of faith in his people skills, but he did have faith in the healing powers of the bay. "You, or we, should come out here for a little while every day," he said.

"You put chairs down here. That's nice." She patted his arm, and they sat in two low wooden chairs that faced the bay.

"Found them in the shed." He'd pulled four of them out, cleaned them off and set them around the old fire circle that looked like it hadn't been used in years. "I can paint them, if you'll choose a color."

"Doesn't matter," she said, and then looked at him. She must have seen his worried expression.

"Gray, maybe?"

She frowned. "No, not gray. I...oh, ask Mellie what she thinks."

That made him smile. "Mellie will have us paint them pink and purple and yellow and green."

"Lime-green at that." Betty flashed a brief smile. "That girl does like color."

"I'll ask her." Although it was easier said than done, when she was avoiding him.

Since their conversation at the store on Wednesday, he'd looked for opportunities to chat with her son. Ryan had been hauling things out of the shed for the past day, hosing and dusting them off, trying to see what was useful and what was junk. Just the kind of project a kid would like, or at least, he would have. He assumed young Alfie would feel the same.

But although the boy had looked over in Ryan's direction with interest a couple of times, Mellie had called him back into the house.

Did she want him to mentor her son or not? It wouldn't surprise him if she was having second thoughts. He was nobody's idea of a good father figure.

"You're right, it's soothing to be out here." Betty's voice pulled him back from whatever brink he was headed toward. "I remember when we had more of a beach here behind the house and used to swim, but that's washed away."

"Are people still looking to build that seawall

Wayne used to talk about?" He now knew that there were alternatives that might be ecologically superior; in fact, learning more about that was a part of his research.

"Oh, you know, it's slow. Look, an eagle." She pointed, and they both watched the majestic bird soar and then land on a giant oak branch that jutted out over the water. A couple of egrets waded near the shore.

All of them relied on the bay's ecosystem. Keeping it from getting more out of balance, or restoring it to former status, was a must.

The grant he was going for had more to do with marine invertebrates, an offshoot of what he'd studied in the Galápagos. But he hoped to also analyze the effect of a seawall on the microscopic creatures, as compared to a living shoreline project. If he got the grant, accompanying publicity might put the bay's problems on more people's radar. Important people; politicians seeking reelection, for example. People who wanted their image to be of caring, saving the environment, helping the little people.

He *had* to get the grant.

He pulled himself back from thoughts of his research and focused on Betty. She wore a sweatshirt and didn't seem to mind the cool breeze. Her hair, brown streaked with gray, was cut in a short style that suited her, and she was slim, fitter looking than a lot of people in their sixties. She had laugh lines, but he hadn't seen her laugh once since he'd been here, and the dark circles under her eyes told him she wasn't getting good sleep.

When he talked to Mellie about paint colors— if he ever *did* pin her down enough to talk to her again—he'd ask her what she thought about Betty's state of mind, see if she had any suggestions of how he could help.

He just hoped it didn't mean delving into Betty's deep past emotions. Doing that might bring up a few too many of his own emotional memories.

"So how's your work going?" Betty asked now.

"It's not. As soon as I get the shed and some office space cleared out, I need to buckle down."

"You're applying for a grant, right? Isn't it a given that you'll get it, being as you're such a star?"

"No." He might be a star in the popular press, but the academic review process was rigorous. And grant review boards were temperamental, unpredictable. "I was turned down for the same grant last year, though it was a close call according to the review committee."

"Did they give you any hints of how to improve your proposal?"

He nodded slowly. "I didn't do well with showing the broader impact of the project. It was mentioned that my application lacked color."

For the second time today, she cracked a smile. "Kind of like your school clothes used to?"

"I guess so." He grinned, too. Back then, he'd always chosen gray or black, until his brothers had told Betty he was getting teased about it and to for heaven's sake get him T-shirts in some other color.

"Who's the audience for this grant application? What are they like?"

"College faculty, mostly. From all different disciplines. Plus some public policy types."

"Nonscientists, then?"

He nodded. "For the most part."

She patted his arm. "Then I feel better about you coming here to stay and help me, because I know you can fix that here. You need photographs, not just of slimy little creatures—"

"I don't just photograph slimy little creatures!" he protested. "Well, not much." He did include some photos of water under the microscope to show the range of microorganisms in a particular locale.

"You need photographs of *people* enjoying the bay. Fishermen making a living here. Kids riding the school boat. And you need stories, examples of how important the bay is. Show something destroyed by a storm and tell how the seawall would have helped that not to happen."

It went against his instincts, in a scientific grant application, but she could be right. The board really emphasized that the project had to benefit society, and while the benefits were obvious to him, he probably hadn't made them clear enough in his previous grant application. "I might give it a try," he said.

He loved his work and was fortunate to have it. Work was where meaning came from in his life, because he couldn't connect with others enough to have love, kids, a family.

There was a crunching sound down the beach, and they both turned to see Alfie making his way to the shoreline. He squatted down to examine a structure that Ryan now saw was something the boy had created out of rocks and sticks, a big square, about six by six feet. Alfie's face creased into a smile and he started carefully checking the structure.

Betty frowned. "I worry about that boy."

"So does Mellie," Ryan said, "but I'm sure you know that. Why do *you* worry?"

"He needs the island, but he's too ambitious to be limited to here." She raised an eyebrow. "Sort of like someone else I know. He'll soon grow beyond us, and I don't know how Mellie is going to handle that. She's pretty much tied to Teaberry Island."

That she was; she was like a colorful plant that only bloomed here. It was hard to imagine her living anywhere else. "I said I'd talk to him while I'm here."

"Good. That's good." She studied him shrewdly. "It's not always biological kids we're called to help, you know."

"Oh, I know." He squeezed her hand, just briefly. "There are a lot of boys, but especially me and Cody and Luis, who would be nowhere without you and Wayne."

Her smile got a little sad. "It was a joy raising you boys." Then she stared out toward the bay, her mind clearly going into the past.

Ryan was encouraged that she'd talked to him a

little, showed an interest. She seemed to have come out of her depressed mood if just for a few minutes. It was a step, but he didn't want to push it and make her uncomfortable. "I'm going to go see what he's up to," he said, gesturing at Alfie, and Betty nodded.

He strolled over toward Alfie. "What do you have there?" he asked.

The boy smiled up at him. "Watch." He pulled out a coffee can and dumped a ghost crab into the pen he'd built.

Ryan sank down to his knees and watched as the crab scuttled at breakneck speed from wall to wall, then wildly dug a hole. "*Ocypode quadrata.* The fastest crustacean on land."

It was clear enough that Alfie was bright, because he didn't question either the scientific name or the offhand fact. Instead, he nudged the creature with a stick, and they watched it run again, spinning, then digging another speedy hole. "I'll let him go," Alfie said as he knocked down one side of his pen. "I like to watch them, but I don't want to hurt him."

"It's interesting that there are ghost crabs here. They mostly live near the mouth of the bay. Salinity of the water is changing." He explained it a little more, putting it in layman's terms, but impressed that he didn't have to simplify the facts too much.

"How'd you learn all that?" Alfie asked.

"Books. College classes. Research."

"I wish I could just skip ahead to college." Alfie's expression darkened.

"You don't like your new school?"

He shook his head. "The teachers and the stuff they know are pretty cool, but the other kids…" He shrugged. "They don't care. They don't listen, and they act up in class, and they don't learn. The teacher in my chemistry class had to go through the whole lesson twice, and even then, most of the kids didn't get it. But it was because they weren't even trying!" He poked a stick into the sand, hard.

"I remember." Ryan sank back to look out over the bay. "I got so mad one time I stood up and yelled at a whole class to shut up because I wanted to hear what the teacher was saying."

"You *did*?" Alfie's eyebrows lifted almost to his hairline. "Did they listen?"

Ryan snorted. "No. They laughed at me and shoved me around and knocked my books off my desk. My brothers had to get involved to get everyone off my case." They'd been a formidable force, three big, streetwise foster kids who didn't fear anything because life had already thrown so much bad stuff at them.

"I wish I had brothers," Alfie said, still poking at the sand with a stick.

"Do you have friends from the island who'll stand up for you?"

"Yeah, but not in my chem class."

"Do you have lunch with them? Let the mainland kids know you're part of a group?" If things were still the way they'd used to be, island kids were strong and unafraid, enough so that most of the other kids didn't give them any flack.

"I eat with them sometimes." Alfie frowned. "Mostly, I like to read at lunch."

"Understandable." Ryan was really starting to like this kid. "But it might be worth putting your book down more often so the kids at the school see you have some friends. Especially big ones."

Alfie grabbed a handful of oyster shells and started stacking them up, making a little tower. "The middle school boys are all showing off for *girls*." He made it sound like that was the worst thing in the world.

That was a problem with being younger than the other kids. Alfie's hormones hadn't kicked in yet. "Girls are okay," Ryan said. "In fact, they can be better at paying attention in class than boys are, in high school. Maybe you can be friends with some of the smarter girls."

"Maybe," Alfie said doubtfully.

There was a shout from the house and they both turned to look. Mellie stood there, beckoning in their direction. Today, she wore shorts and a shirt so pink it almost glowed, even from this distance. "I gotta go have dinner," Alfie said. "You want to come?"

Ryan took another glance at Mellie. She'd crossed her arms tightly across her body and she wasn't smiling. She'd really put up walls. It was no more than Ryan deserved, and for the millionth time he regretted his callous behavior when they'd been teenagers falling in love. If only he'd had the self-awareness and communication skills to let her know that although getting so close to her made him uncomfortable, he cared about her deeply.

He hadn't had the skills, though. Still didn't, when it came to that. "I'm having dinner with Miss Betty," he said. "But thanks for the offer."

"Sure." Alfie ran toward Mellie, and they both turned to the house, Mellie giving Alfie's head an affectionate rub. Alfie leaned in and she put an arm around him as they walked inside.

Ryan felt a hard push of longing in his chest, wishing he could have that kind of closeness with someone.

Not just someone, but someone like Mellie.

He couldn't; it wasn't in his DNA. But in the short time he was here, there was one thing he could do for Mellie. Even though she seemed ambivalent about it, he was going to try hard to make a positive impact on her son.

CHAPTER FOUR

WHEN BETTY SAW who was at her back door on Friday morning, her heart sank.

"Since when do you latch your door?" Peg, her oldest and most interfering friend, rattled the screen.

"I'm coming." Betty pushed herself out of her chair and walked across the kitchen, every joint hurting.

"You're limping," Peg accused as she pushed past Betty into the kitchen and did a three-sixty, her eagle eyes scanning everything.

"I'm old. My bones hurt." Betty waited a few seconds for Peg to reveal her mission, but nothing was forthcoming.

"I thought that genius foster son of yours was helping you clean out this place. Where is he, anyway?"

Instead of answering, Betty poured Peg a cup of coffee and dumped in some milk. "Sit down," she said, and refilled her own cup. Then she sat at the table across from Peg.

They'd done this every week, at least, since they were teenagers. First, when they'd graduated from the little island elementary school to the middle school off-island, they'd hang out at Betty's parents' house. Her mother would be bustling around, and she and Peg would be wishing Mom would leave so they could really talk about what had gone on during the boat ride from school. Then, when Peg was a young mother and Betty was trying to be, but she and Wayne had never been able to conceive. Peg had hugged her through her heartache and shared her kids with Betty, and Betty babysat and tried to control her jealousy. It wasn't Peg's fault that she could make a baby a year while Betty was *barren*, as the old islanders used to say.

Later, after Peg's kids were grown and gone from the island, all except for Ruthie, of course, Betty and Wayne had started fostering kids. Peg had been against the idea, tried to talk them out of it. They were too old. The kids were too troubled.

But Betty and Wayne had known from the moment they'd started talking about it that fostering teen boys would fill the gap they both felt in their lives. And Peg, like the good friend she was, had helped and supported them in the end, counseled Betty on parenting and coached her through grocery shopping and cooking for a crowd.

Once the boys were grown and gone, it was back to just the two of them. She and Peg had talked about flagging libidos and aging husbands and sagging skin. And, of course, they'd kept each other up on who was doing what on the island. And then Peg had lost her husband, and Betty had helped Peg and Ruthie dispose of his things.

She supposed turnabout was fair play, although she really didn't want Peg's help. Didn't want anyone's help, not today.

"Well? What's Ryan doing, if he's not getting your place in order?"

Betty felt a rush of defensive pride. "He's out doing some research. His work is all about the bay, you know. He's making a difference, my Ryan is."

"More power to him if he can help solve our problems." Peg sipped coffee, grimaced. "You never did know how to make good coffee, Betty Raines. Listen. I'm here because if we're selling your things at the church rummage sale, you need to get started. *We* need to get started."

Annoyance flashed through Betty, head to toe. If she'd had another choice of a best friend, she probably wouldn't have chosen bossy, interfering Peg. That seemed mean to even think, except that Peg wouldn't have chosen her, either, had told Betty that more than once. But they'd been the only two girls in their grade on the island. It wasn't like there had ever been a choice, not since their mothers had ridden the boat to the mainland with their two-week-old babies for their first doctor's visit.

Betty leaned back in her chair and propped her feet on the one sitting catty-corner. "I don't have the energy to clean the kitchen. No chance I can start on the rest of the house." She held up a hand. "And before you start in on him, Ryan is doing his best. I put him to cleaning out the shed first, because…" Her throat tightened, annoyingly, and she gulped her own black coffee—which tasted perfectly fine to her—and coughed herself over the emotions. "I'm just not up to doing the house yet."

"Let's just walk through." Peg pushed back her chair and stood. "Do you know it's been five or six years since I saw any room in your house but the kitchen?" She strolled over and peered into the dining room. "You ever going to raise your shades again?"

"No point in it, seems like." Betty didn't stand. "I mean it, Peg. I don't want to go through the house today. I'm not feeling well."

"You weren't feeling well the last two times I came over, either. Let's just do it."

"Peg."

"Come on, you have to. I'm not letting you turn into one of those crazy old ladies with her house falling down around her." She paused, then added, "You need to get back in the swing of things. Run the market. Start putting out *Island Happenings* again."

Betty sighed and pushed herself to her feet. The thought of writing the weekly newspaper she'd created a decade ago was exhausting. So was doing a house tour, but Peg was stubborn. Showing her at least some of the house was the only way to get her to leave.

They walked through the dining room, the table piled high with Wayne's magazines and file folders. Then into the front room, which was so dark that Betty bumped into an ottoman, even though it hadn't been moved in twenty years. Just like when she and Ryan had come in here, she felt tired just looking at the dimly lit mess.

Peggy made her way over to the windows and pushed open the curtains, then turned on a couple of lamps. "Good heavens, it's like Jimmy's Junk Joint in here. Lots of things for the sale."

"We're just walking through," Betty reminded her.

Upstairs, Betty reached in and closed the door to her bedroom, then to the one Ryan was using. Nothing wrong with either of those, nothing to donate to the church.

But the other bedrooms were cluttered with craft supplies and paint cans and boxes. And Wayne's study…

Betty knew she had to get accustomed to being in there sometime, and she might as well take a baby step while her oldest friend was here. Since she and Ryan had looked in here, the door at least moved, and she opened it halfway.

Peg, who was taller, peeked over her. "Worst mess of all! But it would be worth clearing things away to get at that antique rolltop."

Betty didn't speak because she couldn't. She was caught up in the smell.

Pipe smoke and dusty books and some small remaining essence of Wayne.

Her eyes prickling with tears, she forced herself to walk forward. She needed to clean out her house, she knew that. She had to move on with her life. Wanted to, even, for all kinds of reasons.

She picked up the old letter opener he'd used, the one with a handle made to look like a duck decoy. Held it in her hand. It looked bigger in hers than it had in his.

He'd always loved getting mail, opening packages. Even as a young man, he'd always wanted to grab the mail first. He'd bring it up here and sort it, which was fine with Betty because she wasn't good with the bills, not like he was.

She weighed the letter opener in her hand and thought about how he'd never open their mail again.

"What do you think about starting here, with the worst?" Peg said. "We could fill a couple of garbage bags each, just with paperwork, it looks like. You'll feel better making a start. You always did need a push."

It was true. Betty remembered walking into the high school for the first time, fresh off the island, worried about how the mainland kids would be. Frozen by it, until Peg had literally shoved her in the door.

Once she was in, she'd done fine. Got decent grades, joined clubs, even been on the homecoming court.

Where was that girl who could do a new thing with just a little nudge from her best friend? When had she last *done* a new thing?

"I'll go get some bags," Peg said.

"No!" If they threw away all his papers and raffled off his excess furniture, that would be the end of Wayne. He'd be truly gone. Betty grabbed Peg's arm. "No. Not today."

"If not today, when? I'm getting the bags. One each. That's all."

"I'm not doing this!" Betty yelled the words, but the last couple came out twisted and crunched. She sank down onto one of Wayne's multiple boxes of files and let her head drop in her hands. "I can't." She was shaking with sobs.

And Peg, who wasn't the hugging type, pulled up a box beside Betty's and wrapped her arms around her and let her cry and cry.

ON SATURDAY, MELLIE strode into the Bluebird Bakery at 10:00 a.m., and her friend Taylor Harp groaned when she saw Mellie's workout clothes. "I forgot. I can't go."

"No way, you have to." Mellie had a specific agenda; she wanted to talk to someone about her situation, and she'd chosen her relatively new friend, Taylor.

After a little more complaining, Taylor gave instructions to the high school kid who was working the counter and put on her sneakers. They walked outside and headed down the street at a brisk pace.

Taylor would be perfect to confide in. She was discreet; Mellie happened to know that Taylor had been told all about Rich Harris's affair with Connie Douglas, but she had never brought it up. She wasn't a gossip. She was also an outsider, which was good; she didn't know the history of everyone and everything, like island life-timers did. And she wasn't judgmental.

Still, Mellie was unsure if she could do it. She'd never told the truth about Alfie to anyone.

Maybe she could sort of start with the subject, tell half of it?

"Slow down," Taylor complained. "Remember, I haven't exercised in years. Plus, I just sampled about eight muffins."

"Hey, ladies," old Hector Lozano called from his bike-and-golf-cart rental stand. "Pick up the pace!" He made running motions with his arms.

They both smiled at him, but as soon as they were out of the old man's earshot, Taylor groaned. "Why does every male feel like he has the right to advise and counsel every female about everything?"

Mellie snorted. "Right? Old Hector couldn't run to the end of the street if you paid him five hundred dollars." She glanced over at her friend as they walked.

Could she tell Taylor, maybe get some advice?

"I saw your son talking to the hot new scientist in town," Taylor said.

Mellie lifted an eyebrow. "You think Ryan's hot?" Most people on the island remembered Ryan from his rebellious-genius teenage years, when he hadn't been hot at all.

Well, not to most people. He'd definitely been hot to her.

"Hello? He's like this bachelor in demand. Someone paid three thousand dollars for a date with him in a charity bachelor auction."

"Really?" Mellie remembered hearing something about the auction, but three thousand dollars? For Ryan?

"Look, I'll show you the pictures," Taylor said, and stopped to pull out her phone.

Even though Mellie knew this was partly a ruse so Taylor could stop and catch her breath, she couldn't resist it. So she stood by Taylor while she searched through her phone—wonder of wonders, cellular reception was good today—and finally pulled up a news story.

Mellie couldn't pay attention to the words; she was captivated by the photo.

Ryan, wearing nerd glasses and a white dress shirt unbuttoned to reveal impressive muscles. He had a slightly rueful expression on his face that only added to his appeal because it made it clear he wasn't arrogant about his hotness, maybe wasn't even aware of it.

He sure hadn't looked like that in high school. And although she'd seen him a couple of times since he'd returned, had noticed his muscles, he'd been wearing some kind of jacket each time.

"I'm drooling." Taylor looked sideways at her. "I heard you two used to be involved."

"Come on, let's walk." Mellie took a couple of steps ahead, giving herself time to think.

She wanted to talk to Taylor about Alfie. Here was her chance. Once Taylor had caught up and they were walking again, headed out of town on the sandy road that led down toward the beach, she looked over at

Taylor. "Ryan and I were friends ever since he came to the island in high school, and neighbors," she said. "And a little more for a while."

"Ah," Taylor said.

"So it's not like we were in a relationship." She paused. "Anyway, that's not my biggest problem. I need to talk about Alfie."

"Yeah, how's he liking his new school with the big kids?"

"He's not. He doesn't fit in, and some of the kids make fun of him. Which I expected, and we talked about it...but I didn't think about him being totally miserable, too much to really enjoy the classes."

Yesterday, Alfie had come home not crying, but sullen. He hadn't wanted to tell her why, but she'd gathered from a couple of high school kids that had come into the market that the teasing hadn't stopped. She'd spoken to the principal and they'd agreed to give things a couple more weeks and then talk again. "I'm hoping if he becomes friends with Ryan, who was also kind of a genius kid, that he'll figure out some strategies to manage. Because my strategies aren't working."

"That's got to be so tough." Taylor was breathing hard, and she reached out a hand to Mellie. "Slow down, will you?"

Mellie slowed down. Maybe she should just tell Ryan flat out that he was Alfie's father. She wasn't good at keeping secrets, and she hated lying.

But he'd be so angry that she'd kept it from him until now. He had zero respect for fathers who didn't fulfill their responsibilities, based probably on his own biological father, who'd left his mother before he was born. To find out he'd inadvertently been a deadbeat dad would not sit well with him.

Wayne's warnings echoed back in her mind. Ryan wasn't capable of being a parent. His family history was too horrible and too damaging.

Besides, he'd definitively ended things with Mellie. He'd specifically said he didn't want a family, and he'd dumped her, the very night after they'd slept together. He was headed for a career in science and didn't want to be slowed down.

He'd been right, she guessed, because he did have a great career.

But how would he feel about being a father now? Would he still not want to take on the responsibility?

For him to reject Alfie after knowing him would break her heart.

"You don't want to have a fling with him while he's here?" Taylor asked now. "I mean, it's not like there are tons of options on the island."

"No way." Mellie didn't think Ryan would want anything to do with her now; he was totally out of her league. "People pay three thousand dollars to be with him. What do I have to offer? I'm a single mom who runs a small-town market."

"Don't put yourself down. A lot of people would love to have your career and lifestyle."

"Sure they would." Mellie didn't want to go into her insecurities with Taylor, didn't want to talk about how Ryan's rejection had impacted her. It had come at a vulnerable time. She'd lifted her head from the grind that was her life after her mom had left them, and had a short, shining relationship with Ryan… and then he'd dumped her.

She had friends, a great son, a job she liked. She lived in a community that was her heart and soul, one she'd never leave. It was enough.

"So, Mellie," Taylor said as they slowed down to look out at the bay from the elevated bluff. "That time you had a little more with Ryan. It didn't happen to be while you were a senior in high school, did it?"

"Yeah, it was. Why?"

"And you're twenty-eight. Right? And Alfie's ten."

"Uh-huh." Mellie started to feel uncomfortable. She'd planned to tell Taylor, but she was getting the feeling that her friend had already guessed. That wasn't good.

"Because…well, I always thought your husband was your baby's father. But Alfie looks a lot more like Ryan than he looks like the pictures I've seen of Georgie."

All the breath seemed to leave Mellie's chest as she stared at her friend, chagrined, knowing the truth was written all over her face. "You guessed," she said slowly. "How did you guess?"

"Oh, Mellie." Taylor reached out and squeezed her arm. "Come on, let's walk, and you can tell me about it."

But Mellie was stricken silent. If Taylor had guessed the truth, who would guess it next?

Ryan knelt at the edge of the bay, water sloshing around his work boots. Although the heat was the same as summer, he could smell the faintest hint of autumn in the breeze along with the fresh, salty scent of the bay.

It was Saturday morning, and he'd decided to come down and collect some water samples. Feel the sun on his shoulders and try to get people problems out of his mind.

An island dog he'd heard called Spotty for its black, brown and gold spots panted at his side. It seemed like every time he thought about one of his worries, the dog leaned against him or licked his arm. Ryan's logical side knew that it was unlikely the island dogs were especially intuitive, but then again…they'd been living on the island for generations, intermingling with people and thoroughly socialized by them while still mostly living wild outdoors. And animals had different senses than people did, were aware of things people weren't. So maybe Ryan was giving off vibes that concerned the dog enough to cause it to want to comfort him.

Facing into the current, he scooped a surface water sample into a specimen jar and waited for it to settle. Betty was the first problem on his mind. She was up and down these days, but mostly down; in fact, earlier this week, she'd stayed in bed for twenty-four hours straight, and Ryan suspected it had been brought on by her friend Peg's visit and their preliminary tour of the house.

Ryan had taken his own tour and he could understand why the mess would make anyone want to take to their bed. It wasn't a hoarding situation per se, but there were similarities. Wayne didn't seem to have thrown anything away for years.

Mellie was his other concern. She'd wanted him to talk to Alfie, but when he had, she'd looked upset. He supposed he'd have to clarify the situation with her, figure out what he had done wrong.

Maybe she'd never warm to him again. He'd certainly treated her badly when he'd been a troubled eighteen-year-old. He cringed to think of how rudely he'd pushed her away. Never mind that he'd been terrified, his whole inner self out-of-control panicked at the feelings he'd been having.

That wasn't her fault, and yet she'd suffered for it. Exhibit A of why he couldn't get involved in a relationship with anyone.

He rigged up an automatic device to collect a couple of samples undisturbed by the slightest human-created sediment and then splashed through the marsh to the next location he wanted to study.

Behind him, he heard someone moving. He turned, squinting against the bright sun, and saw a dark-clad figure kneeling by the automatic sampler he'd just set.

"Hey! Leave that alone!" He stomped through the mud toward the interloper. Now the thing would have to be reset, its timer adjusted.

The person—small, he saw now, a young boy—put up his hands and scooted backward, eyes wide. It was Alfie.

Shame washed over Ryan when he replayed his own words and tone. He'd shouted just like his step-father used to shout.

He'd scared the kid he was supposed to help.

"I'm sorry I yelled," he said to the boy, who splashed to a safe distance on the shoreline and stood watching him. Spotty sat half in, half out of the water beside Alfie. "Come see. I'll show you why it's important to let the water settle before taking a sample."

"I didn't break it." The boy waded toward him, slowly, but with normal, not excessive caution. Which was good. He must never have been mistreated by an adult.

"Good. Come look." He knelt beside the sampler, gestured for Alfie to join him and explained what he was trying to do.

Being near a boy of this age made him flash back to the child he'd been. At Alfie's age, he'd already been in his second foster family and often in trouble for fighting. His happiest hours had been spent alone, exploring the creek that ran through the wooded area behind their apartment building. He remembered nagging that particular foster mother into getting him a library card so he could learn about the craw-dads and rocks and plants he found.

He'd been a sullen, unpleasant boy, he could see now, always on guard. Hard to love. That, and the fighting, meant he'd been moved to another foster home, and that one hadn't had access to wooded areas and creeks and libraries. That placement hadn't lasted long, either.

Although the foster placements had varied in opportunities and level of care, they had all been worlds better than what he'd come from. Even back then, angry and closed off as he'd been, he'd felt grateful to be alive and in homes with food and clean clothes and freedom.

And then, thank heavens, he'd ended up here on the island, with Betty and Wayne, who understood his issues. They'd helped him work through his anger and had encouraged his academic interests.

Alfie, a smart boy like Ryan had been, had been blessed with a warm and loving childhood that gave him a basic security Ryan would never have. His path to a rewarding adult life would be much more straightforward than Ryan's had been.

Ryan was explaining more about the invertebrates—thousands of them in each teaspoon of bay water—when Alfie turned suddenly, reached into the bay and pulled a tiny blue crab up in his closed palm. He opened it and quickly shifted his hand to hold the creature's body between his thumb and forefinger, avoiding the snapping claws.

"I've been catching crabs since I was little. Mom let me keep a few, as an experiment, but she didn't think they'd do well in the house. I tried to make an aquarium where they could really live, and Mom helped me, but it didn't work too well. All but two died the first week." He pressed his lips together.

"So you ended the experiment?"

Alfie nodded. "I don't like hurting animals."

"Good. I don't, either."

"Don't you have to hurt them in a lab? You know, like cruelty-free products exist because most stuff *is* tested on animals and can hurt them."

Yeah, this kid was smart. "I like being an ecologist because I don't have to do things like that, for the most part," he said. "Animal testing sometimes can't be avoided, but we should do as much as possible to help the animals, not hurt them. That's what my work is all about."

"Cool."

The boy followed him to the next sample site, both of them walking carefully so as not to agitate the water, and by the third, Ryan let Alfie collect a sample himself. Ryan would label it differently, so it wouldn't go to be analyzed with the official samples, but the kid was careful and had better fine motor skills than you'd expect for that age. Ryan had a small microscope set up at Betty's; maybe he'd show Alfie some slides of the sample he'd collected.

He stood from where he was working and smiled to see the child, intent on catching another crab, kneeling in the water, and suddenly it hit him: pictures of a child like Alfie having fun and learning in the water just might be the perfect way to liven up his grant application.

He used the camera on his phone to take a few photos. He'd have to get a release before he could use them, and Mellie might not agree, but it was worth a try. He might even add a little more verbiage to the grant proposal, something on providing education to public school kids about the bay and its problems.

If kids helped with a program to protect the bay, they'd be all the more likely to grow up wanting to continue doing that.

Ryan had already worked with college-age students, but here was a chance to extend into the younger ages, helping schoolchildren get interested in the ecology of the bay. In fact, if college kids, inherently cool, could work with younger ones, everyone would benefit. The bay most of all.

Spotty splashed over to see what Alfie was doing, and Ryan caught a few more photos, then tapped on his notes app to record this new direction. He felt that quickening of his heart that told him this new idea was a good one.

Behind him, he heard more barking from the woods, and turned.

"Alfie! Where have you been?" Mellie emerged from the wooded path, a reddish-gold short-haired dog beside her, and marched toward them. She glared at Ryan. "And why are you taking photos of my son?"

CHAPTER FIVE

MELLIE'S HEART RACED as she hurried to her son. "You know you're not to go off in the marsh by yourself!" She splashed through the water and swooped him into a hug, relief blooming like a flower inside her. "I was so scared! Don't do that to me!"

"I'm sorry, Mom." Alfie briefly hugged her back, then reached down to pat Gizmo, the island dog who hung around their house most often. "Did Gizmo help you find me?"

"He did." Mellie rubbed the dog's sides and ears. "You're such a good dog. I'm giving you so many treats at home."

Only after she'd backed out of the mucky water and sat down on the shore to take off her sneakers did she focus on Ryan, who looked annoyingly care-free. "Didn't you think to ask him if he had permission to be here?"

He shook his head, his face rueful. "I'm sorry, but I didn't. Not much experience with kids. I apologize for the worry."

She shrugged. "It's on him, really." She frowned at Alfie. "You're going to have extra chores, to help you remember that you need to let me know where you're going."

"Oh, Mom." But his attention was caught by something in the marsh grasses and he turned to explore it.

Ryan splashed over to the shore and knelt down beside her. "I really am sorry. And the photos are for my grant application, if you'll sign a release, but you can also delete them right now." He held out his phone.

"I mean, if they're for some valid use...but why do you need pictures of Alfie for a grant application?"

"To keep it from being so boring," he said, his mouth twisting to one side. "It was Betty's idea to add photos of people enjoying or working in the bay. At first I thought it was silly, but then when I saw Alfie and the dog looking at my research stuff, I realized that would really boost the application. Help me show the project's broader impact." His eyes lit up. "And then I started getting ideas about adding an educational piece to the grant. Getting kids involved in collecting specimens and the like, sending some of our college students out into classrooms to teach about the bay. I'm itching to write it all down, actually."

She laughed to cover up her reaction to Ryan, how sexy he was when he was all passionate and excited about his work. "You always were like that, when you got an idea. I remember when you cut out of school in the middle of the day so you could go watch an eclipse of the sun."

"Yeah," he said, "I got a few days of after-school detention for that. Which meant double punishment at home, because I couldn't ride the school boat and Wayne and Betty had to pay extra for me to ride the commuter ferry."

"Mom, you hafta see this!" Alfie beckoned to her, holding up a glass vial. "I think I see some zooplankton! Mr. Ryan told me about them!"

They splashed out to see, and Mellie realized she couldn't punish Alfie too harshly, bring him down from this high, not after how miserable he'd been coming home from school yesterday. He'd begged her to let him just stay in his own grade on the island, and it had nearly broken her heart to tell him no. But she wanted him to give the advanced classes a chance. Maybe she was a single mom, and not nearly as bright as her son—or his father—but what she did have was love. She wanted the best for him with all her heart.

She admired the zooplankton—which to her looked like specks of dirt in the water—and then stepped back to dry land and studied Ryan and Alfie. Did they look so much alike that others would guess what Taylor had?

They both had that strong jaw and the piercing eyes that were a window to their high intelligence. Both were handsome enough to be male models. To her, they were obviously father and son.

But objectively, although they had dark brown hair and blue eyes, that was coloring fairly common on the island. Whereas Ryan was muscular—wow, was he muscular—Alfie was thin and lanky. Their resemblance was far from obvious.

At least, she hoped so.

Fortunately for her secret, Georgie had had similar coloring to theirs. Most people ought to go on making the assumption that Alfie was Georgie's son.

As for Ryan, he was of course bright enough to do the math. But since they'd used a condom, he had to assume that it had worked.

It hadn't.

The other saving grace was that Alfie had been born almost a month early. Even if Ryan counted back from Alfie's birthday, he wouldn't come up with the exact week of their single intimate encounter.

And she'd gotten together with Georgie soon after Ryan had dumped her and left the island. Back together, really, since they'd dated a few times before. She hadn't slept with him, not until they'd married, and he'd known the truth about Alfie. But he'd been just as happy to pretend parentage of him. Having sons was a source of pride in his family.

As Alfie splashed around playing with the dog, Ryan came to stand beside her. "I really am sorry," he said in that deep, rich voice. "Can I take the two of you out to lunch as an apology? Maybe at the Rockfish Grill, for a treat?"

"Yeah!" Alfie said.

Ryan gave Mellie a rueful look, then turned to Alfie. "I didn't realize you were listening, buddy," he said. "Your mom may have other plans for you."

"She doesn't. And she gets tired of cooking,"

Alfie said confidently. "Can we get ice cream after, from the new cart?"

"What new cart?" Mellie was glad to focus on anything other than the flutter she'd gotten, thinking about sitting down to lunch at a nice restaurant with Ryan.

"Goody's Mobile Treats," he said. "It's got all the flavors, not just teaberry."

"Huh." Betty wouldn't be happy to hear that. She prided herself on serving exclusively teaberry ice cream at the market.

Mellie couldn't say no, but she did suggest they eat at the Dockside Diner rather than the Rockfish, considering how dirty they'd gotten in the marsh. And the lunch was easy and enjoyable, kept lively by Alfie's peppering Ryan with science questions. To her own surprise, she was able to follow along and, sometimes, contribute to the conversation.

Afterward, they strolled through town. The trees that lined High Street were just starting to drop a few leaves, and the flower baskets on the lampposts still burst with color. Most of the shops had window boxes filled with flowers, too, an initiative Mellie had spearheaded; she'd helped those who didn't have a green thumb pick out easy-to-maintain flowers, and she watered and deadheaded for Taylor at the bakery and for a couple of others who couldn't be bothered with it. Most of the shop owners had transitioned to fall plantings—flowering kale, mums and coxcombs in fiery gold, red and purple.

The street bustled with tourists, a few families,

some older couples and a group of girlfriends who were laughing and talking loudly—they'd probably come from the Dockside Diner. Callie and Wendell Roosevelt walked their big Airedale terrier—not an island dog, but one they'd brought when they'd moved here from DC—and they stopped so Alfie could pet it. If there was anything he loved more than abstract science, it was dogs.

When they got to the end of the block, sure enough, there was a new ice cream truck. Pink and blue, with a big ice cream cone on top and a window where five people were lined up to purchase their treats. Alfie saw a friend and ran ahead to get in line with him.

"Betty's not going to like this," Mellie said to Ryan as they stood to the side, reading the list of flavors. "Wonder when this place started up. Does she even have a permit?"

"She had to take the car ferry to get that thing over here. Probably a special delivery."

"Alfie, ask if they have teaberry," Mellie urged.

He shook his head. "I'm sick of teaberry ice cream."

That was fair. The bright pink, intensely minty stuff was delicious, but so was chocolate. "I'm going to get in line and ask," she said to Ryan.

"Oh, me, too. I can't be by an ice cream truck without ordering some ice cream."

It turned out that the woman operating the truck—a cranky-looking individual named Goody—didn't carry teaberry ice cream. "It's not a seller," she said.

"I have six flavors. Chocolate, vanilla, cookies and cream, butter pecan, mint chocolate chip and strawberry. The most popular flavors in the USA."

"Makes sense." Mellie ordered a chocolate cone, the same as Alfie, and Ryan got butter pecan. They strolled down the street enjoying their ice cream, which was, admittedly, delicious. "I feel a little guilty," Mellie said. "Like I'm cheating on teaberry."

"I'm hungry enough for a second cone. We could go get teaberry ones from the market," Ryan suggested, grinning in a way that looked suddenly, heartbreakingly, like Alfie.

"Yeah!" Alfie said.

"One ice cream is plenty for one day," Mellie said through a tight throat. She wasn't going to cry for what could have been. Wasn't going to dwell on what it would've been like to raise Alfie with Ryan. For this to be a real family outing, not just a coincidental encounter of near-strangers, unlikely to be repeated.

Alfie pouted for a split second, but they were walking beside the park now, and he ran over to climb to the top of the play structure.

As Ryan and Mellie followed him, Ryan apologized. "I'm not around young kids much. Not used to filtering what I say. Of course a kid shouldn't eat two ice cream cones in a day, but I didn't think before I spoke."

"It's okay. Alfie's pretty easygoing about stuff like that. He follows the rules."

"Good," Ryan said. "Makes it easier for you. You always followed the rules, too, as I recall."

"I did," she said slowly, "most of the time at least."

Except for one hot summer night on a blanket by the bay, when a date to eat sandwiches and watch the sunset had turned into much, much more.

She glanced at Ryan and wondered if he were remembering that same night.

They'd both been inexperienced, but he'd been so caring and honest that it hadn't felt awkward. He'd wanted her to feel good and hadn't pressured her to do anything she didn't want to do, which had left her free to relax and enjoy his embrace, his kiss, his touch.

Afterward, they'd walked home together in a haze of warm romance. He'd kissed her tenderly, standing in front of her house.

The next day...no. She didn't want to think about the next day, how everything had changed.

She wanted, just today, to remember how beautiful it had been, how tender and loving he'd been.

She looked up at him and their eyes linked, locked. Suddenly, she knew without a doubt that he'd been thinking about the same night she had.

He reached a hand for her, touching her shoulder. "Mellie, I... Maybe we should talk more about what happened." He studied her face. "I left the island so quickly, and I said things that I realize now were pretty cold. But I felt anything but cold. I...I've never forgotten being with you, Mellie."

Her heart seemed to reach out toward him. She wanted to hear about how he'd felt good, being with her, maybe as good as she'd felt. To reexperience the beauty of it. But it wouldn't be wise. Not when she was committed to keeping Alfie's parentage a secret.

"No need," she said, forcing distance and coolness into her voice. "What's done is done."

He looked distressed. "I understand if you don't want to talk about it," he said, "but know that door is open if you want to go through." He held up a hand. "And don't worry that I'm asking you to...you know, repeat what happened. I just thought it might help to clear the air."

No way. If the air around that topic became clear, it might be too easy for Ryan to learn the truth. "Thanks, but I'd rather leave the past in the past," she said with a decent approximation of honesty. And then she called Alfie and manufactured a reason they had to go home, now.

Too much time in Ryan's presence wasn't going to be good for either of them.

MONDAY MORNING, BETTY dragged herself out of bed and discovered Ryan was already in the kitchen. Drat.

She hadn't slept well, mostly because she knew they were supposed to tackle some serious house sorting and purging today. She dreaded a repeat of what had happened with Peg. Just going into Wayne's study had derailed her for several days. The last thing she wanted was to lose it in front of Ryan, make him deal with her emotions.

She was supposed to be the stronger one in this relationship. She'd taken on the job of fostering him, and it was up to her to help him through his emotional issues, not the reverse.

"Thanks for making coffee," she said, pouring herself a cup.

"Can't start the day without it. You still up for this?"

No. She looked around the kitchen. It was cluttered and could use a deep clean. "Maybe we should start here," she suggested.

"If you want," he said. His kind tone indicated that he knew she was stalling. "But won't your friend Peg keep bothering you about the rummage sale?"

"You're right. She will. And she wants actual furniture." Betty sipped hot coffee.

They'd decided to start with clearing out the front room. It was a small, achievable goal. Plus, the room was full of furniture that would sell well at the rummage sale, so hopefully clearing it out would appease Peg.

It would also give her and Ryan a good place to sit together and watch TV. She'd realized as soon as he'd arrived that there was nowhere to hang out with him. Her women friends always visited with her in the kitchen, but men wanted a comfortable place to sit and watch sports.

And hopefully, working on the front room would be emotionally neutral for her. Or not neutral—because she had to face facts, if it were neutral she'd have already gotten the work done. But at least not as emotional as Wayne's study.

They walked through the cluttered dining room

and into the living room. Betty hadn't been back in here since Peg had dragged her here, so the shades were still open. The morning sun slanted in through dancing dust motes.

"Wow." Ryan surveyed the room and blew out a breath, staying near the entryway.

She studied him, wondering what was wrong, and then the light dawned. "Still struggling with the claustrophobia?"

"Some. I've gotten better at hiding it, except from you." He gave her a rueful smile. "If we open the windows, I can work in here fine. Kind of a catch-all, huh?"

"It's turned out that way." She looked around and remembered scolding Wayne about letting things get to be such a mess in here. Telling him to keep his books and papers in his study. To stop buying every piece of extra furniture he saw at a thrift shop. They'd argued, and he'd stormed upstairs in disgust.

Her throat felt tight and she coughed, and then it was hard to stop with all the dust.

Ryan patted her back. "Are you okay? Sure you're up to this?" He'd seen right through her pretense and was looking at her with concern.

"I'm okay." She swallowed and looked around. "We used to spend time in here most evenings."

"Continuing on after we moved out?"

"Yes. We got into old movies for a while." When had it changed?

She'd gotten so angry and suspicious for a time, but her suspicions had proven baseless, at least as far as she knew. Still, she hadn't been able to open up to him like before. And he had seemed fine with spending evenings in his office, rather than with her.

"I remember watching movies with you and Wayne and Cody and Luis in here." Ryan looked around, obviously having a different experience of the room than she was. "I'd think, wow, this is what normal families do."

"You boys always did enjoy that. Especially the Hallmark movies. I wasn't even that much of a fan myself, but I could tell you liked them."

Ryan grinned. "Thanks for keeping that secret in the family. It showed us a better world," he said. "Better than real, maybe, but I needed an extra dose of looking at the bright side."

"You did." She put an arm around him, remembering him when he'd come to them. Fourteen years old and so very broken. It had taken a year before she'd realized he was incredibly bright underneath all the anger and hurt.

Now, she studied him. "You might still need that. Why aren't you married or at least dating someone?"

His mouth pulled to one side. For just a couple of seconds, bleakness flashed in his eyes, a look she remembered from that first year he'd been with them. "That's not likely." He moved to an end table. "Does this go?"

"Why isn't it likely? You're a wonderful man. Handsome, and smart, and kind. Any woman would be lucky to get you."

His mouth went flat and he shook his head. "I don't get close to people."

"How can you say that?" She grasped his hand, then wrapped him in a hug. He went fence-post still for a few seconds, then relaxed and put his own arms around her.

That was her Ryan. Hard to hug, right at first, but he needed the physical affection more than any boy she'd fostered.

She'd read the case reports and knew his early years had been horrific. *Ryan has experienced complex trauma and is likely to carry the aftereffects of that for many years, if not for a lifetime.* The few details given had nearly broken her heart.

But she didn't believe the lifetime aftereffects prediction, never had, with any of her boys. You couldn't, and keep doing the work. "You don't get close to people *easily*," she said as she released him. "But your capacity to feel and care about people is as big as that bay you love so much."

He smiled down at her. All of her boys had turned out tall and strong and healthy, and it satisfied her. Everyone complained about the huge appetites of teenage boys, but she'd loved cooking the big batches of wholesome food they'd needed. Plenty of treats, too. When Ryan and his brothers—for she called each of the several generations of boys she'd fostered through the teen years brothers—had been here, she couldn't make less than three pies without having a fight on her hands. Ideally, four, because Wayne had been a good eater, too.

It was a way to show love, a concrete way that men understood better than pretty words.

"You're ever the optimist," he told her now. "Let's use that power to get some of this stuff outside."

So they carried out a long, low coffee table, a couple of end tables and an empty dresser that had somehow made its way into the wrong room. When they got to an old desk, though, she raised a hand to slow Ryan down, her throat tightening up.

This was the desk Wayne had worked at when they'd first married, before they'd cleared out the upstairs and built on the addition. It had been in the kitchen, and she remembered him sitting there writing his sermons while she cooked, quiet as a mouse, the good smells and steamed windows and sense of love and possibility all around them.

That was before they'd learned she couldn't have children. Before he'd taken on extra jobs off the island so they could pay for the fertility treatments that hadn't worked, except for making her incredibly moody.

"This is hard for you." Ryan slid an arm around her and side-hugged her close against him. "We can stop for today. The floor's visible now, and your friend Peg will have a few pieces for the rummage sale."

"No. Let's get this out of here." She put her hands on one end of the small, old-fashioned wooden desk. It was no use to think fondly back on those early days; she'd just spiral further into depression, not just for the present-day loss of him, but for all they'd lost along the way.

Wayne, oh, Wayne. This farmhouse, this marriage, this life, *it was all supposed to last forever. So why did you have to up and leave?*

They lifted the desk and something rattled, so after they'd carried it outside, Betty opened the drawers. Inside was a small, locked wooden box. She shook it. "Papers, sounds like."

"What do you think it is?" Ryan was going through the other drawers. "I don't see a key."

"That's Wayne. The most secretive man you'd ever want to meet, especially for a man of the cloth. Very annoying."

Ryan's eyebrows drew together. "I thought you two had a perfect marriage."

That made her laugh. "No, indeed," she said. "It was miles and miles better than what you came from, but there are problems in every marriage." Maybe more than most in hers, but she wasn't sure. Had no way of finding out, now that he was gone.

Tears pushed at her eyes, but she took slow, deep breaths to calm herself. She wasn't going to distress Ryan by breaking down. "We've probably cleared out enough for one day," she told him, her voice only faintly husky. "Thank you for helping me. You're a good boy."

"Of course." He frowned, probably sensing that she was upset but not sure what to do about it.

"Let's get this load to the rummage sale and then we'll be done." She shook the box in her hands, wondering what it held. She'd keep it, but the trouble was, there were several such boxes in the house.

Why had her husband been so secretive? He'd been the kindest and most loving man she'd ever known. Surely he hadn't been hiding something awful that he'd done. Had he?

CHAPTER SIX

RYAN WAS DEFINITELY out of his element at a church rummage sale, or rather, among the group of women preparing for it.

The church hall was basically a big warehouse. Long tables lined every wall, and eight or nine women lifted boxes and sorted clothes and talked, talked, talked.

Ryan had never been very good at small talk, so he smiled and carried things and tried not to slow down enough to get into an extended conversation with these women he hadn't seen since he was a gawky, angry teenager.

Betty didn't look any more enthusiastic about the scene than Ryan was, probably for different reasons. He'd guess that she'd known these women for much of her life, but the way they all looked up when she and Ryan came in…they were curious about her, probably too curious for her taste. Despite her annoyance about Wayne's secrecy, she could be a private person, too.

As he carried in a couple of wooden chairs, he heard one of the women talking to Betty.

"I sure miss *Island Happenings*," she said. "Are you starting that up again soon?"

"Don't know."

"When are you going to start working at the market again?" another woman asked.

"When I'm ready." Betty spoke tartly.

"Mellie can't do it forever, you know. Especially not with that son of hers needing so much attention."

"He's a strange one, that Alfie."

"He's not strange, he's smart," Betty snapped.

The woman who'd called Alfie strange raised two hands in the air. "No need to be so touchy," she said, sounding offended.

"Betty's always been touchy," another woman offered.

Betty looked more than touchy; she looked like she was about to explode like a lethal bomb. "Hey, Betty, could you help me with something?" he asked, and led her outside to the truck. There, they both leaned against the tailgate, looking at the small white church and the bay beyond.

"Thanks for rescuing me."

"Figured you could use a break."

"They're my friends, but they're as noisy and nosy as a bunch of blue jays."

"I could see that." He hesitated to show her the other thing he'd found, but it was her right to know. "I found this taped to the bottom of the dresser," he said, and held out another small, locked box.

She looked at it and frowned, her face going to stone. Only then did Ryan realize that it was a jewelry box of some sort. Whatever it was, it seemed to have significance for Betty.

"Do you want me to…hold on to it or something?"

She shook her head, staring at the ground. "I'd like to go home."

"Okay. Get in the truck and I'll just carry the rest—"

"Now, Ryan. Please." Her voice was low and desperate.

"Right." He slammed the tailgate on the remaining items and strode up to the driver's side, and within minutes they were back at the house.

She got out before he could help her, gently pushed his hands away and walked slowly inside. Her shoulders were slumped.

Ryan blew out a breath. He wasn't good at the kind of confrontation that was probably needed here, but he was the person on the ground. He walked after her. "Betty," he said as she marched toward her bedroom. "We need to find you someone to talk to. There are psychologists who specialize in—"

She held up a hand and kept walking. "No therapy."

"I know." He'd already brought that up with her. He himself was a fan of therapy, which surprised his brothers, who weren't. But he'd read the psychological literature when he'd been a teenager. He was very aware that he wouldn't have made it through adolescence and young adulthood without it. "Hold up. How about Peg? She's your oldest friend."

At her bedroom door, she paused. "Not Peg. None of the women we saw today."

The good thing was that she wasn't denying she needed help.

He looked around the cluttered dining room off which her bedroom was located. It was overwhelming and depressing just being in here, and that was to him. To Betty, the clutter held memories he was starting to realize weren't all positive.

"The new pastor?" he asked.

"That man is younger than you are!" Betty sounded outraged. "I can't even believe they hired him to replace Wayne, honestly. He's a good man, but too young to counsel me."

Ryan nodded as the possible helpers got whittled down. No one who was from her age group on the island, yet no one too young and from off the island. "How about Mellie?" he asked. "Would you talk to her?"

"I *do* talk to her."

"I mean on a deeper level. Would you try it? She's so practical she could help with the house, but she also understands a little about what you're going through."

Even as he spoke, he was scolding himself inside. What was he doing, suggesting more involvement with the woman who made him positively ache for what he couldn't have?

She heaved a sigh. "Her I can stomach. Maybe."

It's for Betty. "Okay if I ask her over to look

around, and talk to you? See if the two of you can sit down together and talk about how you're feeling?"

"All right," she said grudgingly. "I'd pay her to help with the house, too." She withdrew into her bedroom and closed the door with a firm click.

So Mellie was coming over. Clearly, it was the only way to help Mama Betty, so it had to happen. But what would Ryan do, in close quarters with the only woman he'd come close to loving?

ON TUESDAY EVENING, Mellie stood at her kitchen window, washing baking sheets and looking over at Betty's house.

Why had Ryan invited her and Alfie for a meal?

The sun was low, casting golden light across the bay. Pretty and romantic, like always.

But she felt the romantic part more, thinking of having dinner with Ryan...and that made her mad at herself.

She should never have agreed to go to lunch after finding Alfie with Ryan. That was what had started her feelings waking up.

If she were honest with herself, her feelings had reawakened the moment she'd seen him, that first night on Betty's porch. They'd only grown since then.

But having feelings for Ryan was a mistake. If she got closer to him, even in a friendly way, she'd risk revealing the truth about Alfie being his son.

She moved the cookies she'd baked from the cooling rack to a serving plate. Chocolate chip—Alfie's favorite and, as she recalled, Ryan's, as well.

Of course, it could be that she was wrong to keep the secret. After all, Alfie deserved to know who his father was, and Ryan deserved to know he had a son. Especially since the two of them were growing fond of each other, hiding their relationship felt wrong.

But Ryan didn't want children. And Alfie assumed, like everyone else, that he was Georgie's son. Why rock that boat when Ryan was just here for a short time? Why open Alfie up to being hurt and rejected by his biological father?

"Mom, can I go help Mr. Ryan?"

She looked out the window and saw that Ryan was carrying a tray down to the picnic table by the bay. "Yes, go help."

He ran over, and Mellie watched with misgiving as he approached Ryan and started talking fast, the way he did when he was excited. Alfie was getting attached to Ryan. And while she wanted Ryan to help Alfie adjust to being so smart, how to live in the world with it, she didn't want him to get hurt.

She wouldn't have agreed to go over for dinner tonight, except that Ryan had said it was for Betty's sake, that Betty needed her.

When Ryan and Alfie reemerged from the kitchen, each of them carrying a plate of something steaming hot, she couldn't delay any longer. She grabbed her plate of cookies and the mason jar of cut flowers she'd fixed up for Betty, and walked over.

"Mom! Ryan made crab cakes!"

Not an uncommon meal on the island, but it was Alfie's favorite.

"'Made' is stretching it." Ryan lifted the plate. "Mrs. Fernwood made these. I just fried them up."

"Good plan, hers are delicious," Mellie said. And it was nice to support the Fernwood family, who had little. Her crab cake business was their only source of income now that her husband had become disabled. "Where's Betty?"

Ryan set down the plate. "She isn't feeling well. She backed out."

Mellie pressed her lips together to avoid saying what came to mind. She was now roped into another meal with just Ryan and Alfie. Another little family-like meal that might evoke emotions she didn't want to have, and worse, to make Alfie feel more connected to Ryan.

"Sorry, it's pretty simple." He gestured to the plate of corn on the cob and the crab cakes, then looked at her covered plate. "I'm hoping that's dessert."

She set the flowers in the middle of the table and then lifted the towel from atop the plate. "Chocolate chip cookies."

"Definitely my favorite cookie," Ryan said.

"Me, too!" Alfie sounded amazed.

"Chocolate chip are everyone's favorite," she said, deliberately depersonalizing it, or trying to.

They all sat down. "I'll say grace," Alfie volunteered, reaching out a hand to take each of theirs, unselfconsciously.

Which meant that Mellie had to hold Ryan's hand.

Bigger than hers, calloused, and she had a sudden memory of holding hands with him during the brief time of their high school romance.

"God, bless our food and us. And please take care of Miss Betty, because she's sick and sad and needs help. Amen."

The simplicity of Alfie's prayer tightened Mellie's throat. Alfie knew what was important. He was a wise kid.

They bit into crab cakes and ate corn, and it was all delicious. The sun sank lower into the bay, painting the sky with purple and pink and gold.

It felt idyllic, like every dream of family she'd ever had. She lifted her face to the breeze and sucked in the fragrance of crab cake and bay water, and let herself pretend, for just a minute, that they *were* a family.

She glanced at Ryan and saw him watching her, maybe reading her mind, and she snapped out of it. She needed to ask what this was all about, this dinner allegedly for Betty's sake. But he hadn't brought it up in front of Alfie, which probably meant it was something Alfie shouldn't hear.

Finally, an island dog named Princess for her tall, poodle-like beauty, came over with a stick in her mouth, and Alfie excused himself and ran toward the bay, where he threw the stick for the dog, repeatedly.

They both watched him, and when she glanced at Ryan, she saw he wore the same fond smile on his face that she had on hers.

Again—as if they were legitimately his parents.

Which, of course, they were.

And she needed not to think about that, but to get down to business and get this too-domestic meal over with.

"What's this all about—?" she started to say.

"You're probably wondering—" he said at the same time.

"You—" they both said at once again.

Cue awkward laugh. "You first," she said.

"Right. Good. You're probably wondering what this is all about."

"I am."

"It's Betty. She's not getting better, not really moving forward."

Mellie frowned. "I've been worried too, but are we overanalyzing things? It's only been three months since Wayne died."

"Right. And I could be wrong. But to me it seems like she's off somehow."

Mellie winced and nodded. For all Ryan's scientific bent, she knew he was pretty sensitive to emotions. "I've been worried about her, but I was hoping for a quick fix. Do you think it's depression?"

"She's avoiding people. Keeping stuff inside. It's like she turns into a robot, and that's not Betty."

"No, it isn't." Mellie sighed. "She doesn't have near the number of friends in and out that she used to have. Almost nobody."

"I noticed. And we're finding some weird stuff in the house, which seems to upset her more. Locked boxes, two of them, with no keys that she knows of.

She says Wayne was always secretive, but..." He lifted his hands, palms up. "Like I said, it seems off."

Mellie nodded and pretended to be just contemplating what he'd said, but inside, her thoughts raced.

Wayne was definitely secretive, more than Ryan knew; he'd encouraged her to keep her pregnancy a secret from Ryan. And then there was the money...

"—not like you'd be counseling her. She hates the idea of counseling. But I got her to agree to talk to you a little, while you help her clean out the house."

"I thought that's what you were here for."

"Believe me, there's plenty of work for both of us. She said she'd pay you."

The thought of cleaning out Betty's house as a joint project between her, Betty and Ryan filled Mellie with dismay. She already lived next door to Ryan, and against her better judgment, she'd enlisted him to help Alfie adjust to school. If she added another togetherness activity, her plate would be full of an unending diet of Ryan, Ryan, Ryan.

She was strong, but not that strong. She lit on the next truest excuse. "I'd like to help Betty," she said, "but I just don't see how. It's not money I'm short of, at least no more than anyone else. It's time. With Betty not being able to come back to work, I'm running the store by myself."

"She's not working at all, is she?"

Mellie shook her head. "I told her I'd run things for as long as she needed, but the truth is, there are decisions that I make on a daily basis that I'm not sure about. I wish she'd come for a few hours a day. A few hours a week, even."

Ryan looked thoughtful. "Cut her a deal," he suggested. "If she comes back to work some hours, you'll work an equivalent number of hours with her on her house."

She nodded, reluctantly. "That would make a certain amount of sense, but will she go for it? Having us bargain with her about her mood, her grief?"

They looked at each other for a minute and a snap of understanding came into both of them at the same time. "Yes. It's the only thing she *does* understand."

Mellie felt a sense of impending doom. "It's not going to work for me to declutter the house while she's at the market," she said, picturing hours of close quarters with only Ryan. "You don't have to be there, but Betty should."

He looked at her for a little longer than was necessary, his eyes thoughtful. Maybe a little hurt, but it was hard to tell. She only recognized it because she'd seen the same look on her son's face.

Man, were they alike.

"I might be around some," he said carefully, "because I'm living there. And as you pointed out, helping Betty clean out her place is really why I'm here."

"Of course." She felt terrible that she might have hurt his feelings. Which was ridiculous, really, considering how badly he'd hurt hers.

On the other hand, the secret she was keeping from him comprised a monumental hurt. "I didn't mean you can't ever be around when Betty and I are working," she said. "It's just that, sometimes, she might want to talk about something without her son being there."

"I get it," he said, his voice neutral. "Anyway, the main thing is, find some time to talk with her about Wayne, her loss, how she's managing. She seems to be struggling, and I just don't know if it's normal or if it's worse than normal. You're a widow, too, so you can understand more than I can."

Mellie blew out a breath. She was a widow, and she'd grieved Georgie's loss, far more than she'd ever dreamed she would. At the same time, their relationship had been nothing like Betty and Wayne's.

In large part, it was because of the man in front of her. He'd twisted her heart inside out and then thrown it away, and it hadn't been whole enough to give entirely to Georgie.

She'd tried her best to be a good wife, and he'd never complained. People had seen them as a happy couple, and certainly, Alfie had benefitted from Georgie's steadying influence on their lives.

"I'll talk with Betty," she said, "and I'll help some, as much as I can, with the house. But you're not off the hook, not with any of it."

"I never asked to be," he snapped.

Great. Now she'd hurt his feelings and agreed to work with him, both. A good evening's work.

If it would help Betty, of course it was worth it. She just hoped it wouldn't be a disaster for her and her son.

CHAPTER SEVEN

AT NOON ON THURSDAY, Ryan climbed the steps to the outdoor deck of the Dockside Diner and seated himself at the table the waitress waved him to.

There hadn't even *been* an outdoor deck when he'd lived here. Now, there was a striped awning and brightly painted picnic tables topped with umbrellas. A great view of the docks and the bay. Tables mostly full of talking, laughing diners who looked like tourists, the white-haired crowd who were free to travel in the fall.

He was here to meet with his old advisor, and he welcomed the opportunity. It would help him stop thinking about Mellie and how pretty she'd looked as she'd bit her lip and considered his request that she help Betty.

Even in shorts and an old T-shirt, Mellie was a stunner. And kind. She had the kindest heart of anyone he knew. He got the sense that her heart had gotten deeper, more soulful, through the trials she'd experienced as a wife, a mother and a widow.

What had he done by comparison, really? In some ways, although he was a little older than she was, he was far less experienced.

"Ryan!" Charlie Fisher waved from the dock, trotted up the stairs and strode to the table, hand extended. "Beautiful day on the island. Hate to leave."

Ryan stood to greet him. "Did you find what you were interested in?"

"Got a feel, got a feel." Dr. Fisher was near retirement and was checking out possible places to settle down. "Beautiful place."

"It is. We could use someone like you as an advocate."

"We?" The man raised an eyebrow. "I didn't know you identified that closely with Teaberry Island. You're not thinking of settling here yourself, are you?"

Ryan wasn't, but his mentor's words created a vision in him. Settling down in one of the new houses on Betty and Mellie's road.

Settling down in *Mellie's* house. Cooking with her, exploring the island with her and Alfie. Waking up with her every morning.

An end to his perennial loneliness—a life full of love.

Charlie, fortunately, was a lighter-hearted person who didn't pick up on Ryan's impossible daydreams. "You could do worse. I like it here, always have. I'm seriously thinking about buying here."

"Do you want to be this far from the university and your friends there?"

Charlie waved a hand, his can-do grin lifting Ryan's spirits. "An hour's drive, then a short boat ride. Not a problem. I'm starving. What's good here?"

Their waitress, Miss Chantel, overheard and ambled to their table. "Everything's good, honey," she said. "You look like a fried oyster kind of guy."

"Or get the whole seafood platter," Ryan recommended. He knew it wasn't the purest form of Eastern Shore food, but he loved anything fried.

"We'll take two of those," Charlie said. "And a couple of beers."

She shook a finger back and forth. "Day drinking?" Then she smiled. "Kidding. Beer's perfect with the seafood platter. Coming right up."

They chatted for a few minutes. The sun warmed Ryan's face and the presence of his old friend and mentor warmed his heart.

"How's the work going? The application?"

"I'm getting it done," Ryan said. "Although I'm also keeping busy with Betty."

"How is she?" Charlie's expression sharpened, and Ryan remembered that Betty had known Charlie, that he'd been Wayne's friend and then a friend of them both. Betty had been the one to suggest him as a mentor for Ryan way back when Ryan was in high school and Charlie was a striving midlevel professor. Of course he'd take an interest in her still.

"Losing Wayne has been hard on her. She's struggling, but she'll get by."

"Good, good." Their beers arrived, and then their food, and they dug in. Steaming hot crab cakes, shrimp and deep-fried oysters from the bay, fresh and flavorful, occupied their full attention for a few minutes.

When they sat back, Charlie interlaced his fingers over his stomach and studied Ryan. "I'm glad you could meet me today. I wanted to talk to you about what I've been hearing."

Something in his voice told Ryan this wasn't going to be good news. "What is it?"

"You know Bryce Carrington?"

Ryan nodded. The man was a new hire at Charlie's university and was considered a rising star.

"He's going for the same grant you are."

Ryan put down the piece of fried rockfish he'd been about to eat. "Chances?"

"Very good." Charlie frowned. "He's going to conferences, guest speaking, meeting the right people."

All the stuff Ryan hated. It was shallow, meaningless, and besides, he knew he was bad at it. "How's he finding time for research?"

Charlie waved a french fry. "He's the new generation. More about style than substance, honestly."

"But yet you think he has a chance."

Charlie hesitated, then nodded. "Yes. A good chance."

Ryan pressed his lips together and stared out at the bay. Charlie didn't have to say that this Bryce character had a better shot than Ryan did; it was written all over his face.

"I don't need the glory of winning," Ryan said slowly, "but I really, really want to help save this island. And not just the island. The way of life, the community. In a small way, the research I'm working on can help."

"I agree with you." Charlie pushed his plate away. "I love it here, too. Just wanted you to know you have some tough competition."

Ryan blew out a sigh, and they were quiet while Miss Chantel took their plates away.

Then Ryan saw something—someone—that surprised him. Betty, walking down the street toward the market. He called out to her, and she trudged up the steps, only seeing Charlie when they both stood to greet her.

She started visibly, staring at Charlie. She looked so shaken that Ryan put a hand on her shoulder, steadying her. Seeing Charlie must bring Wayne to mind, since the three of them had spent a lot of time together. He wished he hadn't called out to her if it was going to set her back. "You're going to work?" he asked.

She looked away from Charlie, took a breath and then held a hand flat, tilting it back and forth. "Mellie's talked me into spending an hour there. Desensitizing myself, she calls it."

"I've told you before," Charlie said. "But I'm sorry for what you're going through, losing Wayne. He was the best."

"Thank you."

"Sit down and have a coffee. Or a beer." Charlie held a chair for Betty.

She shook her head. "No, I'd better get over there before Mellie sends out a search party."

Charlie took her hand. "I'm glad for the chance to have seen you," he said, his expression sincere.

Betty pulled her hand back and didn't return the pleasantry. "I'll see you tonight," she said to Ryan. She nodded at Charlie and hurried away.

They both watched her leave, Charlie with a bemused expression on his face.

Interesting.

MELLIE HAD RESIGNED herself to encountering a lot more of Ryan than she would have liked, over at Betty's place. But now, ridiculously, she found herself walking down the sandy road to Jimmy's Junk Joint with him and Alfie.

She didn't want Ryan here. Being around him was rousing all kinds of longings in her, longings she thought she'd purged from her system when Georgie had died.

She'd always known that people liked her best when she was doing things for them, taking care of them. That was what she liked to do, anyway. She'd accepted not getting a whole lot of love aside from that, or at least she'd thought she had.

But Ryan. Ryan didn't need caretaking. He was confident in himself. He could be an actual partner.

His presence made her realize she wanted that. She shouldn't have wanted it, shouldn't need it. She had Alfie to raise, a good job and plenty of people who relied on her on the island.

Ryan, serious, scientific Ryan, made her feel strangely like a kid again. It was as if she'd been a prisoner for years without knowing it, and suddenly here was this amazing man offering her freedom.

Except he *wasn't* offering her that. He was being kind to Betty and to her son, kind to her, and that was all. To even think about more was a huge mistake when she was holding on to a terrible secret.

A better woman would manage to stay polite and distant, a friendly neighbor.

But, of course, Ryan had been her first love. That heavy set of emotions tended to stick with a woman.

She blew out a sigh and looked across the bay. Some islanders, especially the younger ones, saw freedom that way, getting off the island to the mainland. Ryan had himself. Her sisters, as well.

But for Mellie, freedom was here. Living on her beloved island, among people she cared about.

Alfie ran ahead to a marshy area where he'd once found a nest of just-hatched red-bellied cooters. Every time they walked in this direction he checked, hoping to see more of the shy little turtles.

Mellie looked over at Ryan. "Sorry you got roped into coming along on your day off," she said. "I don't know why he was so insistent that you come. Maybe he wanted you to help him identify a subspecies of plankton." She was joking, but not.

He narrowed his eyes at her, a slight twitch of his lip the only sign that he'd recognized the humor. "First of all, plankton don't have subspecies. And second, they're not visible to the naked eye."

"I was misinformed." She smiled. "Just like I was misinformed that there was a swamp creature out here," she added, waving her arm to the adjoining marsh. "I think I believed in it for the first ten years of my life."

Ryan snorted. "Someone probably invented that story because they were scared to come out here and didn't want other kids having fun without them."

"You were never afraid."

"Of the marshland? No." He looked around, his eyes thoughtful. "I'm not sure why this place felt like such a refuge. It was completely different from Philadelphia where I grew up. But the smells and the sounds, all the water…it was like it took up all my attention, so I didn't think about the bad stuff when I was out here."

She studied him thoughtfully. He never talked much about his childhood before coming to the island. Everything she knew came from gossip and his foster father, and that was pretty horrific.

His face was peaceful now, and she didn't want to bring the ugliness of his life into the marshland he loved.

He looked over at her, put a hand on her shoulder and squeezed. The touch was light, minimal, and she felt it all the way up her arm and into her chest, her heart. "Thanks for being the person who never asked about my past," he said. "And I don't mind coming out here for Alfie's sake. I have the feeling that there's something else going on with him. I'm just not sure what."

Of course he was here for Alfie's sake. The thought deflated her. As did the fact that he'd basically told her he didn't want to talk about his childhood with her.

She walked quietly, no longer trying to make conversation, until they got to the Junk Joint. Jimmy, the owner, didn't respond when Mellie called his name from the door. "He's probably around back," she said.

They walked around the building to where a ragged canvas roof on metal poles housed the larger-size junk: a couple of rusted-out motorcycles, a refrigerator, a dishwasher and a bunch of tires. A truck was parked on one side, half-dismantled, hood up, missing a door and a passenger seat.

Alfie liked the natural world best, but still, a place like this was a playground to a ten-year-old boy. He kept his hands to himself but wandered over to peer at the motorcycles and then squatted to look at the inner workings of the dishwasher.

"Hey, yoo-hoo, Jimmy," Mellie called again.

Jimmy emerged from behind the rusted truck, wiping his hands on an oily rag. He was a forty-something guy she'd known all her life, who'd always lived out here away from others. At one point, he'd left the island and come back with a young boy, his son, who was now a couple of years older than Alfie and who seemed to keep mostly to himself, just like his father.

Jimmy nodded at Ryan and lifted an eyebrow at Mellie. "What's up, hon?" His eyes flicked her up and down, but not rudely.

She introduced Ryan, and was impressed when

he reached out a hand to shake the other man's still-dirty one. Jimmy waved it away.

"Don't get dirty," he said. "I remember you. Spent some time out here when you were younger, didn't you?"

"I did. Your father put me up during a storm once."

"Sure, and Betty and Wayne went near out of their minds with worry. Bet you got a whaling when you got home."

Ryan tilted his head to one side. "I was punished."

Mellie got the sudden insight that Ryan didn't want to even joke about his foster parents beating him. Had he been beaten in earlier years, as Wayne had said?

"And now you're some big scientist."

"I'm Betty's foster son and I'm here to see that she gets the best price for her things." He was asserting his intention to be sure Betty didn't get ripped off, but he didn't need to do that. He was unused to island living these days. Jimmy, rough around the edges as he was, wouldn't do anything to hurt a neighbor.

She'd better clarify their purpose, frame it in nicer terms. "Listen, Jimmy, we're cleaning out Betty's house some. We're going to have a lot of stuff to get rid of. Want to take a look before we ship it off?"

"Always. One man's, or woman's, trash is income for me."

"Oh, the trash is mostly Wayne's. I brought a list of the big stuff."

"Come on in," Jimmy said.

So they traipsed inside and wove their way through Jimmy's small, low-ceilinged shop, where the shelves overflowed with, well, *junk*. On an island, where it was hard to get things, not much was thrown away; instead, it ended up here, where others could find something they needed.

She was surprised to see that Ryan looked uncomfortable, a fine sheen of sweat on his forehead.

"Are you okay?" she asked him.

He nodded. "Not much for closed-in places," he said. "I'll stay by the door. Get some air."

That brought back a memory of the time that Ryan's brothers had built a clubhouse in the marsh. They'd talked her into going in, but she hadn't liked the dark, shut-in feeling of the place and she'd known her father would yell at her if he knew she'd gone in.

What her father didn't know was that Ryan stood outside, waiting, and had walked her home as soon as she'd said she wanted to leave.

He'd ignored his brothers' teasing him that he was afraid of the dark. But maybe it hadn't been the dark he was afraid of; maybe it had been the small, airless enclosure.

Jimmy sat down behind the counter and started reading through the items on her list. "Desk, dresser, those'll go fast. Toasters…really, Betty has three of them? I'll take 'em, but I have a surplus right now, can't give you much for them." He continued in this vein through the whole list.

Alfie wandered the aisles, fingering old clocks and toy trucks, looking at books with yellowed pages.

Jimmy's son, whom everyone called Junior, emerged from the back of the shop, gave the adults a quick glance and then headed toward Alfie, who stiffened. Mellie pretended to keep paying attention to Jimmy's musings, but from the corner of her eye, she watched the boys' interaction.

"How come you're at the middle school when you're just a kid?" Junior asked.

Alfie picked up a truck, not looking at the other boy. "Teachers wanted me to go up a couple of grades."

"'Cause you're a genius?"

Alfie shook his head quickly, still not looking at Junior.

"What's a million times a million?"

Ryan glanced over at the two boys and, as Alfie opened his mouth to answer, shook his head slightly. Alfie pressed his lips together and went back to examining the toy truck.

"How many countries are in the world? What's a...a quadratic equation?"

Mellie was pretty sure Alfie knew the answers to those questions, too. He looked from her to Ryan, almost pleadingly. He wanted to answer.

But again, Ryan shook his head.

"Aw, you're not a genius," Junior said, sounding disgusted.

Alfie walked over an aisle and knelt down to study something, clearly withdrawing from the other boy.

Jimmy looked up. "Shut up, son, he just don't want to talk to you," he said. "Ain't nothing wrong with a genius. We could use some of them to fix our island. And our country, too." He looked at Ryan. "You going to do that?"

"I can't fix the country," Ryan said, "but I'm trying my best to figure out how to fix the island, or at least to help it. I love it here."

Mellie's heart filled with pride. If anyone could do it, Ryan could.

She glanced over at the boys and was relieved to see that Junior was showing something to Alfie. Maybe they'd start to get along.

Jimmy nodded. "Good. You keep working on that and leave the junk job to me and Mellie here." He looked at her. "I can drive my truck over and haul things whenever you're ready."

"That would be great. Thanks, Jimmy. I'll put everything you checked off in one place so it'll be easy to get to." The rest, she'd package up for the dump off-island.

As they headed down the road, Alfie ran ahead. He didn't seem upset by his encounter with Junior, which Mellie counted as a win.

"That went pretty well," she said to Ryan.

"It did." He hesitated, then added, "Still, I don't think you should go there alone."

"What do you mean, to Jimmy's? Why?"

"Just... Look, I know guys. Just don't."

She squinted at him. "You know guys?" What did that mean? And then it dawned on her, what he was saying. "You think that *Jimmy* is going to hit on me?"

"If he gets the chance, yes."

"It's *Jimmy*," she said. "I've known him all my life."

"And you don't know your own appeal." He held her gaze with his own.

Her heart rate sped up. Was he saying *he* did know her appeal? Was she appealing to him?

The way he was looking at her suggested that maybe, just maybe, she was.

And her heart flipped way too hard at the thought. This was Ryan. He was forbidden to her. She was keeping a terrible secret from him.

She tore her gaze away from his, waved a hand to dismiss his concern and sped up to catch Alfie.

Somehow, she was going to have to make her heart settle down and behave.

CHAPTER EIGHT

ON THURSDAY AFTERNOON, Betty handed a crab salad on rye to a tourist and sneaked a glance at her watch.

This was exhausting. She'd agreed to come work at the store for a whole afternoon just to get everyone—Mellie, Ryan, Ryan's brothers—off her back, but it felt like a mistake.

Either she wasn't ready to come back, or she would *never* be ready and should sell the market and retire.

That was what Ryan's brothers thought. They'd pooh-poohed her money concerns, saying they would help with any shortfalls. Which was an offer she had no intention of accepting; she didn't take charity. Help was supposed to flow downhill, from parents to kids, not the reverse. That was true of foster parents and kids, just like natural ones.

Anyway, she could probably manage on Social Security and her savings and Wayne's insurance payout. Yes, that was what she should do: retire.

Then she wouldn't need to agree, as she had done in a conversation with Ryan yesterday, to pay Mellie for extra help cleaning out the farmhouse. She could do it herself.

But will you?

"It's so great to have you back," Mellie said, leaning on the deli counter and smiling at her. "This place has been lonely without you."

She couldn't truthfully say it was good to be back, but she smiled at Mellie. "I've really laid a lot on you, haven't I? You've been a wonderful, wonderful help during this time."

"Aw, Betty, you know I'm glad to do it. It's just that I don't want to make your business decisions for you, and I'm bad at doing the books."

Betty didn't particularly like doing the books, either; that was something she'd left to Wayne, one of the few areas he'd helped with in the shop, because he knew how much she disliked working with computers and numbers.

If she sold the shop, she wouldn't have to worry about that.

Wayne had wanted her to sell the place, too, once she'd turned sixty. He'd said it was too much for her. They'd even talked about traveling after retirement, although that had been a long time ago. She'd always hoped, in the back of her mind, that they'd get closer again and maybe take a trip or two.

But now, that wouldn't happen. Tears prickled the backs of her eyes and her throat tightened. *You always thought you had forever to fulfill your dreams. Turned out that wasn't so.*

The bells on the market's door jingled, and Betty looked up through blurry eyes to see Peg marching in.

Betty bent down like she was getting something from the cupboard below the deli case, swallowed hard and wiped her leaky eyes. No way was she crying in front of Peg. The woman would take it as confirmation that Betty needed more interfering help from her and would never leave her alone.

"You back there, Betty Raines?" Peg was peering through the glass at her.

She stood, her irritation chasing the last of her sadness away. "Yes, I'm back here. Working. What are *you* doing with your life?"

Peg's mouth twisted to one side. "Ruthie needed some air."

Peg's daughter, Ruthie, was a sweet girl. Not a girl, really; she was nearly, what, forty now? How time flew by. Ruthie didn't speak but a few words, and she stayed home with Peg most of the time, helping with housework and some simple cooking, watching her videos. But occasionally, Ruthie got frustrated and emotional, and nothing would do but to get her out of the house. Today must be one of those days.

Compassion for Peg pushed away the last of Betty's annoyance. "Sit and have a cup of coffee," she said. "Ruthie can help me back here."

"Mellie's already got her breaking down boxes." Peg ran her fingers through her short-cropped hair. "I'm just going to pick up a few things while I'm here. Like some of that crab salad."

Betty scooped her a container of it while Peg surveyed the rest of the meats and salads in the case.

"You all need to modernize," Peg said. "Get some of that quinoa salad, maybe some kale. Cute stuff the tourists like. And new flavors of ice cream."

"Tourists like teaberry," Betty said, handing her the crab salad. "You and Ruthie want a scoop?"

"No, thanks. I promised her we'd stop at the new ice cream truck after this."

"Traitor." Betty walked out from behind the counter and looked out the front window. Sure enough, there was the new ice cream truck. And here Betty had three freezer containers of teaberry near their expiration date.

"You need to bring things up-to-date if you want to keep the market strong," Peg said. Peg had always wanted Betty to keep the market, rather than retiring. In that, like in so many things, she'd been opposed to Wayne. She'd never liked him a whole lot. No real reason, just different personalities and, if the truth be told, some competition over Betty's attention and time.

The feeling had been mutual, and now, Betty thought back on all her arguments with Wayne over Peg. Why had they wasted time on that? What had it all come to?

Peg and Ruthie left, and a few tourists came in. When they'd finished shopping, Betty went to the cash register to check them out. But she made a mistake with giving change, and the customer in question spoke sharply to her like Betty was trying to cheat her on purpose. Betty felt her chin quivering.

After they left and the store was empty but for her

and Mellie, Mellie put an arm around her. "How's this first day back going for you? You okay?"

"Fine, but I might be close to my limit." She looked up at the old clock and realized she'd only been here for two hours. This was more exhausting than she'd remembered. Maybe she *should* sell the store and retire.

"It's hard, it's your first day." Mellie gave her shoulders another squeeze and then stepped over to the candy rack, straightening a few crooked items. "If you want to talk about anything, you know I'm here for you."

"Thank you, honey, I know that." She probably should talk to Mellie. She'd told Ryan she would, and it was better than talking things through with Peg, or some counselor. But she didn't want to, so she grabbed the push broom and started sweeping. Amazing how much of a mess the store got to be within a few hours. "How's Alfie doing with the new school?"

Mellie shook her head. "I think it might be getting better, a little, but he still doesn't like it much. Maybe I was wrong, keeping him on the island for his whole childhood. Maybe I should have been getting him out doing things and meeting people on the mainland when he was younger."

"That's a tough call." Betty frowned, leaning on her broom, remembering. "Some of the boys we fostered benefitted from being out in the wider world. Some seemed to need the incubator of the island to get up to speed and launch out into adult life."

"Which was Ryan?" Mellie asked, and her cheeks flushed pink. "And Cody and Luis?"

Betty watched her, musing. She *hadn't* meant Cody and Luis; she wanted to know about Ryan. Mellie and Ryan, huh…they'd be good together, maybe. "Ryan had such a terrible childhood. He was exposed to things he should never have seen, did things he should never have done."

Mellie nodded. "I got that impression, though I never knew the details."

The details weren't Betty's to tell. "He was isolated, abused… If anyone needed the space to heal, it was him. He had to go to school off-island, but other than that, he stuck close to home. Seemed to need it, after what he'd been through."

Mellie looked like she wanted to talk more, but Hector Lozano came in. "Ladies! I heard the rumor that Miss Betty was here and I had to see it for myself. Welcome back! It's about time you gave this sweet young thing a break!"

"Coffee and a pastry, Hector?" Mellie asked, shooting Betty a wry look.

"*Con leche*, sweetheart. Betty, you look gorgeous as usual! What are you trying to do, drive all the men on the island crazy?" He smiled and gave her a long, soulful gaze.

Hector had never spoken to Betty like that before, never acted like that. Was he actually flirting with her? Hector? She cringed, feeling vulnerable and exposed, and realized that now, without the safety of Wayne protecting her, any man could feel entitled to hit on her. And she'd thought her age would prevent it, but apparently not with the older crowd. Ugh.

Fortunately, Ezra and Deacon Wells came in. No way would the lifelong bachelor brothers think of approaching a woman, and they tended to have a daunting effect on others. Both taught at the elementary school and were known as the toughest teachers there; both were older than Betty but seemed to have no intention of retiring anytime soon.

Hmm. Maybe she should talk to them about why they kept working, get some advice.

The market door's bells jingled again, and this time, an older woman Betty hadn't met appeared. She walked around slowly, almost like she was casing the joint.

Betty fake-swept as she moved from aisle to aisle, keeping an eye on her. They'd never had much shoplifting here, but there was a first time for everything.

"Where's your ice cream?" the woman asked, her voice abrupt.

"Right over here," Betty said, since Mellie was still talking to Hector. "Have you tried teaberry?"

"Why aren't you eating your own ice cream?" Ezra Wells asked the woman. "The chocolate is the best I've had."

"Better than teaberry?" Betty asked indignantly.

"Everyone's sick of teaberry," the woman said, and then it dawned on Betty. This old woman was Goody from Pleasant Shores. That was who'd brought that gaudy ice cream truck to the island.

The nerve! Of course, Betty had been to Goody's

ice cream shop a few times over the years, during visits to Pleasant Shores. Goody, who'd been the proprietor for years now, had never been a friendly person. Apparently, she'd retired and come here to compete for Betty's business.

Come to think of it, Goody was her own age. Did Betty look that old? "You're trying to put me out of business," she said, propping a hand on her hip and glaring.

The woman shrugged. "If you can't take the competition..." She turned without buying anything and walked out of the market.

She really had just come to look around and stir up trouble.

Betty frowned. She was tired and didn't want to come back to work. Didn't want to face people and deal with their questions, let alone something ridiculous like Hector's flirting.

But she also didn't want to lay this whole burden on Mellie. And she definitely didn't want to lose business to that unpleasant Goody.

So, for now, she guessed she'd have to come back to work, for real.

THE SATURDAY AFTER Betty returned to work full-time, Mellie was thrilled to get a day off to spend doing home chores and being with Alfie. Truthfully, she was also thrilled because he was having a friend over, meaning that he'd be a little out of her hair.

She'd spent her day off last week cleaning out one of the spare bedrooms of Betty's farmhouse, getting rid of old magazines and knickknacks, washing down the walls and windows. With the clutter gone, the painted shiplap walls and wood plank floor presented a farmhouse style that people tried to emulate in cities and suburbs these days. She'd dusted off the iron bed frame and located a cream-colored comforter, and she'd washed and rehung the white curtains. The room looked great, ready for guests. Ready to be a guesthouse, really, if Betty would ever choose to go in that direction.

She'd enjoyed the cleaning, just as she was enjoying the yardwork today. It gave her time to think.

It was officially fall now, but as hot as ever on the island. The sun beat down, making the bay sparkle beyond the browning yard. Even the dogs were quiet, two of them, Gizmo and Spotty, sleeping on their sides under a tree.

Mellie put on her gardening gloves and started pulling out the last of the marigolds. They'd held up well through late summer and fall, but were beginning to look scraggly. She stacked the uprooted plants by the corner of the house. Later, she'd pull seeds for next year from the deadheads.

Alfie ran with his friend Junior and the dogs, looking carefree. She was trying not to look next door, but she'd seen Ryan carrying things out of Betty's place and knew he was on his cleaning and decluttering mission. Good. Betty was working, and she was sure Ryan thought he could get a lot more done now.

Should she be over there helping him? But he'd

said he was fine, and Betty had urged her to take an actual day at home, so she tried not to feel guilty about it. Tried, too, not to admire Ryan's muscles. He was lanky but strong, and in his T-shirt and jeans, he looked more like a hot local construction worker than a brilliant scientist.

And she didn't need to be thinking about that. She refocused on her task, pulling the dried-up plants and the weeds, leaving the still-thriving coleus and goldenrods in place.

She *needed* to think through whether to tell Ryan the truth about Alfie.

As she'd spent more time with Ryan, she'd been trying to figure out whether what Wayne had told her was true. *Was* Alfie at risk if the truth were revealed? Obviously, Alfie had to be her priority.

But she had seen no evidence of Ryan being violent or destructive. She'd never heard his voice raised in anger. It was hard to even imagine him yelling, let alone striking out physically.

Meanwhile, whenever Alfie was around Ryan, he lit up. He clearly felt a kinship to Ryan, something that had to do with their shared intellects even though neither knew they were related.

Could she ethically deprive Alfie of having that benefit as an ongoing part of his life?

And yet, if Ryan did carry some secret darkness inside of him, she couldn't expose Alfie to that full-time. Couldn't risk leaving them alone together, and definitely couldn't trust Ryan to help raise Alfie.

Ryan brushed his forearm across his forehead and

waved to the boys, who were playing down at the bay. Alfie immediately ran over, leaving the other boy behind, and started talking a mile a minute to Ryan. He was clearly crazy about the man.

And it was breaking Mellie's heart.

If she'd made a mistake, she needed to set it right, and soon, before they got closer and more vulnerable to being hurt by the revelation.

Her brain cycled, back and forth, back and forth. She got a ladder and laid it against the apple tree. She'd pick some apples, make a pie. Baking always calmed her.

She'd just filled a bucket with apples when she heard a crash, followed immediately by a shout from Ryan.

An angry shout.

She descended the ladder as fast as a firefighter, dropped her bucket of apples and ran over.

The stack of junk that Ryan had brought from the house had toppled over, and the guilty-looking boys stood staring at it all.

An old feather pillow had broken open, and feathers flew in the wind. A jar of marbles—no doubt the inciting incident for the boys—had broken, making a double hazard of broken glass and rolling marbles underfoot. A stack of old *National Geographics* had fallen over, pages fluttering in the wind.

Ryan's nostrils flared and his legs were planted wide as he glared at the boys. "What did you do?"

The very thing she'd feared: Ryan's rage. She reached the boys and stepped in front of them, noticing for the first time how *big* Ryan was. She put one arm around Alfie and the other around Junior. "What happened?"

Although looking at the mess made it all too obvious. Was that...oh, it was. A can of paint, on its side, making a river of paint down toward the bay.

Ryan took a deep breath and let it out, and she could see the anger dissipating. "Boys, I asked you to stay away from these things. You could have been hurt."

"I'm sorry," Alfie said miserably.

"It was my idea," Junior said, to her surprise.

Ryan glanced at her. "Since the two of you thought you were old enough to deal with this, I guess you're old enough to clean it up. Wait here." He headed into the shed.

What was he getting in there? Mellie trailed after. She was *pretty* sure he wasn't going to hit or beat them, but after all, Wayne had warned her that he might be violent...

She stood beside the boys, ready to protect them if needed. When Ryan emerged, he looked surprised to see her.

He'd brought out heavy work gloves and big cloth sacks, plus a bucket and sponge, no doubt to clean up the paint.

Mellie sagged with relief. Ryan wasn't going to hurt Alfie or Junior.

She looked at Ryan, whose jaw had clenched as he studied her.

She was pretty sure he was reading her mind.

She'd thought he was going to hurt the boys.

One look at Mellie's concerned face, and he knew why she'd followed. Even, when he forced himself to be logical, understood it.

An angry adult man, two young boys who'd done mischief...it wasn't surprising she'd be concerned.

He lifted his two hands like stop signs, showing her that he wasn't holding a weapon, a stick or a club. "Is it okay with you if they clean up the mess they made?" he asked. He was proud of how steady his voice remained.

Overhead, an eagle soared and landed in the top of a twisted oak tree. He watched its flight, its freedom, its solitude.

From there, he let his eyes descend, testing himself. The Virginia creeper twining up the oak's trunk, leaves just starting to turn red: *Parthenocissus quinquefolia.*

The cordgrass that covered the ground, in clumps: *spartina*, but was it *spartina alterniflora* or *spartina patens*? The energetic chickadee—*poecile carolinensis*—landing on a bush beside them.

As always, the thinking and classifying and naming settled him. He took another deep breath and met her eyes, pushed the corners of his mouth up into a smile.

"Yes! Of course! They should clean up!" She knelt in front of Alfie. "But first, you need to apologize to Mr. Ryan for undoing all his hard work."

Alfie looked miserable. "I'm sorry," he said.

"Me, too," Junior, the other boy, chimed in. "We'll clean it up."

Compassion twisted Ryan's heart. He steeled himself against it. Boys needed to be tough; hadn't he been forced to learn that lesson, over and over? "I expect it to be neater than it was when you first saw it," he said, frowning and glaring. Might as well lay it on thick.

The boys' eyes widened and they both nodded, then ran over toward the mess.

Once the boys were out of earshot, he turned to face Mellie. "I wasn't going to hurt them," he said. "I would never hurt a child."

He'd made sure of that years ago by deciding he'd never have children. He'd heeded the advice given by his foster father. Knowing his own weakness was key.

"I...I didn't think you'd hurt them." There was doubt in her voice.

"Really?"

She shrugged. "I mean...I never knew you to hurt anyone, unless you were protecting someone else," she said. "But..."

"But what?" He noted the pink of her cheeks, the concern in her eyes.

It was quiet, quiet enough that he could hear the sound of water lapping against the stones at the bay's edge and the lonely caw of a gull.

She shrugged. "It's just...the way you grew up. I know it wasn't great."

He frowned. "You knew me."

"Not when you were younger. Alfie's age." She looked curious, more so than he'd have expected once she'd ascertained her child was safe. "I guess your parents were hard on you."

"At that age, it was my mom and stepfather." He tried to make light of it. "Let's just say I wouldn't have dared to do something like what Alfie just did." There. That sounded like he'd just come from an extremely strict family rather than the ugly reality.

"Or else what?"

Did she want details? Why?

He suddenly remembered a ripped velvet couch, a tile floor, a lamp toppling. He couldn't have been more than three.

What had happened next... He swallowed and looked away, letting his eyes settle on the bay. Its blue-gray waters, the mysteries beneath. Mysteries that could be unlocked and understood, unlike the mysteries of the human mind.

"What happened?" she asked gently.

Her touch on his arm made him flinch. He'd flinched when his mother had finally come to rescue him from the dark closet in which he'd been confined, bruised and beaten.

It had been the first of many such beatings, many such confinements. He tried not to think about them. Why had Mellie pushed him in that direction?

Oh, right. Because she'd thought he might hurt her son.

"Ryan? Do you want to talk about it?"

"Not. Your. Business." Hearing the sharpness in

his tone, and seeing her hurt expression, he added, "It's not important." Because what was important about a clumsy little kid who kept making mistakes until his own mother had abandoned him?

She looked confused, concerned. "But if—"

"Leave it alone," he interrupted. "It's past history. I'd better go keep an eye on them."

"I'll tag along," she said, her voice cool as she fell into step beside him.

But an arm's length away.

And who could blame her? Even the memories of those days evoked so much pain and hopelessness that he couldn't seem to see anything else.

Couldn't see anyone so good and kind and *normal* as Mellie. Which was why he couldn't get involved with her, or anyone.

CHAPTER NINE

THAT EVENING, AS the sun sank into the bay, Ryan walked across the yards to Mellie's. In his hand was a bottle of wine.

Is this a good idea?

Maybe it was. Maybe it wasn't.

He'd seen her standing outside on her deck, looking west, her shoulders a little slumped, her hair blowing back in the breeze. She'd looked lonely. He felt doubly bad seeing that, because he'd been a jerk to her today.

So he'd gotten her number from Betty and texted. This is Ryan. Can I come over?

The answer back had been noncommittal. Okay.

At least she hadn't said no. He'd not only been rude, he'd scared her today, and he wanted to make up for it, to explain.

It put a burning feeling in his gut just thinking about it. This was why he tended to keep people at arm's length. He didn't want to hurt or scare them, and he didn't want to feel the guilt and pain and disappointment in himself that was the inevitable result.

But with Mellie…it was just hard to stay detached.

Doubly hard with her son, who reminded Ryan of himself.

But true to form, when he'd let them get close, he'd screwed up. Hence this visit tonight.

His goal was to clarify to her that while he was unable to be close, he was aware of his deficiencies and wouldn't hurt Alfie or her. He'd remain a distant friend.

And taking over a bottle of wine will help you keep your distance?

Right. Maybe he was fooling himself. But maybe the wine would make his little speech easier, both to say and to hear.

When he climbed the steps to her back deck, she turned to him. The gold of the sunset lit up her hair like fire. Her eyes were huge, like always, and so pretty. Involuntarily, he stopped at the top of the steps and just looked at her.

Until she looked at his hands and her eyebrow lifted. "Wine?"

Her questioning tone brought him out of his trance. "We don't have to drink it. I, uh, I thought—"

"I'm not objecting. I'll get glasses." She went inside, called something up the stairs and then came back out with two squat wineglasses and a corkscrew.

He opened the wine, poured it. "Where's Alfie?"

"He's in his room reading. He has to be in his room by seven thirty on school nights, but he's allowed to stay up and read until nine."

"Smart mom."

She half smiled. Good, she was softening. "Saves my sanity as a single mom. You might have noticed, he has a constant string of questions. I need time to chill, and he needs to read, get some of those answers for himself." She raised an eyebrow. "It's a strategy I learned from Betty. She used it on boys like you."

"Yes, she did." To him, it had been wonderful, miraculous almost, to have a quiet room in which to read. But it had also been a blessing to gain some real brothers. Luis and Cody and he had fought for a couple of weeks and then bonded, tightly, against the world. And it had been shocking, happily so, that Betty had the patience to listen to his questions and answer them. Once he'd ascertained that she was sincere and wouldn't hurt him, he'd bugged her, and later, once he'd come to trust him, Wayne, asking them everything he wondered about the natural world.

Around them, the sound of crickets rose and fell in waves. The sun was down now, but pink streaks remained in the sky.

They sat in two white rocking chairs, looking out at the bay, sipping wine. It could have been a romantic scene, but that wasn't his mission. "Today, I was short with you," he said. "I'm sorry. I came over to explain."

"You don't have to," she murmured, looking at him over her wineglass. "You're allowed to get cranky, like anyone else."

He got a little tangled in her eyes and then forced himself to look away. He blew out a breath and tried to recall his planned speech. "I tend to keep my distance with people for good reasons. But I want you to know you don't have to worry about me with Alfie."

She studied him. "I don't think of you as someone who keeps his distance, particularly. I mean, you didn't used to. When we were younger."

Her words brought back that last disastrous time he'd gotten close to her. "I know. And look, Mellie, I'm sorry—"

She held up a hand, stopping his words. "I didn't mean you should apologize. I just mean you didn't seem to have any trouble getting close. Although maybe that was just teenage hormones?"

He couldn't let that idea hang in the air. "It was that, sure, but it was more. I felt for you, Mellie. I felt for you a lot. I just…" He shook his head, tried to put it into words. "I was too young to understand. That there'd be ramifications from the way I grew up. What it would mean when I tried to have close friends, relationships…" He spread his hands. "I've realized I'm just not cut out for it."

She leaned forward, her brow wrinkling, and put a soft hand on his arm. "That's not true. You've been hurt, maybe, but I've seen how close you are with your brothers, and with Betty."

He tried to focus on her words and not her touch. "Luis and Cody get it. They're the same way."

"And Betty?" she probed.

He lifted his hands, palms up. "Betty…who can explain her? She's incredible. Was incredible to a whole bunch of boys, saved us."

"She *is* incredible." Mellie pulled her hand back and rocked, gently.

He could almost hear the question in her voice: *You brought wine over to tell me this?*

"Anyway," he stumbled on, "I know you were worried today, when I yelled at the boys. And I did get mad. But look, I know the hard limits with a child, and I would never hurt one."

"Like you were hurt." She said it matter-of-factly.

"Like I was hurt." He nodded.

They both looked out at the bay a minute, rocking. "Do you ever talk about it?" she asked finally.

He shook his head. "Not much."

"Ryan." Her tone made him look at her. "I'm your friend, or I hope I am. And I would really like to know, if you'll tell me. What happened to put you into foster care and land you on Teaberry Island?"

The direct question surprised him, especially since she'd known him throughout his teen years and never asked. "I... Look, the details aren't important. My dad didn't stick around, and my mom got together with the wrong man, that's all."

"An abusive one." It wasn't a question.

"Yes." Unbidden, an image of Cueball arose in his mind. Cueball, who was huge, an ex-con, who commanded fear on the street. Fear in Ryan's heart, too, from the moment he'd seen him.

"What happened?" she asked quietly.

Maybe it was because her tone was so gentle and nonjudgmental. There was none of the avid curiosity that sometimes arose when people learned he'd grown up rough. Mellie was asking because she cared.

So maybe he'd tell her, at least a little. He couldn't get close, but he could let her see a small corner of himself.

"You don't have to if it's too painful."

He looked at her briefly and then stared out at the bay. Easier than looking right at her.

He rarely thought about those days, never talked about them, and the words came out slowly, brokenly. "Cueball got angry at the least little thing. Noise when he wanted quiet. A mess when he wanted neat. Questions when he wanted peace. And he didn't have a logical way to get what he wanted, so…"

She looked at him, waiting, not saying anything. There was compassion in her eyes.

"As you might guess, I was continually making him angry and paying the price. But the last time…" He paused. Could he really talk about this?

He glanced over at her. There was no dread or disdain on her face, only kind encouragement. "One day, I decided to surprise my mom by making some biscuits. We didn't have much food in the house, but we had flour and lard."

Or so he'd thought.

"I was scooping out the flour when Cueball came in and started yelling. I jerked, and a bunch of white powder flew around the kitchen." He could still re-member the puffs of it, and Cueball's red, furious face. "Apparently, that wasn't flour. He'd just gotten in a big shipment of cocaine and he hadn't divided it up yet. He'd hidden it in the flour canister."

She sucked in a breath, audibly. "If there was enough for you to think it was flour…"

"Right. It represented a lot of money. He freaked out."

Just saying the words made his stomach go sour. Not so much because of the pain he'd experienced, but because of what had come next.

"I'd like to know what happened," she said, "but only if you want to tell me."

He shook his head, his own mind swiping through the details, quickly, never pausing to contemplate any of it too closely. "Thanks. It's…not fit for you to hear. The worst was when I heard my mother's car in the driveway. By then Cueball had stopped beating on me and was trying to gather up the cocaine. I crawled out to warn her not to come in, to drive away. But of course, when she saw me…" He swallowed. Looked over, not at her, but in her direction.

She leaned forward into his line of sight. "She loved you, like any mother loves a child."

He nodded slowly. "In her own way, I guess she did. But…apparently, she'd gotten a ride home with another guy. She left him in the car and came to try to get me, and Cueball came out and dragged us both inside." The man had been so big and strong that he'd just grabbed Ryan's arm with one hand and his mother's with the other, kicked open the door and hauled them both inside. He rubbed his shoulder reflexively, remembering how much it had hurt.

"Anyway, she was screaming, and the other guy came in, and they were all fighting. I went for the phone to call the police and Cueball threw me into the basement and locked me there."

Counseling had taught him that the whole situation hadn't been his fault, but he still got a sick feeling in his stomach just talking about it.

He remembered intense pain and a vague awareness that fighting was going on upstairs. And then silence, and darkness, and aloneness.

A day later, tipped off by a neighbor who'd heard him calling, the police had come and found him, along with the drug evidence Cueball had had to leave behind.

He'd gotten taken away in an ambulance, with a broken arm and various sprains and bruises.

Mellie was looking at him expectantly and he realized he needed to make a long story short. He couldn't remain in this mental space very long. "I survived, with some injuries, but I never saw my mother again." That, really, was the worst part: that she'd never come back for him, never sought him out. That he didn't know whether that was on purpose, or whether Cueball—or some other guy—had prevented it. He wouldn't be surprised if she'd ended up dead at some man's hands. He'd tried to find her, later, as an adult, but without success.

He shook his head rapidly and blew out a sigh. "And that's how I got into foster care. I bounced around some—I was pretty angry—but eventually I was lucky enough to land here."

"Oh, Ryan." Her voice broke a little, and when he looked at her, those big eyes were swimming with tears.

"Don't." He softened the sharp word with some kind of smile. "I didn't tell you to make you feel sorry for me. It's just so you can understand why I'm the way I am. Maybe why I ran away, before, after we started getting close. But I'd never hurt a child. My memories are too vivid."

She looked troubled. "Did you get counseling?"

He nodded. "A lot of it, both before and after I came here. It helped."

She wiped her eyes. "I can't imagine a child going through that."

"It had an impact. I'm not whole."

She got out of her chair and came over to him, and the next thing he knew, she was hugging him. "I'm so sorry, Ryan."

Of course she was, because Mellie was a kind and giving person. But reliving his own memories reminded him: getting close would be a big mistake.

"I appreciate that. But…" He shook his head. Gently, he disentangled her arms from around his neck, allowing himself just one quick inhale of the light, flowery perfume she wore. "Drink your wine," he said gruffly. "Like I said, I wasn't asking for sympathy." And he needed to stop those warm eyes from looking at him that way. "You had a rough childhood yourself, with plenty of losses."

"Nothing like what you went through."

"Everyone's different." He reached out for her

now, took her hand. "Mine was bad, but then it was over. Yours was ongoing. After your mom left, you were basically in charge, right?"

"Well, I mean, Dad was in charge," she said. "I took care of the house and my sisters. Not so bad."

He wanted to ask more questions, but she held up a hand. "Hang on," she said. "You told me a lot, and I don't want to talk about me right now. I just want to say…you're pretty amazing."

He lifted an eyebrow. "That's not the interpretation I'd put on what I told you." The truth was, despite all his therapy, he was ashamed of what he'd been, what his family had been, what his mother and Cueball had thought of him.

"You went through all that, and yet you were strong and you survived. Not only that, but you made something of yourself. Made a lot of yourself." She looked him up and down and nodded. "I'm impressed with you."

"Aw, shucks," he said, waving a hand. Because he had to say something, and a joke seemed more comfortable than the other complicated emotions he was feeling.

Mellie didn't despise him or even pity him. She thought he was strong for surviving his rough childhood. And because he cared what she thought, it sank in, a little bit. He felt a little…lift, or something. He guessed he *had* done pretty well, given what he'd come from.

They both reached for the bottle of wine at the same time, and their hands brushed together. The feeling of that shot through Ryan, making him want to hold on.

He grasped the bottle instead and saw that it was nearly empty. When had they refilled their glasses? "Just a little left," he said, and divided what remained into their nearly empty glasses.

She held hers up and clinked it against his. "Here's to happier days ahead."

"Amen." They both finished off their wine. "And I should go," he said, standing.

She stood, too.

He looked down at her. And all of a sudden, he was a high school kid again, close up with the neighbor girl he'd been crushing on for two years. Just like back then, he reached out to touch her hair. Just like then, it was soft and shiny.

She was looking up at him. Her big eyes somehow got even bigger. Her lips fuller, softer. She seemed to sway toward him, and he froze to stop himself from pulling her close.

She took a step back. "I should go in. Thanks for the wine." He could hear her trying for a steady tone, but there was a little quaver at the end. She walked to the house and went inside quickly, more quickly than good manners would recommend.

And he was left staring after her, his heart pounding.

He'd failed at his goal of explaining his intention to keep his distance. Instead, he'd spilled his guts, and in showing her a part of who he really was, a part most people didn't see, he'd gotten closer to her.

At least, that was how he felt. Did she?

THE DAY AFTER sharing wine with Ryan, Mellie skipped church, something she almost never did. But she was freaked out about the conversation they'd had.

Ryan had faced ongoing abuse, confinement and, basically, abandonment by his mother. Did that mean, as Wayne had said, that he could never be close to people without hurting them, a child especially?

A little tipsy internet research last night hadn't helped. The cycle of abuse was powerful, hard to break.

She'd resigned herself to that; it was no more than Wayne had said.

But she'd felt so close to him. He'd trusted her with his story, which she knew he didn't share with most people. When he'd touched her hand, she'd felt that physical spark that had always been strong between them.

She'd wanted him to kiss her.

The exact opposite of what should happen, given what he'd said, given what she knew.

She needed to get the whole thing out of her mind.

Luckily, she had a way to make that happen: the community crabfest. She'd promised to help, of course. It was a fundraiser for the church, to help families on the island who were struggling, and it was an end-of-summer celebration.

She and Alfie attended, as they always did. This year, he immediately went off with Junior, Jimmy's son. Mellie took charge of the side dishes people had brought, setting out hot plates for the ones that needed to stay warm and ice baths for the ones that needed to stay cool on this warm day.

She couldn't help looking around for Ryan, but he wasn't there. What a relief, she told herself, ignoring the pang in her chest. She needed to forget about him, at least forget about these feelings she'd started to have. Despite how open he'd been with her, she couldn't share her own truth in return. Not without putting Alfie at risk.

But he wouldn't be at risk! Ryan would never hurt a child!

That was what he'd said. But Wayne, and now the internet, told a different story. The cycle of abuse. She was sick of hearing about it, but it also terrified her.

Corn on the cob was stacked high, with a Crock-Pot full of hot butter to dip it in. She helped children fill their plates and dip their corn, and gently limited them to two each of Minnie Johnson's cheddar-dill biscuits.

Which made her think about Ryan's biscuit cooking story, which knotted her stomach, but she pushed that aside.

Peg Harris had brought her famous Old Bay potatoes, and Hector Lozano his equally famed Spanish rice. The dessert table was weighed down, too, with various versions of teaberry pie and Smith Island cake.

"Mom, where's Mr. Ryan?" Alfie came to her side and leaned against her.

"He might not have come, honey."

"But we told him about it."

"I know." And his not coming could be directly related to last night. Good heavens, had she really swayed against him?

The truth was, it had been him who'd shown restraint, not her.

He told you he couldn't do relationships. You need to listen.

But with Alfie beside her, she couldn't put Ryan's sad story out of her mind. He'd been about Alfie's age when the worst had happened, and it hurt to think about it. As close as Alfie was to her, losing her would gut him. Even the idea of it made her pull him closer, and ruffle his hair, until he got annoyed and ran to the table where the men were dumping steamed crabs.

"Woolgathering?" It was the pastor, her old friend David.

She smiled at him. "Kind of. Can I serve you some potatoes or rice?"

"No, thank you. You can come sit down and relax. There are others who can take over."

"But—"

"You don't always have to help," he said. "You didn't come to church this morning, and you looked worried just now. So sit down and let's talk while we eat crabs. Look, they're starting a new table."

Indeed, Hector was unrolling brown paper over the second big picnic table and taping it on.

She followed Pastor David to the table and sat down across from him. She *did* want to talk to him.

She needed to figure out how to put things in God's hands more, to stop all the worrying.

Maybe, though she wouldn't say it to the pastor, she could get Ryan out of her head. It was good, really good, that he wasn't here.

They each took a big crab and started breaking the shells, spurning the wooden mallets. The more delicately you treated them, the more sweet, delicious crabmeat you could glean.

"Nothing better," David said, wiping his hands. "Now, tell me why you're looking worried and why you didn't come to church."

She gave him a side-eye. "You don't miss much, do you?"

"It's my job to shepherd my flock." He dipped into Hector's rice, took a bite and sighed with pleasure. "Such good cooks on this island."

"You have one of the best at home."

"I do, but I'm trying to keep her from cooking every day. She needs her rest, and I need to stay in shape."

Mellie smiled. "It won't be long, right?"

David's face lit up. "Couple of months. We're so excited, I can't tell you. But this isn't about me. What's going on with you?"

"Alfie, for one," she said. "He's struggling at his new school."

David looked over to where Alfie and Junior were headed off from the table, Alfie wiping his hands on his shorts. "I *think* it'll be good if those two become friends," he said. "Jimmy's son suffers from an excess of cool."

"And Alfie suffers from the lack of it. I know." She smiled. "I'm keeping an eye on them, but I think you may be right."

"I suspect there's something besides Alfie that's got you worried." David studied her. "Is it your new neighbor, Ryan Hastings?"

Immediately, her face went hot. She focused on extracting a piece of crabmeat from the shell, not looking at him. "Maybe. But that's just me being silly."

David chuckled. "That's about the last word I'd use to describe you, Mellie. You're colorful, and hardworking, and dedicated to your son. But silly? No."

She shrugged. "Silly of me to think of him when there's no potential there. We have a bit of history, but there's no way we could be more than distant friends."

"Is that so." He looked at her skeptically, and then his eyes traveled upward. "Speak of the devil…"

Mellie looked up at the same time she felt someone sit down beside her, just a little too close. A tingle warned her of who it was before she heard that resonant voice. "Pastor. Mellie. Mind if I join you?"

CHAPTER TEN

RYAN NEEDED TO get Mellie away from the pastor, and fast.

That was the primal thought in his mind as he sat down beside her. There was no logic to it. It was pure, possessive male instinct.

The day was bright and warm, no humidity, perfect for a picnic. He'd encouraged Betty to come, brought her down in the old truck and made sure that she was settled with her friends.

And then he'd spotted Mellie. With her red hair glowing in the sun and her bright purple sweater, it was hard to miss her.

She was having a close, seemingly intimate conversation with *David* of all people, the kid he and his brothers had loved to hate. David had been the island golden boy, thought of as a Boy Scout, always helping the elders, earning good—but not *too* good—grades. More than once, his behavior had been held up as a model for Ryan, Cody and Luis to emulate. Just a little older than the three of them, he'd been kind to them, offering to show them around the island and introduce them to people at school.

Which, coming from the environments the three

of them had come from, had spelled teacher's pet or wimp to them, and they'd let him know it, Luis with his fists. Surprisingly, David had held his own in the fight, and the three of them had settled into a grudging respect for him. He'd continued being kind and helpful, annoyingly so.

David left the island after graduation, just as Ryan and his brothers had. When Wayne had died, David had returned to Teaberry to take on the job of pastor for the one church on the island. And now he was hitting on Mellie. Why else would he have her off to one side, talking intently as they ate a messy, delicious meal together?

Now, the pastor raised an eyebrow. "The prodigal appears. Good to see you, Ryan."

Mellie scooted a few inches away from him. Fair enough, but he didn't have to like it. "Have a crab, Ryan," she said, "and give me some elbow room."

"Make sure you try some of Hector's rice, too," David said.

"Got some." Ryan took a few bites, watching the dynamics between Mellie and David. Were they a couple, or at least drawn to each other?

If they were, he told himself, that would be a good thing. David lived on the island, had grown up here. He was a man of the cloth, a moral and upright person presumably. Not just presumably; Ryan knew the man was a good guy.

He had no trauma in his past, not that Ryan knew of. He'd be a far better mate for Mellie than Ryan was, and he ought to encourage them. "I didn't mean to interrupt your conversation," he said.

Mellie didn't say anything. Was she that upset about last night?

David was jovial. "Stay, stay. I'd like to hear about your work with the bay."

"It's pretty technical." When he realized he was implying the pastor couldn't understand, Ryan softened the statement. "Boring to most folks."

"I always liked biology in school," David said mildly, "though I was no star at it like you were. Are you studying the problems with the water quality?"

"In part. I work on the whole ecosystem and how it affects the animals." He held up a crab to illustrate. "I study the microscopic organisms to understand how pollution affects the bay. And I'm working on a project to figure out what erosion management system is best for the bay's ecosystems."

"Heard you won a big award. In fact, I saw you on a magazine cover."

"Yeah." He never knew what to say when people mentioned that. It was true he'd been chosen for the award, because he'd been so young when he'd gotten his PhD. But to his own mind, being young didn't mean anything special, so the award didn't feel earned. It also didn't feel like his own work, since he hadn't been the lead scientist on the project in question. "In science, you're only as good as your last discovery. That's why I'm cranking hard on a grant application while I'm here."

David nodded. "I wish you the best. Although…" He trailed off, looking thoughtful.

Mellie looked up, her eyes narrowing. "What?"

"Well…" David looked at Mellie, then Ryan, then back to Mellie.

"He's about to give you some spiritual advice," she said. "I can read him like a book."

Ryan had to admit the man was a better match for her than he was. And he knew his tendency toward jealousy was something he needed to work on.

But he also knew his own limits, and he was nearing them. "I'll take a rain check on that," he said, and stood. "I promised Alfie I'd help him find a marsh fiddler." When David looked blank, Ryan resisted showing off by using its Latin name. "It's a kind of crab."

He put a hand on Mellie's shoulder as he left. "Enjoy your lunch," he said.

"I am." She looked up at him, her expression puzzled.

He waved at the pastor and left. Great. He'd been awkward. Rather than separating the two, he'd probably pushed Mellie into the pastor's eager arms.

BETTY HAD GONE back to work basically full-time last Thursday, but she was still finding it tiring and, to be honest, annoying. So she juggled the calendar to get herself off on Wednesday. Her excuse was that she wanted to do some cleaning alone, while Mellie was working and Ryan was busy with his grant proposal. And that was true, or at least she made it true by dutifully going through a bedroom and gathering two big garbage bags of trash, as well as a small stack of useful stuff to take to Jimmy's Junk.

Once she'd carried the bags to the pickup, she felt a little lighter. But she didn't feel like cleaning anymore. So she made herself a sandwich and walked down toward the bay.

Having lunch outside, just what she wanted, just because she wanted to, gave her a glimmer of the self she used to be. Way back, before she and Wayne had married, during those brief years when her sisters had been grown and her father gone, and she'd had only to run the market and fend for herself.

The entire time she'd been married to Wayne, she'd never allowed herself to look back fondly on her single days. But now, she admitted to herself that it had been nice to be so carefree.

Finishing her sandwich—no napkin, wiping her hands on the sides of her jeans—she spotted the old rowboat and got an idea.

Before she'd married Wayne, she used to go out in the boat by herself. Had loved being surrounded by the water on all sides, the peace and solitude of it. But Wayne hadn't liked it and had felt it to be unsafe, and so she'd stopped. Keeping the peace was more important.

Maybe now, with a day off and no one worrying about her, she could reexperience that pleasure.

She did a quick visual inspection of the boat, even though she knew Mellie and Alfie used it sometimes and that it was basically sound. She checked the oarlocks, threw in a lifejacket and floatation cushion and rowed out onto the water.

The exertion felt good. A different kind of exercise than she normally got, and she knew better than to push it by going out too far. You didn't have to, to feel that peace and solitude. The boat rocked her, gently, and after fifteen minutes of rowing, she propped up the oars and just sat.

She inhaled the saline scent and felt the breeze cool her sweaty face, lift her hair. Off in the distance, she could see the outline of trees and buildings on the mainland. Behind her was Teaberry Island, home.

She could still see the farmhouse, and now she studied it. From this distance, it was just a house, and from this angle, it didn't hold quite the emotion that the street approach always evoked in her.

The sadness, really. The house that she'd longed to fill with children and then *had* filled with them in a different way than they'd planned, teenage boys who'd taken all her energy and mind and heart to guide toward independent adulthood. It had been worthy work, and while she'd been doing it, she hadn't really had time to lift her head and look around her and think.

Once she and Wayne had grown older, and he'd decided they were too old to foster, it had been a different story. She'd gotten used to the slower pace, the quiet house. And, of course, she'd still worked almost every day at the market.

And she'd had Wayne. Wayne, who, with all his quirks and complexity, had been the love of her life.

Now, she had none of that. Her life was a blank book, and she had no idea of how to fill the pages.

The ferry came by, and she waved, then steadied the rowboat in its wake.

Everyone on the island was familiar to her, and she to them.

It would be interesting to take a trip, something she hadn't done often, and then only with Wayne. Not just to the mainland, but to another state. Another country, even; she'd always listened to Hector's stories of Mexico with interest, had been patient to look at pictures of his extended family even when others rolled their eyes and sidled away.

Maybe she'd go to Acapulco or Mexico City. She wasn't rich, but with Wayne's life insurance, she could afford a splurge or two.

The possibilities, when she thought about it, were endless.

When she realized she was smiling, feeling excited for the first time in months, guilt washed over her. She looked heavenward and uttered a prayer of apology. She'd loved Wayne so much, would have rather she'd gone before him. Would give anything to have him back.

"Hey! Betty!" The voice was accompanied by the revving of a powerboat, and she pulled herself back to the present reality. Those things created a wicked wake, and she needed to be alert and handle it.

"Betty!" The figure piloting the boat became clearer, and…oh.

Charlie Fisher.

He looked agitated, shouting and waving, and she straightened and rowed toward him. Was something wrong? Had something happened to Ryan, or Mellie, or Alfie, or maybe to Peg?

He got closer and cut the motor.

"What's wrong?" She kept rowing toward him, her boat bobbing in the waves he'd stirred up.

"There's a storm coming!"

She looked at the sky, the horizons. Aside from a few puffy clouds, it was blue. "Sure about that?"

"The weather service says so." He held up a cell phone.

She restrained an eye roll. "I have a weather service in here," she said, tapping the side of her head, "and it's not predicting anything within the next hour or two. Thanks for the warning, but there was no need. You can go on back now."

He pulled the boat closer to hers and cut the motor. "That's a small boat. And you shouldn't be out alone."

She sighed. She'd met Charlie years ago, since he had been Wayne's college roommate and they'd remained close. She had been grateful for the help he'd provided to several of their foster boys, Ryan in particular. Charlie had come to Wayne's funeral and had made a nice donation to the island church in Wayne's name.

He'd sent her a note of condolence, just like many of Wayne's friends. A few weeks later, he'd followed up with a phone call. As best she could remember from that dark time, she hadn't been especially nice to him.

The thing was, he'd always looked at her in an *interested* way. As a happily married woman, she'd thought it kind of funny. Wayne had seen it, too, and smiled about it; he'd said it was a compliment to his taste in women. And there had been no question whether Charlie would do anything inappropriate. He was a good man, and a good friend to Wayne, and that was that.

Now, though, Wayne wasn't here as a barrier, and Charlie had chased her out into the bay, for heaven's sake. "I'll be fine," she told him. "I've been boating on the bay since I could walk. You're more at risk than I am."

"I wouldn't feel right leaving you out here." The assurance with which he said it told her he wouldn't change his mind.

Wasn't that just like a man, trusting his own inexpert ideas over a woman's actual knowledge. "I'm fine. I'm about to head back."

"I can give you a tow." He held up a rope.

"I don't need a tow!" But she wasn't going to stay out here for hours to prove a point. Charlie had destroyed the peace she'd felt, squashed down that glimmer of independence. Annoyed, she started rowing toward the shore.

And then had to face the additional irritation of him puttering along beside her, making a wake she had to contend with and shouting inane observations about the weather and the seabirds and why he was on the island. She rowed faster, ignored the half of it that she could hear.

Finally, tired and sweating, she got close to the public dock and waved Charlie away. "I'm safe, see? I'll take it from here." She gestured toward her own dock, several hundred yards down the shore.

"I'll see you home," he said, probably thinking he was being gallant.

There was a shout from the deck of the Dockside Diner. Peg leaned over the railing, a fruity drink in hand. Beside her was Tammy Granger, the nurse. "Hey, Betty! We're day drinking! Come join us!"

She wouldn't have done it when Wayne was around, because he'd disapprove of her coming home tipsy. And after he'd died she hadn't accepted any invitations. Today, though, it seemed she was doomed to having somebody's company. She'd rather spend time with her women friends than with an annoying, disturbing man. "I'm fine," she said to Charlie. "I'm going to join them. You can get on with your afternoon." Then she tied her boat to a piling, sloshed out through shallow water and headed up toward the Dockside Diner.

THURSDAY AFTERNOON, increasingly frustrated with the island's spotty cell phone service, Ryan walked down to the market. He'd get a soda and ask Mellie if there was an area with better reception somewhere else on the island.

While she was ringing up his drink, her afternoon replacement came in, so she walked out with him.

Good. She didn't seem to be annoyed with him.

He hadn't seen her, except at a distance, since the crab bake last Sunday. He also hadn't seen the pastor hanging around her place, and yes, he had to admit he'd been watching. It wasn't his business, and he had no right to interfere, but he was still glad they didn't seem to be an item.

He explained his problem with cellular service, and she nodded. "Come with me."

She led the way to a trio of short piers down the shore from the big main dock. Each of them had a fishing hut attaching them to the shore, one bigger than the rest. Two men sat outside the big hut, one with long white hair, smoking, and a younger one repairing a crab trap. The several benches and chairs indicated that this was a gathering place for island fishermen.

She introduced Ryan—or reintroduced him, really, since they both claimed to remember him from his teen years—and he greeted them. "He's here for phone reception," she explained, at which point he checked his phone and was thrilled to see the texts and emails pouring in. Some just work, but several that he needed for the current stage of his grant application.

One demanded an immediate callback, so he stepped to the side and returned the call. After speaking with his colleague in California, he ended the call and realized that the men had both been listening.

"Quite important, you are," the white-haired smoker, Jed, commented.

"Gonna save the bay without ever getting his hands dirty." The younger man, Tim, spat into the water.

Mellie bit her lip, her forehead wrinkling. "He's got to get his work done."

At that point Ryan realized he'd been a jerk, not showing the fishermen the proper respect before taking his call. He blew out a breath, sat down on the dock and pulled another broken trap toward himself. "I'd like to do my part to save the bay," he said, studying it. "The island, too, since it's eroding so bad."

"So would I like to," Jed said. "But wishing don't do much good."

"Ryan's taking action," Mellie said. "He's working on a grant to study the bay." She gestured toward the two fishermen as she turned to Ryan. "They're taking action, too. Tim actually testified to the Maryland State Legislature, and Jed's a letter-writing genius."

"Much good as it does," Jed said, but there was a little smile under his beard.

"It takes everybody." Ryan leaned forward to study how Tim had tied a twine closure onto the crab pot, then mimicked the action on the broken trap he was holding. He'd always been good at mechanical things, and the repair went quickly. He picked up another trap.

"That one's probably beyond repair," Jed said.

"I can—" Tim said.

"It's fixable—" Ryan said at the same time.

Jed laughed. "There's no shortage of broken traps, if the two of you want to have a contest." He stood and walked over, eyeballed two from a heap and brought them over, his arms rippling with working-man's muscles.

Tim's eyes narrowed. "Who picks first?"

"Flip a coin." Jed produced one from his pocket. "Smart guy gets heads, the guy that works his tail off gets tails."

Mellie laughed. "Truth is, they're both hardworking and they're both smart."

"You know what I mean." Jed flipped the coin, and Tim won the flip and chose his trap. Ryan took the other one, broken more badly. Jed fumbled around and found a net repair needle and more twine for Ryan.

Mellie waved her phone. "I'm keeping time. And…go."

Ryan grinned and started enacting the repair that had already appeared in his mind as he'd looked at the broken trap. His hands flew over the wires and corners, twisting, tying, stitching, repairing the holes. He finished and looked over at Tim.

Tim had propped his feet up on the deck railing, his finished trap below. "It's not pretty, but I beat ya," he observed.

Ryan grinned and nodded. "Owe you a beer at the Dockside Diner."

Tim glanced over at Jed. "There's another bar on the island. Of sorts."

"The Floating Fisherman?" Mellie's eyes widened.

"You might could pay us a visit," Jed said.

"I've heard of it," Ryan said. He and his brothers had tried to find it a few times, but the fishermen moved it from cove to dock to cove. That, and the fact that it was reputed to look exactly like all the other fishing boats, made it hard to locate.

Unlike some of the other Chesapeake islands, Teaberry wasn't dry. Places could serve alcohol with a liquor license, which the informal Floating Fisherman probably didn't have.

All the same, he felt good to be invited. "Drinks are on me."

"Donations only, but make a good one," Jed said. "It's put toward the families of those who lost their lives on the water."

Both men glanced over at Mellie.

"It's a real blessing," she said quietly. Then, looking at her phone, she jumped up. "I have to meet the school boat!"

"Bring the young one back if you want," Jed said.

"Maybe I will, if he doesn't have too much homework."

All three of them watched her hurry off. "Fine lady," Tim said.

"That she is." Ryan looked from one man to the other. "Did her husband die on the water? An accident?" He'd been curious what had happened to widow Mellie so young, but no one seemed to talk about it. Either that, or Ryan was just out of the loop, which would be no surprise.

"Well…" The two men looked at each other.

"You might say that," Tim said. "A squall came up while he was fishing, but… Georgie was a drinker, see. If he hadn't been drinking, he wouldn't have had a problem, most likely."

"There was question of whether to give her anything from the watermen's fund, and she tried to turn it down, but we wouldn't hear of it." He waved a finger to indicate himself and Tim. "That gal's had a hard row to hoe."

"Probably wouldn't have married Georgie," Tim added, "but she didn't have a choice."

Ryan had wondered about that. He'd thought about the math of Alfie's birth and knew that Mellie must have been with Georgie not long before the few weeks Ryan had been with her.

She wasn't the sleep-around type, had the opposite reputation, in fact. But apparently she'd jumped directly from Georgie to Ryan.

And apparently, Georgie hadn't been as careful as Ryan had been. So when she'd discovered she was carrying Georgie's child—and after Ryan had left the island—she'd reunited with Georgie and married him.

He wondered if the marriage had been happy. And as he continued to shoot the breeze with the fishermen, he thought about how she'd listened to his story.

He wanted to hear hers. Maybe, someday, he'd ask her about it.

CHAPTER ELEVEN

As she and Ryan walked into the school building on the mainland on Friday, Mellie's stomach churned. What had she been thinking?

"Whoa, flashbacks," Ryan said. "You, too?"

"Yeah. This takes me back." Anyone would be nostalgic, she guessed, returning to their old high school, now a combination middle school and high school. The squat yellow-brick building looked really old-fashioned now, although she knew that was just the exterior; the inside had been renovated. The new science labs were part of the reason why Mellie had agreed to have Alfie attend the school. He'd gotten so excited when he'd seen them. He'd begged to be allowed to go to the school where he could take serious science classes.

That excitement had disappeared during the difficult first week, but his attitude had been steadily improving. He seemed so much happier that Mellie had hoped this conference wouldn't even have to take place, but the principal had said it was important. She'd suggested that Mellie bring another family member or someone else involved in Alfie's life.

That had been fine with Mellie, because she felt

she needed an ally. Not just because Principal Martinez, who'd been the principal when Mellie had gone to school here, could be intimidating.

But also, she'd wanted to bring someone who would understand Alfie, and understand the nuances of being a gifted kid in school. Betty had been her first choice, but Betty had to work and really wasn't up for leaving the island these days. The best she could offer was to watch over Alfie after school.

So, mostly against her better judgment, she had chosen Ryan. And being kind, he had immediately agreed to come.

They were getting along well. They might be on their way to having a regular, nonromantic friendship. She hoped so, because Ryan was really good for Alfie.

"I'm trying to remember why we actually graduated at the same time," she said. "Why didn't you skip ahead and graduate early?" He'd been way too smart to follow the traditional pattern.

"Because Betty wouldn't let me," he said. "She told me she didn't want me to move on that quickly, acted like she would miss me too much and I would miss out on too much. The truth is, she knew I was an immature mess. She knew I needed more time in the family and on the island, and she wanted me to stay with my brothers. So she found me advanced classes, college-in-high-school stuff."

Principal Martinez approached them, smiling, her heels clicking on the concrete. "I remember you," she said. "Ryan Hastings. The bane of my existence back in the day."

"Thank you for putting up with me," he said, shaking her hand. He glanced over at Mellie. "Since Betty insisted that I stay for my full four years here, I took every class the school had to offer. Unfortunately for Dr. Martinez."

The principal's eyes went from Mellie to Ryan and back again. She opened her mouth. "Is he Ryan's—"

"A friend," Mellie interrupted quickly, her face heating. She must've been crazy to invite him. This was the sort of situation where he might very well guess the truth about his own relationship to Alfie.

"Good," the principal said. "I'm glad you brought someone along. You have some decisions to make, and it's good you have someone to discuss them with."

Oh. That didn't sound good.

They followed the principal up the school steps and down the hall. She was obviously still respected by the students; those hanging around the halls, most likely for after-school activities, quieted their noise and shenanigans while the woman walked by. They greeted her with respect. And just like when Mellie had gone to school here, Principal Martinez knew every student by name.

Mellie breathed in the familiar smell of sweat and disinfectant, and unbidden, the not-so-great memories rose inside her.

School hadn't been awful for her, but it hadn't been a place she liked to go. She hadn't had much time to study, and she'd even been held back a year in fifth grade, earning some teasing from the other kids. That was right after her mother had left and she'd been reeling with pain and scrambling to manage everything at home.

But even before that, she'd never been more than an average student. Just not much for sitting at a desk with a book.

That was what made it almost ironic that she had a son like Alfie.

They walked into the glassed-in main office. Two kids sat slumped over phones, probably either waiting for rides home or waiting for discipline. The principal nodded at both of them, took a small stack of message notes from the secretary and swept into her office. "Have a seat," she said.

Mellie's heart was pounding. The principal hadn't been forthcoming over the phone about what she wanted to discuss, and Mellie wondered what she would say. And how it would compare to what Alfie had been saying. He seemed a lot happier now, seemed to be finding his footing. He had become friends with Jimmy's son and talked about other kids at the school. Mellie had hoped that would be enough.

"In some regards," Principal Martinez said in her no-nonsense, get-to-the-point way, "Alfie is doing well. But in other ways…" She paused, propping her elbows on her desk and steepling her fingers.

"Tell me. I want to know." Had the bullying gotten worse?

"He's doing surprisingly well now, socially," the

principal said, "but he's falling behind in his academic classes."

Mellie's jaw dropped. That was the last thing she had expected to hear. "What?" she managed to say.

The principal nodded. "He's apparently started to be accepted by the other kids. He sits with various different groups at lunch and seems to get along well with them. The bullying has dropped way off."

Some of Mellie's tension eased.

"So what's going on with the classes?" Ryan asked.

"Apparently," the principal said, "he's being accepted by being a class clown. He's not paying attention. And I hear he has a wicked wit."

"That he does." Mellie smiled, glad that her son was at ease enough to show that side of himself at school.

Dr. Martinez frowned. "He's at risk of failing biology."

"Oh, no." Mellie shook her head slowly, staring at the woman. "He loves science."

"I don't know whether to attribute it to emotional immaturity or emotional maturity," the principal said. "He's acting immature, but he also seems to have the desire to be accepted by peers that's characteristic of middle school age. In a way, he's advanced by having that desire at age ten."

"Is he showing interest in the subject matter?" Ryan leaned forward, elbows on knees, chin propped on his hands.

Mellie was so relieved to have Ryan here. He

could slow things down, ask good questions, giving Mellie time to figure out how to address the issue.

"He was. But now, according to his teachers, I think the social side is occupying all of his time."

Mellie restrained an exclamation of dismay. "That's what he did back at the island school. He figures out how to fit in and then he does it. Even if that means acting out."

The woman nodded. "It's a characteristic of gifted kids. They don't all do well in school, you know. If they're not challenged, or they have other priorities, school can actually go quite poorly for them."

"So what are you saying?" Mellie gripped the arms of the chair, worried not only about what she was hearing, but about Dr. Martinez, who wasn't known for being easy on kids. "Are you kicking him out?"

"No. Not at this time." To Mellie's surprise, she smiled, her expression sympathetic. "But we need to find a way to engage him, or he'll have to go back to his home school. I can't have an optional student creating chaos in the classroom. The teachers are complaining."

"Let me talk to him." Mellie sat up straight. "He needs to understand that he can't do that. He was raised better than that and knows how to behave."

"I have no doubt of that, Melanie," the woman said.

"And I'll work harder to get him interested in the science." Ryan looked at the principal. "I'm doing some fieldwork for a grant proposal, and partly because of Alfie, I started to think about proposing something to share in the schools. Maybe if Alfie gets involved in that, it will help."

"If you ever want to try anything out on middle or high school students, contact me," Principal Martinez said. She studied Ryan. "You know, there are a lot of similarities between you and Alfie. Students like you come along maybe once in a decade."

Mellie's whole body heated and her heart pounded impossibly fast. Surely, now, Ryan would guess the truth.

But as they said their goodbyes to the principal and walked down toward the docks, Ryan's face remained open, not suspicious.

And then he said it. "I want to ask you something."

Here it was. Mellie steeled herself for the inevitable conflict to come. "Go ahead."

He looked at her quizzically. "Since we're here in Pleasant Shores, and Alfie is staying with Betty this evening, how would you like to have a nice dinner?"

Mellie stared at him. That was the last thing she had expected. Was he asking her out on a date?

IT *WAS* A DATE. At least it felt like one. And Ryan never dated.

The restaurant was a nice Italian one with white tablecloths and a view of the sunset-streaked bay. The waiter spoke in low tones.

Since they were riding the ferry later—he *had* had the foresight to arrange a late-evening trip—Ryan ordered a bottle of wine. That, he knew how to do, having been out at plenty of professional gatherings with sophisticated people.

"It smells wonderful." Mellie offered a hesitant smile. "Thanks for suggesting this."

"It's my pleasure." He wasn't lying. Just being here across the table from beautiful Mellie felt like a dream.

But it was a dream he didn't know quite how to handle. Did he converse differently than usual? Should he compliment her dress, one of the most conservative things he'd ever seen her wear?

She was looking at him strangely. "Is everything okay?"

"Uh...look, I don't usually date." Could he be any more awkward? "So I'm not sure what to talk about or how to act."

"Ohhh." She considered. "It's not really a date, right? So can we just have fun together and eat great food?"

"You're a genius," he said as relief washed over him. Along with a tiny bit of disappointment.

The thing was, he *wanted* to date Mellie. But he guessed he'd have to settle for a friendly dinner with her. There was a reason—a boatload of them actually—why he didn't get into romantic relationships, and this social awkwardness was just a minor part of it.

The wine came, and he tasted it and nodded, and the waiter poured them each a glass. Mellie raised an eyebrow but didn't comment.

"So, what do you think about the meeting with the principal?" he asked.

"Honestly, I don't know what to think. It's the last thing I would have expected."

He wished he could lift away her burdens, soothe her anxiety. "You said he'd acted out before, right?"

"He did." She ran a finger around the top of her wineglass. "It was because he was bored at school. Now, if he's also acting out at the new school…" She shook her head. "Sometimes I just don't know what to do."

He reached out and touched her hand, squeezed it quickly and let go. "You're a great mother, and Alfie's a great kid. You'll figure it out."

She drew in a breath and let it out in a sigh. "I will. I just hoped this new school would solve all his problems, you know?"

He laughed a little. "I'm sure you did, but…does school ever do that?"

"No. No, of course not, but I hoped it would help." She picked at her salad.

"It will." He thought back on his own childhood, how school had been a sanctuary. "It's what you do at home that's the most important, but school is a close second."

She bit her lip. "People warned me that he could struggle socially, thrown in among older kids. They were right."

He poured a little more wine into both glasses. "It's early days, Mellie. He's finding his way, figuring out how to navigate middle school. It could take a little time."

"You're right." She sighed. "It's just…that kind of goofing around will work a little, and Alfie can be really funny. But it's not ultimately the way to make good friends."

"He's been seeing a lot of Jimmy's son," Ryan said. "Do you think he's an okay influence?"

"Yeah, well…I don't know. I was just glad he had a friend at the new school, but maybe…" She looked at him. "Parenting is hard."

"And like I said, you do a terrific job of it." He buttered a piece of steaming-hot bread and then offered her the basket.

This was going fine. She'd been right to remind him that it wasn't a date.

"Thanks." She lifted the linen cloth covering the bread and inhaled. Then she took a piece of bread, bit into it and closed her eyes. "Delicious."

Ryan's mouth went dry and heat swept through his entire body. He put down his own bread to watch her enjoy hers. His heart seemed to warm and grow.

She opened her eyes and caught him staring. Her cheeks went pink and she put down the bread and cleared her throat. "Anyway. As far as parenting, I do my best. It's hard to have a gifted kid when you're the opposite of gifted yourself."

He didn't like the sound of that. "Don't put yourself down. You're very smart."

She snorted. "Right."

"There are all kinds of smarts, Mellie. And you've

got a lot better of a mix than I do. I'm one-sided, all about the science."

"Maybe."

"And you're raising Alfie to be well-rounded, too."

"I hope so. Like I said, it's hard."

"I can't even imagine, not being a parent myself."

She looked at him strangely, but then their food came and the goodness of homemade pasta and fresh vegetables and sauces overwhelmed any other thoughts.

They ate for a couple of minutes and then Mellie leaned back. "Thank you for this," she said. "The food's good, delicious, and it's nice to have an evening out with another adult."

"Agreed." And with Mellie, it was comfortable, too, once he'd stopped feeling weird about the dating angle. Everything was better with Mellie; it always had been.

After that evening when he'd shared some of his childhood history with her, he'd talked some with Betty, and some with his brother Luis. Both of them seemed to think he was selling himself short in the love department.

He would always have issues. He knew it, and Betty didn't deny it. Neither did Luis. They both knew about his past, and that there was no way he'd have come out of his rough childhood without psychological wounds.

He'd spent formative years made to feel like scum. Now, although he knew logically that he wasn't what

Cueball had said he was, he still carried that uncomfortable feeling of being wrong, inadequate, bad.

That was why he loved the outdoors, especially the bay: because he felt freedom there. He could escape the inner ache that he got around people.

Well, most people. Eventually—it had taken years—he'd gotten to where he was comfortable around Betty, Wayne and his foster brothers, Cody and Luis.

The only other person who'd ever made him feel free from his inner demons was Mellie.

Betty had been encouraging him to try building deeper connections with people, especially with Mellie. She seemed to think he would be a decent person in a relationship, that he wouldn't end up hurting the person he was involved with.

He still doubted it, but there was a glimmer of light through the clouds in his mind.

Maybe he *could* do it, have a relationship.

It was worth a try. And to be close emotionally, they needed to talk about real things. Like *her* past, her marriage. "Did you and your husband go out much?"

She paused, her fork in midair. "Me and Georgie? No. Not like this." She thought for a minute. "We went out for a beer every now and then. And when the Dockside Diner opened, we went there for an anniversary dinner, I remember."

"Was it a good marriage?" That was what he really wanted to know.

She hesitated. "It was," she said slowly, after a pause. "It grew to be."

"Not at first?"

She looked down.

"I'm sorry. It's not my business to pry."

She changed the subject. "It's okay, but...what about you, Ryan? Any women in your life? Because you say you don't know much about dating, but I noticed you have the nicest manners. Holding doors, pulling out chairs, standing when women enter the room. Not to mention you're a pro at ordering wine."

"The manners part was drilled into us by Wayne," he explained. "He said it would serve us well."

"And has it?"

He shrugged. "I'm probably more comfortable socially than some of my colleagues."

"So do you socialize with women?"

He shook his head. "Not really."

"Ryan!" she scolded. "Why wouldn't you date? I heard you won a lot of money for charity at a bachelor auction."

He laughed. "That was ridiculous. But a good cause."

"So then why don't you date?"

"Because...I'm just not cut out for it." He didn't want to talk himself down, but truth was truth. "You saw how it was, back in high school. As soon as we got close..." He made a chopping motion with his hand. "I was out of there."

Her mouth twisted to one side, just a little. "You did back away pretty fast."

"Exhibit A. Backing away isn't something you should do. Right?"

"You were young." She tilted her head to one side. "Maybe you've worked through it enough to commit to a relationship as an adult."

What was she saying? Was she offering to be in a relationship with him?

He got his answer when she blushed. "I don't mean with me, if it sounded... I just mean generally. You're a great person. You should find love."

He heaved a sigh, exaggerating it. "I think 'you're a great person' means you'd be a horrible romantic partner, doesn't it?"

"In your case, no. No, I don't think so. You have a lot to offer." A shadow passed over her face then.

The waiter returned to tell them about the featured dessert: dark chocolate cake with whipped cream and raspberries. Ryan remembered something Cody always said: if you want your way with a woman, feed her chocolate.

He *did* want his way with Mellie, although he hated to even think about her like that. But he ordered the cake, of course. A piece to share.

When it arrived, she took a bite and then rolled back her eyes in exaggerated pleasure. "Taste it."

He did, and she was right; it was an explosion of rich, chocolate goodness. But Ryan couldn't even concentrate on that. He was focused on her face. The pleasure there mesmerized him.

As they shared the cake, their eyes met. He remembered that from years ago, when they'd been together so briefly: she'd made the most intense eye contact he'd ever experienced in his life, and it had been a good thing, not a bad thing.

"You eat the rest," he said when only a few bites covered with dark frosting were left.

"Help me, or I'll have to buy all new clothes. This is a million calories."

He opened his mouth to say "not a million" but instead what came out was, "You look perfect the way you are."

She lifted an eyebrow for just a second and then finished off the cake. "So delicious."

"It was." He reached across the table and hooked his fingers in hers. He meant to just give a quick squeeze, sharing in the pleasure, but then he couldn't resist hanging on.

She didn't pull away.

He waved for the check without ever looking away from her. Her lips, full and pretty, drew his attention completely. He wanted to kiss her.

It would be a mistake, wouldn't it? He wasn't sure if he could do this. The last thing he wanted was to hurt her again.

The check arrived, and he reached for his wallet and she for her purse. "Let me get it," he said.

"No, Ryan, there's no need—"

"Mellie. I want to." He looked at her and was pretty sure she got the message of what that meant: whatever they'd agreed on before, he now saw this as a date.

As they walked out, he put a hand on her back,

gently steering her past a crowd waiting in the restaurant's foyer. Outside, they walked along the bay toward the docks.

The water shone bright around them, lit with moonlight. He held out his arm in invitation, and she took it. As they walked together, Ryan felt like he was holding his breath.

He didn't want to push. He wanted her to have the space to say no.

But she didn't say no. She snuggled against him, shivering, and he put an arm around her.

They got to the dock and the ferry was waiting. As the boat left the dock, they stood outside, the water surrounding them, encased in their own private world of the bay.

He kept his arm around her as he thought about kissing her.

He wanted to. He really wanted to. But it would be a change in their relationship. They'd become friends, and this would alter that. Push it in the direction of those few glorious, romantic high school days he kept remembering.

She might have been thinking the same thing, because she turned to him, her forehead creased. She opened her mouth, looked up at him and didn't say whatever she'd been planning to say.

Instead, she reached up and ran a hand down his cheek.

Her touch was like igniting a flame. He stroked her hair as he'd longed to do, tugged her a little closer and kissed her.

CHAPTER TWELVE

MELLIE FELT LIKE she was dreaming, so breathtaking and tender was Ryan's kiss, there in the middle of the bay.

Dizzy, she kept a hand on his face, half wanting to bring them back to earth, but he closed his eyes and deepened the kiss, and she was lost. Lost, as she'd been when she was a teenager. Lost to the way their bodies fit perfectly together and their breathing was in complete alignment.

Finally, he lifted his head. Waves lapped against the gently rocking ferryboat and he kept her close, pressing her cheek against his chest, stroking her hair. "Mellie." His rich, deep voice was low, almost a growl. "I've wanted to do that ever since I came back to Teaberry Island."

His words were a balm to her soul. "I'm glad," she said, because she couldn't quite admit that she'd wanted it, too.

"I care about you," he said. "It's more than physical." He brushed her lips with his again and then she felt him smile. He lifted his head a little. "Is that wrong to say? I don't want to pressure you, but… I'm

not just some guy who wants you in the moonlight.
I like you all the time."

He knew her so well, and it was the reassurance
she needed.

"You saved me as a teenager, you know," he continued, punctuating his words with tiny kisses. "I
was so lost. You were something to grab on to. You
anchored me."

Something about that didn't sit so well. She didn't
want to be an anchor. That was why she'd cut him free.

She should think about it, but the back of his neck
felt so good beneath her hand. The warmth of his
body enveloped her, and she felt safe, especially if
she didn't listen too closely to the words.

His kiss deepened then and she could feel the
moment when he started to want more, because the
same happened for her. And that was the danger:
they knew how good it could be for them. So after a
reluctant moment, she pulled back. "Ryan," she said,
and he finally opened his eyes.

When he looked at her, he loosened his embrace,
studying her, his expression concerned. "You okay?
I didn't mean to get…intense."

"It's okay. It's just that…just because we went further before…that door's not open now."

He studied her face for a long moment, and she
forced herself to keep her eyes clear and open, showing him she meant what she'd said.

Finally, he spoke. "I understand." He stepped back
and seemed to physically withdraw into himself.

And Mellie felt a sense of cold and loss.

On Saturday, Betty rang up a line of customers at the market, bagging, chatting and helping old Mr. West carry his groceries out to his golf cart. Finally, when they had a quiet moment, she went hunting for Mellie.

She found her in the produce area, wearing jeans and a neon green sweater with an apron protecting her outfit. The woman could definitely pull off bright colors.

There was a box containing wilted lettuce and a couple of pieces of fruit past their prime. Mellie was absently looking over the vegetables, but mostly, she seemed to be staring into space. Like she'd been doing all morning.

Like Ryan had been doing back at the house, when he and Betty had had coffee in the kitchen early this morning.

Something had happened between the two of them when they'd gone to the mainland last night, Betty was sure of it. She just couldn't tell from either of them whether it had been good or bad.

"Earth to Mellie," she said.

"Sorry," Mellie said. "I was daydreaming. And I'm about done going through the produce. Do you need a break?"

"I do." Betty was back in the rhythm of working at the market, and she had to admit, it felt good to have a place to go and meaningful work to do. She was no more sure about where she was going in her life overall, but she was pretty sure she wanted to stay on at the store. Maybe cut down, though.

"We talked about you cutting down your hours," Mellie said as if reading her mind. "I know you put on the schedule that you'd work all day today, but if you want to take off—"

"Just a break. I'm actually going to take a lunch, run over to the library." She didn't need Mellie coddling her and worrying about her, not as much, anyway. "I'll be back in an hour and then you can head out—how does that sound?"

"Terrific. In fact, if you see Alfie at the library, tell him to come on over here when he's done. We have big plans to clean the house today."

"I'm sure he'll love that." Betty waved and headed out into the sunshine. Speaking of cleaning, she *wasn't* doing enough of that in her own house. Mellie had been helping some, for pay, which was good. They'd even had some good talks.

But Betty was letting Ryan do too much of the work. Which he kept assuring her was fine, but she knew he didn't plan to stay with her much longer. She really should work with him, take advantage of his presence to get more done.

She would ask him about his plans, but right now, she was going to see if their little library had any books about women of her age, retirement, the golden years.

She walked into the library and immediately felt the boost of happiness she always felt here. The place was small, just a front-facing public area with magazines and computers and the librarian's desk, flanked by an adult book room on one side and a children's book room on the other.

There was Alfie, sitting at one of the computers, rapt. And, of course, the good smell of old books. She inhaled and felt even better.

She heard noise coming from the children's room and peeked in.

Linda Iglesias, the librarian, was just finishing up her Saturday morning kids' book group. Five or six kids sat on carpet squares and a couple of parents sat on folding chairs. The rest, she assumed, were taking the opportunity to browse the adult books, use the computers or play a quiet game on their phones.

Moving on into the adult book room, she bypassed her usual favorites—science fiction, fantasy and mystery—and started looking through the nonfiction. She'd checked out a couple of books on gardening in the past, a few cookbooks. But now she was going into the way-back machine.

Back when she'd been figuring out how to raise and deal with foster kids, she'd read several books on child development and psychology. She had a dim memory that there had been some books on adult development, too, books on aging. Back then, she'd skimmed right past them.

Now, she found the section on psychology and life stages and started browsing. She bypassed anything that included *geriatrics* in the title, just on principle. She didn't want some young psychologist classifying her into a group.

What she really wanted was advice from women her own age, and she didn't know where to find it.

She pulled out her phone, but reception was bad here today. So she went over to the computers. She sat next to Alfie and logged on. While she waited, she nudged him and told him to go over to the store when he was finished.

He wrinkled his nose. "Mom's making me help her clean."

"That's good. You're a strong boy and a big help to her." She paused, then added, "Like my Ryan is a big help to me. He's a good cleaner."

Alfie sat up straighter. "I guess."

She searched "aging" and "women growing older" and "senior women" and came up with a short list of titles that the library had. She knew they could get more, through the interlibrary loan system, but she'd start with these. She found an account by a woman who'd walked the Appalachian Trail in her sixties, a short book on fashion and beauty as an older woman—pretty ridiculous, because who was she primping for? But the pickings were slim. The third volume was called *Sailing into the Sunset*, published in 1940 and written by a woman who'd reinvented herself as a sailor after losing everything during the Great Depression.

After locating all three books, she took them to the circulation desk, spines facing in and the beauty book sandwiched between the other two. No need for anyone she encountered to know her business. Linda wasn't there, so Betty walked over to find her in the children's room, cleaning up scraps of paper and carpet squares.

Linda saw Betty, waved and got to her feet, wincing. "Getting old's not for sissies," she said. "My knees and back are complaining today. Are you ready to check out?"

"Yes." Betty followed her back to the desk and produced her library card.

"Oh, I've read both of these," Linda said, holding up the Appalachian Trail book and the one about sailing. She smiled at the beauty book. "I probably *should* read this one."

"If I walk in here looking like Miss America, you'll know it's worth reading," Betty said with a snort. "Why are you reading books about getting old? You're not thinking of retiring, are you?"

Linda shrugged. "Maybe. I can't do this forever, and some young ideas would only help this place. Plus, I get tired. I'd like to cut back. But candidates for the job aren't exactly thick on the ground here."

Betty mentally scanned all the young people she knew on the island. "There are some bookish kids. Take Alfie there."

"He'd be a great librarian," Linda said. "In about, oh, fifteen years. I was thinking of retiring sooner."

"I hear you. I go back and forth about it myself. We should talk about it, get a drink sometime."

Linda looked startled but pleased. "Uh, sure!"

Why hadn't Betty ever asked Linda to get together before? Busy with Wayne and with her other friends, she guessed.

Linda handed her the checked-out books. "Since I'm trying to cut down a little," she said slowly, like she was thinking it through as she spoke, "would you want to take over leading the book club?"

"Me?" Betty frowned. "I'm no teacher."

"You're one of the biggest readers on the island."

"Sure, but I don't read book club books." She put the words in air quotes.

"You could lead us in a year of science fiction and fantasy. We need a change. We might even get some men to join the group that way, and some young people."

In the act of opening her mouth to refuse, Betty thought of having a group of people to talk about her favorite novels with and paused. "I don't know how to lead a group," she said.

"At least come to the next meeting. See if it's something you might be interested in." Linda handed her a flyer. "This month's book is magical realism. Which is at least somewhat close to fantasy. And I happen to have an extra copy you can borrow." Without waiting for Betty to answer, she walked back to a shelf of reserved and held books and started scanning it. "Here it is," she said, pulling out a book and handing it to Betty. "We meet next Thursday night. As fast as you read, you'll be able to finish it easily. And don't worry, I have a guest leader for this one. You can just sit back and listen if you want."

Betty took the brightly colored book. "Just what I need in my life, another pushy friend," she said, softening the words with a smile.

She was thinking of retiring, or at least offloading some of her duties, and here she was contemplating a new activity and even a new responsibility. Was she out of her mind?

But as she left the library, hustling to get back to the market, she found that she was smiling.

CHAPTER THIRTEEN

SATURDAY AFTERNOON, AFTER they'd eaten sandwiches she'd brought from the market, Mellie set Alfie to cleaning up his books, action figures and games while she stripped and remade his bed.

She'd been thinking all morning about how to address his school issues, and she'd decided the talk would go better if they were both doing something, not sitting down facing each other.

Anyway, his room was the usual mess. The kid had a lot of stuff. He *needed* a lot of stuff to keep him entertained. The tall bookcase was full to overflowing, including the shelf she'd designated for library books. Clothing half-covered the floor, predominated by dirty, smelly socks. By the window were his plants; she'd never been able to get him as interested as she was, but he had a couple of weird-looking succulents and, of course, a Venus flytrap. So far, she'd managed to keep actual reptiles to a minimum; he had a chameleon and a hermit crab.

"Look at this book I got on snakes, Mom!" He opened one of his new library books to a colorful picture and held it out.

She cringed and held an arm in front of her eyes

to block out the orange-and-white snake. "Get that out of my sight!"

He laughed, but did so, and started picking up and reorganizing the rest of his books.

She needed to address his academic issue, but she didn't really know how to start. He'd never struggled in school before. And Lord knows, she herself had struggled plenty with schoolwork, but it was a different sort of struggle than Alfie's. She'd been genuinely lost; Alfie most likely was just bored.

A sudden wish tugged at her: for Ryan to be here, sharing the responsibility for his son. She had the feeling he'd know just what to do.

But just thinking of him made her get hot, then cold.

They'd kissed. They'd kissed and it had been so romantic and beautiful, there on the boat in the moonlight. But all too quickly the beauty had been tarnished.

He'd said he had clung to her, back in high school, because he was lost. Not out of real, romantic love was the implication.

And besides, she was keeping a terrible secret from him. If she told him he was Alfie's father, would he even be willing to help, or would he run away in anger and hurt?

Even worse, was there a chance he would do something abusive to Alfie, as had happened to him?

No. It was impossible to imagine, as she came to know Ryan better. Wayne must have been wrong.

But can you take that risk?

Alfie hummed to himself as he organized his action figures, stopping often to act something out with them, little bursts of "Hah!" and "Take that!" interspersed with his cleaning. She hated to ruin his good mood, but she had to. She was a single mom, and the responsibility for working through his problems rested on her alone.

"Alfie," she said as she threw the dirty sheets out into the hall, "I heard from Dr. Martinez that you're struggling in school. Not only that, but she said you've been acting up."

His mouth opened and he took a breath, obviously planning to argue, and then he seemed to think better of it. "Yeah, I got in a little trouble."

"And you failed a test," she said as she tugged the fitted sheet onto the last corner of the mattress. "And got a D on another one."

He shrugged. "It's easy stuff. I can learn it."

"Well, but if you don't show that on the test, you'll fail your new classes. You'll have to come back to the island full-time. Same if you keep misbehaving." All of a sudden something dawned on her. "Hey. You're not getting in trouble on purpose so you'll get sent back, are you?"

"Noooo." He looked thoughtful.

Uh-oh, genius. You just put that idea into his head. "Is Junior trying to get you in trouble?" she asked, mostly to chase away any notion Alfie had just gotten about manipulating things to get back to the island full-time.

"No! He's my friend!" Alfie's tone was loud, indignant.

"I know he's becoming a friend, and I'm glad about that," she said as she spread the top sheet and tucked it in at the bottom. "I just don't know if he's the right influence, school-wise. I've heard his dad say that he doesn't like school."

"He's. My. Friend." Alfie glared at her, his lip curling. "I don't care what you think." He ran out of the room. She heard him clattering heavily down the stairs, then stomping through the kitchen. The back door slammed.

What had just happened? She'd never seen that expression on her sweet boy's face before.

It shouldn't shock her that he was taking a snarky teen attitude. He'd always been precocious, and now he was surrounded by teens at school.

She sighed and followed him down the stairs and outside. He'd kept running and was almost down to the bay. "Alfie!" she yelled. "Get back here!"

He turned, made a one-fingered gesture he'd definitely learned at school, then started running toward the bay again.

Mellie froze.

From next door, Ryan came striding over. "Is everything okay? I heard you yelling."

She was still staring in shock at her son, who'd apparently morphed into a troubled teen overnight. "Oh, Ryan," she blurted out, "I have no idea what to do with him." She walked over and stood close beside him, wanting comfort, and receiving it when he draped an arm around her shoulders.

RYAN WANTED NOTHING more than to pull Mellie into his arms.

And not because she looked so pretty, even in that glow-in-the-dark sweater, although she did. Not because she smelled like summer flowers and fit so perfectly against his shoulders, although she did. Not because her closeness brought back the beauty of their kiss, although it did.

But because he couldn't stand to see her hurting, to hear the pain in her voice. "What happened?"

She lifted her head and looked at him, eyes shiny with unshed tears. "He flipped me off!"

"What?" Ryan had enough distance on the situation to think that was a little bit funny, but he also felt bad that Alfie had disrespected Mellie.

"He's my baby," she said, and a tear rolled down her cheek, undoing him. "He's never done anything like that before."

His heart ached for her. And he reached out and brushed back her hair, thumbed away the tear. "Hey. I'm sure he didn't mean it. It's obvious how close you are and how much he loves you."

She met his eyes, nodding, and again he wanted to hold her.

Some remnant of his logical brain reminded him that getting too close would only hurt her in the end. The kinder thing was to avoid involvement.

He needed to help Mellie with Alfie and then disengage. Immediately.

She was only leaning on him because she felt
hurt, anyway.

"I'll talk to him," he said.

"No, I should." She wiped her eyes on the sleeve
of her sweater. "But…come with me?"

"Of course." He left his arm around her for a minute, letting a temporary fantasy build in his mind.
That he lived here, with her and Alfie. That they
were married. That they were walking down to the
bay to have a word with their son, together.

But that was not ever going to happen. She'd said
as much when she'd pulled away from him after their
kiss, and she had been right. Maybe Ryan wasn't
the complete loser at relationships that he'd always
thought he was, but he was no prize.

Deliberately, he let go of her as they walked toward the bay, slate gray and choppy today, the sky
hanging low with threatening clouds.

Alfie was kneeling, poking a stick in the water,
not looking at either of them. But Ryan had seen the
kid's quick glance back. He knew they were there.

"Alfie." Mellie's voice was stern, with no trace of
tears. "You need to apologize for that gesture you
made to me."

He poked at the sand a couple more times. "I'm
sorry," he said, his voice barely audible.

Ryan watched Mellie, and it was like he could
read her mind. She was trying to decide whether a

weak apology was acceptable, or whether to push Alfie to a more sincere one.

Finally, she nodded. "Okay. Now, let's talk about this school situation."

Alfie looked at Ryan and his face reddened.

"He knows about it. What made you run out here, just now, when we were talking about it?"

Alfie's lower lip stuck out. "Junior's my friend."

"I get that. But we were talking about—"

"I need him at school!" Alfie's words burst out.

Mellie was quiet a minute, clearly thinking through what Alfie had just revealed.

Having been a boy in a situation similar to Alfie's, Ryan could understand. Having a friend who was more popular could save you, at a new school.

"Even if you're hanging around Junior," Mellie said, "you can't act out in class."

Alfie dug at the sand, not answering.

"What's going on in your classes?" Ryan asked.

Alfie shrugged. "Everyone else is bad, so I am, too. But I'm the one who gets caught."

Mellie and Ryan glanced at each other. Of course Alfie got caught; he was less experienced at misbehaving than the other, older kids.

"The stuff you're studying," Ryan said. "Is it interesting?"

"Yeah." Alfie used his stick to splash some bay water onto the sand.

"Is it hard?"

Alfie nodded. "A little bit." Then he flushed.

"Sometimes really hard," he added in a barely audible voice.

Ryan was beginning to understand, or at least partly so. "You know," he said, "when I came to Teaberry Island, I had to learn how to study."

Alfie glanced up, and Mellie looked at him. "What do you mean?" she asked.

"I skated through my other schools without studying," he said. "Here, I got bad grades and I got in trouble, until I learned to be *really* smart."

"I heard you're a genius," Alfie said.

The designation usually made Ryan uncomfortable, but coming from Alfie in that matter-of-fact way, it didn't bother him so much. It just required clarification. "There are all kinds of smart," he said. "One kind is knowing *how* to learn, and in that, I was a mess. I didn't know how to focus. I had to learn to sit down and read carefully and take notes. I had to pay attention when there was something I didn't understand, and slow down rather than just skipping over. I had to get some patience." He smiled at Alfie. "That's hard when you're bright, but it's important."

Alfie was staring up at him with what looked like real admiration. "I'm bright. But not that way. I don't know how to study."

"I can show you," Ryan said. "It's not that hard." And then he had a sinking feeling.

The words had come out before he realized what he was saying. Showing Alfie how to study would be more than the kind of light conversations they'd had about how to fit in. It would mean some regular study sessions.

Working with Alfie meant being around Mellie a lot more.

"Would you, Mr. Ryan?" Alfie's eyes shone with hope.

Ryan took a breath and looked at Mellie. On her face was the same mixture of emotions he felt in his own heart.

Desire to help her child.

Concern about spending time together.

"That's up to your mom," he said. "She makes the decisions, buddy, and she may have other plans for you. You did something to her that wasn't very nice."

Alfie looked ashamed. "Can he help me, Mom?"

She bit her lip and studied her son. "You can have a few after-school sessions if Mr. Ryan has time," she said.

"I have time," Ryan said. Whether he had the emotional chops was another thing, but he couldn't say no to this pair.

"But you also have to behave in class," Mellie went on, looking seriously at her son, "or there will be more consequences."

"I know," Alfie said, low. "I will."

"As for now, you're on dish duty for a week because of what you did. At school and to me."

"Oh, man…" The complaining tone was light, though, and Alfie's expression had brightened, too. He scooted over and leaned against Mellie. "I'm sorry I did that to you, Mom."

She cuddled him against her, a fiercely loving expression on her face. "You're forgiven. But you still have to do the dishes. And I'm going to cook some things that make a bi-i-ig mess."

He laughed. "No, do hot dogs!"

Watching their interaction, Ryan was charmed by how they could fight and make up. Their connection was one hundred percent real, and one hundred percent loving. Not something you saw very often.

She looked up at Ryan, and he realized that beneath the confident mother there was a concerned, unsure woman. And who could blame her?

Not only did she have a challenging child—because bright kids could be every bit as difficult as those with cognitive or emotional impairments—but he, Ryan, had gone hot and cold on her. He knew he couldn't handle a relationship, but he also couldn't stay away.

He definitely couldn't resist saying yes when her son asked him for help.

Their gazes met and it was as if lightning, bright and dangerous, flashed between them.

It *was* like lightning. This connection could really hurt someone, hurt all of them. Most importantly, it could hurt the innocent child who now leaned against Mellie, if he got close to Ryan and then Ryan left them cold.

He'd agreed to help Alfie, which meant he had to walk an emotional tightrope. Not something he was good at, but there was no choice in the matter.

"Can we start our study sessions tomorrow, Mr. Ryan?" Alfie asked.

Ryan looked at him and then at Mellie. "We'll see," they both said at the same time.

"I'll talk to you later," she added to Ryan.

"And I'll see you after school next week." Alfie smiled with all the confidence of a well-loved, slightly spoiled child.

"Maybe," Mellie reminded him. "For now, let's go back and finish cleaning that mess of a room."

"Okay." Alfie jumped up and Mellie got up with her usual grace, and they headed toward the house holding hands.

And Ryan sighed. Far from disengaging as he'd planned, he was now more involved than ever with the pair. What's more, he was looking forward to it.

He would just have to keep his emotional distance.

Yeah, right.

CHAPTER FOURTEEN

ON WEDNESDAY AFTERNOON, Betty was on her way to work when she spotted Goody Whatever-her-last-name-was opening up her ice cream truck.

The sight annoyed her. Wasn't it common courtesy to visit the other business owners in a town before you came in and started encroaching on their territory?

But, oh, well. The market was doing fine, and Betty was slowly getting back into the swing of things, listening to Mellie's ideas, making a few changes, taking charge again.

She'd also been reading the books she'd gotten at the library. The woman who'd walked the Appalachian Trail had inspired and shamed her. At sixty-seven—older than Betty—and after bearing and raising eleven children, she'd hiked the entire Appalachian Trail.

If Grandma Gatewood could do that, Betty could surely manage to take up her life again.

She'd also paged through the book about style and beauty for older women. Most of it had been impractical for someone living in a remote place and with an outdoorsy lifestyle, but it had made her think about the fact that she'd worn nothing but ragged T-shirts and jeans since Wayne's funeral. Her own form of mourning, she supposed. But today, she'd put on a newer shirt, patterned and hippie-ish, and had braided her ponytail rather than leaving it ratty. Sure enough, the small changes made her feel a little better.

She waved at Goody, who was still puttering around in the back of her truck, and the woman nodded but didn't wave back. Irritating. Why Goody had chosen Teaberry Island—Betty's turf—to set up a new business, Betty had no idea. Not to mention that she was old to be starting over.

As old as I am.

As Betty continued on toward the market, an idea came to her, full-blown. She turned back toward the woman and her gaudy truck.

She strode up to the woman, pasting on a smile. "Hi! Even though we chatted that once, and I've seen you over the years in Pleasant Shores, we were never officially introduced. I'm Betty Raines."

"Goody." Goody held up her two hands, encased in disposable gloves, presumably to show why she couldn't shake hands.

"No problem," Betty lied. "Listen, in addition to owning the market—"

"Thought that Mellie woman owned it."

"No!" Betty felt heat rise to her face. "It's my place."

"So *you're* my rival," Goody said.

Betty's mouth hung open. *Rude!*

She definitely wanted to find out what the woman was doing here, what her background was. Lord knew she didn't have any customers. It was the middle of the week, off-season. If it were her, she'd only open the truck on weekends during this part of the year.

She could give Goody that advice, but then again... maybe days of low or no business would run the unpleasant woman out of town sooner.

The mean thought gave her a twinge. If Goody were new to the island and didn't know anyone—and she certainly didn't have a lot of charm, to make friends easily—maybe she didn't have anything else to do.

Again, she forced herself to smile. "In addition to owning the market, I also write *Island Happenings*. It's a little weekly newspaper." Honesty compelled her to add, "More like a newsletter, really."

"Been here six weeks and I haven't seen it."

Betty studied the woman. Maybe this went beyond rudeness. Maybe she had social issues, similar to what Betty's foster sons had had, especially Ryan. Maybe something had happened to her in the past.

Or maybe she was just awkward. "I've been on hiatus," she said. "I lost my husband recently."

"Oh." Goody frowned. "I'm sorry for your loss."

The words sounded begrudging, but maybe that was just Goody's style.

"Thank you," Betty said. "I'm starting up again, and I wondered if I could interview you."

Goody's eyes narrowed and Betty could almost see the word *rival* spinning through her head.

"It might drum you up some business," she said sweetly.

"I'm doing just fine."

"Really?" Betty looked around. There were a few people on the street, walking from here to there, but nobody seemed to be stopping.

"Really." Goody crossed her arms over her chest.

Betty's curiosity rose. "So why did you make the switch from your shop in Pleasant Shores?"

It looked like Goody wasn't even going to answer. But then she shrugged. "Needed a change."

Hmm. This was like pulling teeth. Then again, maybe Goody had an interesting story. Was this another Appalachian Trail walker right here on Teaberry Island? "What made you decide to come here, specifically?"

Goody looked uncomfortable. "I came here as a child and liked it."

"Do you know anyone here?"

Goody got very busy pulling up bins of ice cream. "Look, I'd rather not be featured in a story. I tend to keep to myself."

"That's obvious. But a word of advice. You really *can't* keep to yourself in a place like this, so you might want to shape the gossip that's going around about you."

"There's gossip going around?"

There wasn't, not that Betty knew. Then again,

surely *someone* aside from her was interested in the island's newest inhabitant. "Of course there is."

Goody shrugged. "It's nothing interesting. I have nothing interesting about my life."

"Everyone has something interesting to share."

"Maybe everyone doesn't want to share it."

"Fine." This woman really was annoying. Betty put her hands on her hips. "Then I'll just ask you point-blank why you're trying to compete with the island specialty of teaberry ice cream."

"Because there was a market for it. Nobody likes teaberry ice cream."

"You're crazy!" The words burst out of Betty, loud. A couple walking down the street glanced back at her and Goody.

"I'm a good businessperson," Goody said, raising an eyebrow. "Chocolate is where it's at."

"Forget the story in *Island Happenings,*" Betty said. "I'm a good businessperson, too. No sense giving publicity to someone who's trying to hurt my business."

"Fine. I didn't want a story, anyway."

But, Betty thought, there was such a thing as freedom of the press. She was going to find out the woman's background and write a story, whether Goody wanted her to or not.

MELLIE FOUND HERSELF smiling as she waited for the school boat Thursday afternoon. It was a gorgeous Chesapeake day, with strong breezes whipping her hair out of its usual messy ponytail and autumn sunshine heating the back of her shoulders. The fishermen, including Jed and Tim, waved, and Betty's friend Peg gave a shout from the deck of the Dockside Diner.

Mellie had gotten a good report from Alfie's principal when she'd checked in earlier today. Alfie hadn't gotten in trouble all day. And she'd been able to assure Dr. Martinez that she'd discovered the root of the academic problem and found a way to help Alfie do better in his classes.

She'd never have guessed on her own that Alfie didn't know how to study. She had always had to work hard to learn her school subjects. It had always amazed her that Alfie didn't need to read things over and over, make notes or ask for additional explanations.

No doubt, with his sharp mind, he learned much differently than she did. More like Ryan. His *father*.

The idea sent nerves skittering up and down her spine, but also good feelings.

"Here he comes," Jed said, bringing her attention back to the here and now. He was right; the school boat had appeared and was chugging toward them.

But Jed was pointing the other direction, toward the road.

And there was Ryan, his own hair blowing, his jacket flapping open. He wore the khaki pants and blue shirt he always wore, a uniform that must be an attempt to blend into the woodwork.

Everything inside Mellie warmed up. He was

probably the most gorgeous man she'd seen in years, and he could dress in sackcloth and still get noticed.

And he'd kissed her. *Her.* Right here on the bay, and the memory of it made her press the back of her hand to her lips and then drop it, quickly, as he got closer. No need to embarrass herself by letting him guess what she was thinking about.

He'd been such a help when Alfie had been acting out, so insightful about the studying problem, so kind to offer assistance.

She couldn't help being excited that they would spend time together at her house. She'd stay out of the way of the tutoring session, but then maybe she'd ask Ryan to dinner as a thank-you.

He reached her just as the boat got to shore. His smile was a distracted Ryan smile, which meant he'd been working.

Alfie came off the school boat in the midst of seven or eight other kids, shoving at Junior in a playful way and laughing when he was shoved back. Typical boy behavior. A relief.

"Hi, Mom." He didn't hug her, but looked up at Ryan with an eager expression. "I have a *lot* of homework."

A cold hand gripped Mellie's stomach. Alfie was getting attached to Ryan. What would happen when Ryan left?

And how could she go on keeping the two of them apart, now that they'd made such a strong connection?

She shoved the thought aside as the three of them

walked off the dock. Other kids ran and walked, and Mellie couldn't help noticing she was the only parent who met the boat. It wasn't strictly necessary. Maybe that apron string should be untied.

But not today. "Come on, let's go home and get you a snack and then you two can get set up for your study session. Maybe the dining room table would be the best—"

"I'd rather work with him at the library," Ryan interrupted.

Oh. Not so cozy, then. "That's fine," she said, "but he needs a snack first."

"I thought of that." Ryan fumbled in his pocket and pulled out two sticks of jerky. He handed one to Alfie and started opening the other one for himself.

No way would Alfie eat that when there were Betty's cookies waiting at home. "He doesn't like…"

But Alfie was opening the jerky and biting off a hunk of it, just like Ryan. "This is good!" he said through a mouthful.

They turned toward town instead of the bay, along with the three or four kids who lived on the other side of the island. On High Street, Taylor waved from the bakery window, where she was creating a new display featuring mouthwatering cinnamon buns and pumpkin muffins along with a scarecrow and fall leaves and a hay bale. From the vent strategically placed over the door, fragrances of baked goods made Mellie's stomach rumble.

Ryan hadn't brought any jerky for *her*. Not that she'd have wanted it.

She didn't need to let her mood sink. "Hi, Goody," she called to the older woman who was scooping ice cream for a couple of the schoolkids.

The woman gave her a nod. She wasn't exactly brimming with small-town friendliness.

They approached the small brick library. Alfie's steps quickened—he loved the place—and Mellie was glad she'd started bringing him here for baby lap sit when he was small. She'd even checked out the occasional book herself, waiting on him, mostly ones about gardening or cooking.

As Alfie pulled open the door, Ryan spoke. "You don't have to come in if you have other stuff to do."

"Yeah, Mom, it's fine."

She opened her mouth and shut it again, feeling breathless.

"Run in and find us a table where it's okay to talk," Ryan told Alfie. When the boy was out of earshot, he faced Mellie. "Look, I'm glad to help him learn to study, but I think it's better if I do it here, alone. I can pick him up at the boat and drop him off after."

"Oh." Now she really couldn't breathe.

Her son was growing up, that was part of it. And Ryan didn't want her around.

Double ouch.

"Sure, that's fine," she forced out, hearing her voice as shaky. She swallowed hard and turned away so she wouldn't have to look at Ryan's handsome, closed-off face.

"I'll have him home by five," Ryan called in a businesslike tone.

She couldn't speak, couldn't trust her voice, which was utterly ridiculous of her. She waved and nodded and hurried away from this place where she obviously wasn't needed.

CHAPTER FIFTEEN

MELLIE TRIED TO keep her head down and avoid people, walking home. But on Teaberry Island, that was impossible.

Hector called out to her from the bench in front of the post office, his main hangout weekdays during the off-season, when there were no customers for golf carts and bikes. "Hey, Mellie, chin up! You okay?"

"Fine." She forced a smile, waved and kept walking.

But her grandmother, who'd been locking up the post office, turned around at Hector's words. "Why, Mellie Anderson. What's that sad-sack expression all about?"

"I'm fine, nothing, I'm fine." She turned out of respect but kept walking backward. "I'm, um, I'm late to meet up with Taylor."

She gave a little wave, spun and headed toward the bakery, barely escaping the concern of two other friends along the way.

It was fine that Alfie and Ryan didn't need her as a part of their tutoring session. It was good that Alfie was getting more independent.

Her whole goal in life was to help Alfie grow up

strong and happy and safe. Ryan's tutoring him was a step in the right direction.

She ducked into the bakery, where wonderful fragrances of cake and pie and fresh chocolate chip cookies assailed her nose.

Taylor was still working on her window display. She looked up, saw Mellie and came out toward her. "Mellie! What's wrong, are you okay?"

Her friend's sympathetic face brought back the emotions she'd been trying to stifle. She nodded. "Fine," she croaked.

"Sit down while I get you a snack." She guided Mellie to one of the tables that lined the shop's windows, covered in a blue-and-white gingham tablecloth.

It was a comforting space, but the mention of a snack made Mellie think of Ryan giving Alfie jerky, and of Alfie eating it. That brought her emotions even closer to the surface for some dumb reason.

A white-haired couple came through the door, wanting a dozen teaberry muffins to take back home to the mainland. Taylor waited on them and then brought over a plate with a giant, steaming chocolate chip cookie and a cup of tea, set them down and turned back to the counter. "Be right back."

Mellie was sad, upset inside, and yet the wafting fragrance of warm cookie was a temptation and a comfort she couldn't ignore. She broke off a piece of the cookie and ate it, and the explosion of flavor in her mouth made her smile despite what had happened.

"You're so talented!" she told Taylor as the woman approached with her own cookie and tea. "These are amazing. How did we get so lucky as to have you here on the island?"

A shadow passed over Taylor's face, and then she sat down. "Good, they turned out, then?" She took a bite, nodded. "Just a little oatmeal in the batter. Gives them body."

They ate for a minute, sipped tea. Mellie looked at the beautiful pastries in the glass case, the hanging baskets of plants, the fall flowers in boxes outside the windows. Taylor had taken a run-down, empty building and made it a tremendous asset to the island.

Taylor was using her gifts to make a contribution. Mellie felt like her chance to contribute was shrinking fast as her son grew up and needed her less.

"Where are Alfie and Ryan?" Taylor asked. "I saw you three walking by a little while ago."

"They're at the library," Mellie said with a creditably serene voice. "Ryan is teaching Alfie how to study."

"I thought Alfie knew everything there was to know about studying."

"I did, too." Mellie explained the situation. "Ryan got it, because he was the same way, so he offered to help."

Mellie's grandmother came into the shop. "Hi, ladies," she said, walking over to the table. "Taylor, if you could get me a couple of your bran muffins, I'll have one for dinner and one for breakfast. Saves me cooking."

"One sec."

As Taylor headed to the counter to fulfill her request, Gram stage-whispered, "Keeps me regular, too."

"I hope you're going to have some protein along with the muffins," Mellie said, reaching a hand up to squeeze Gram's. "I could bring you over some chicken."

"Don't you fuss over me. I'll make myself an egg."

"For dinner and breakfast? That's not enough nutritional variety."

Gram rolled her eyes. "I've fed myself for almost eighty years and I'm still going strong." She put a hand on a hip and studied Mellie. "You look a little better, but I could have sworn you were about to cry when you walked past the post office. You okay?"

"I'm fine, Gram. Thanks."

"And Alfie?"

"He's doing really well."

"Good to hear," she said. She wasn't the warm and fuzzy grandmother type, but Mellie knew she cared.

"Here you go, Ms. Tanner." Taylor brought over the bakery bag. "That's a dollar fifty."

Gram handed Taylor a one-dollar bill and then counted out fifty cents in a combination of dimes, nickels and pennies. "They're pricey, but they're worth it."

"You charged her seventy-five cents each?" Mellie said after Gram left. "For those giant muffins? They'd be four or five dollars on the mainland, wouldn't they?"

Taylor sat down, shrugged and smiled. "She's on a fixed income."

"And you need to *make* an income." Taylor had sunk every penny she had into the bakery.

"We're not talking about me, we're talking about you. If Ryan's helping Alfie, why are you so sad?"

Mellie contemplated denying it and decided there was no point. Taylor was too perceptive. "They don't need me."

Taylor tilted her head to one side, studying Mellie's face. Then she took the last bite of cookie and brushed her hands together. "Keep talking."

"I know," Mellie said. "It's stupid. I should be glad Ryan's helping Alfie, and I am, really."

"Well, then, why…" Taylor's eyes narrowed. "Did something happen?"

"What do you mean?"

"I mean, there used to be something between you and Ryan. Is there now?"

Mellie blew out a breath. There was no hiding anything from Taylor. She was Teaberry Island's equivalent of a bartender-slash-psychologist, and she'd already gotten to know Mellie well. "Kind of the same thing as before."

"You slept with him again?" Taylor sounded genuinely shocked.

Mellie almost choked on her tea. "No, no, no," she said. "We *kissed*. And then he kicked me to the curb."

"What?"

Mellie nodded miserably. "And it's bringing back

all the feelings I had back then." Only as she said the words did she realize that was what was going on.

It had been more than ten years ago now, but she remembered it like it was yesterday. It had been a one-two punch. Ryan had told her he couldn't continue the relationship, didn't want to, had other things in his future. That had broken her heart, but it hadn't shocked her. She'd known deep inside that the romance with Ryan was a short interlude, set apart from real life.

Real life had slammed into her, though, when the pregnancy test had come back positive. That had added a huge layer of worry on top of her feeling of abandonment.

Taylor's fists clenched. "Man, if that gorgeous nerd hurt you, he'll have me to answer to."

"He doesn't owe me anything. It just seemed for a little bit that…" She paused. "It seemed like we might, you know…" She couldn't even say the words.

The bells on the shop door jingled, and Taylor jumped up to wait on a couple of teenagers while Mellie tried to compose herself. She was a grown woman, a mother. She'd been in charge at home since she was twelve, had started working at the market at sixteen, had run it on her own for three months now while Betty recovered. All kinds of people relied on her for all kinds of things, and she managed well.

She couldn't let this minor hit to her ego derail her. It shouldn't even upset her.

"I brought us another cookie to share," Taylor said. The teens had left and the shop was empty again. "Now, tell me what happened today to bring on the blues. Tell me everything."

So Mellie explained the whole encounter, from the boat docks to the library door. "It was a double whammy, you know? Alfie's growing up. He won't need me forever, which is a good thing, but—"

"But he's your baby and your world. I get it."

"Exactly. And then there's Ryan, basically telling me to get lost. Which, again, should be fine. I mean, I'm not exactly lovable, not to a man like Ryan, anyway."

"You're *so* lovable!" Taylor sounded indignant. "Look how you brought me homemade chicken soup when I was sick, that first week I came to the island. Look how you introduced me to everyone. Look how you take care of everyone like a little mother hen."

Mellie felt her mouth go into a straight, flat line. She *did* take care of people and she loved doing it. But if she didn't go overboard for people, who knew how many friends she'd really have?

Taylor seemed to read her mind. "And you're not just lovable because you bring chicken soup. You're fun and funny and colorful, and everyone feels comfortable around you. You're incredibly talented with your flowers, and you're super pretty, as I'm sure Ryan is well aware."

He'd said as much, but that had been when he'd wanted to kiss her.

Taylor checked the time on her phone and then went over to the door. She locked it and flipped the sign to Closed. Then she came back over to the table.

"I don't know how to convince you that you're the greatest. You have to come to see that for yourself. But there's one area where you're very screwed up."

"What's that?" Mellie was ripping her napkin into shreds, but now she looked up.

"You need to tell Ryan and Alfie that they're father and son."

Mellie's hands went still.

If she told them the truth, it would push them even further away from her. And who knew what it would do to Alfie, to gain a father and then lose him when Ryan inevitably left the island?

"There's that saying, the truth will set you free. From the Bible, maybe? Or Shakespeare. Anyway…" She stood, hugged Mellie and put her hands on her shoulders. "At least think about it, okay?"

"I will." But Mellie had already thought about it.

She was starting to believe that telling the truth wouldn't expose Alfie to danger, as Wayne had said it would. She was seeing so much evidence that Ryan was a good man, that he had control of himself and that he wouldn't do anything to hurt a child. She had always held out the hope that Wayne was wrong, and now she felt surer than ever that he had been.

And telling the truth would confuse Alfie and probably upset him, but he'd manage the truth okay. What he wouldn't manage was losing another father.

And then there was the fact that revealing her lie would turn Ryan against her, irrevocably. Even if he *did* care for her now, at least somewhat, she wasn't lovable and appealing enough to overcome having made that big of a screwup.

He'd be so furious that he'd leave forever. Which was no more than she deserved.

But Alfie was another story. He deserved more, so much more. If he couldn't have Ryan as a father, he could at least retain him as a friend and mentor who showed up occasionally, who might unknowingly boost his chances in life, give him a helping hand, teach him how to handle himself as a highly gifted man in an ordinary world.

She wanted that for Alfie, more than anything. Wanted more for him than she, given that she was no genius herself, could provide. Wanted him to grow up happy and successful and at ease with himself, surrounded by friends and love.

That wouldn't happen if she told the truth. In fact, she thought as she gathered her things and headed home, all she could see from telling them both the truth was disaster.

RYAN HAD MANAGED to focus on teaching Alfie some study hacks during their hour in the library, but now, as they walked through town toward home, he couldn't push out of mind the sight of Mellie's stricken face.

He'd acted cold, distant. He'd refused her invitation to snack and work at her house. He'd told her he wanted to work with Alfie alone.

Junior, the son of Jimmy the junk guy, ran over to

them from the small park at the central crossroads of town. "Did you figure out your homework, genius?"

"Some of it," Alfie said cheerfully. "It's hard."

"No kidding it's hard." Junior fell into step beside them. "I'm in dummy science and I can't even do that."

What did you say when a kid put himself down like that? Ryan wasn't sure how to combat the dummy label. Because, obviously, *he* was a dummy at social interaction.

"Maybe I can help you sometime," Alfie said. "Hey, and you can teach me to shoot free throws, okay?"

"Sure." Junior punched Alfie in the arm, but gently. "You're crap at them."

As the boys walked, darted and pushed at each other, doing a very mild form of trash-talking the whole time, Ryan smiled. Alfie was a great kid. He'd instinctively known the right thing to say to Junior. He was going to be all right, that kid; he was going to make plenty of friends.

Ryan couldn't wait to tell Mellie about it. She'd be so proud.

And then he actually stopped walking. He'd forgotten, for a second, that he couldn't stay and interact with Mellie. That he'd messed everything up by kissing her and then pushing her away.

He couldn't get close to her, not anymore. He couldn't risk hurting her that way.

"You want to come in for dinner?" Alfie asked.

The invite was thrown out casually to both Junior and Ryan.

"Yeah!" Junior said. "Anything beats my dad's cooking."

"Doesn't your mom need some advance notice?" Ryan asked Alfie.

"No. I can invite anyone, anytime. She always makes extra. You coming?"

Ryan looked at Mellie's house, its windows lit up in the twilight. Mellie was inside, moving from stove to counter, chopping and stirring.

Longing hit him square in the chest.

He wanted that home, that shared meal, that family life.

He wanted *her*.

"I can't come in, but thanks, buddy. See you next time."

"Okay." The two boys ran toward the front door, and Ryan turned toward Betty's house.

As he reached out to open the door and go inside, Betty came out. "Hi, honey," she said, reaching out to give him a half hug. She had a big purse over her arm and a plate of cookies in her hand.

"Mmm, those smell good," he said.

"I left a little plate of them for you." She patted his cheek. "I'm going to check on a few things at the market, and I'll grab dinner there. Then, for whatever reason, I agreed to go to a book club meeting at the library." She made a face.

"Have fun." He kissed her cheek and watched as she bustled out to the truck. It was just a two-minute drive, but it would be dark when she got home. He was glad she was driving.

And he was thrilled that she was going out voluntarily. That bespoke a level of healing he'd barely hoped for.

He went into the dark kitchen, flipped on a light and looked around appreciatively. Betty and Mellie had spent a recent morning cleaning and decluttering in here, and it was looking more and more like a magazine. The big farmhouse sink, the white appliances, the wood plank table—all of it had been buried under clutter when he'd arrived, but all was visible now. There was a mason jar of flowers on the table, tied with a bright red ribbon. Mellie's touch for sure.

He opened the refrigerator, then a cupboard. He settled on a can of soup, dumped it in a pan, turned on the gas burner.

While the soup heated, he went to the window and looked out on the bay, reflecting the pink and gold and violet of the sky.

When he'd come to Teaberry Island, the view had mesmerized him. The bay's beauty had been the only thing big enough to fill him up completely, pushing out the pain of his past.

It still had the power to comfort him. He was truly fortunate to have his work.

Truly fortunate to have food and a place to stay. It was so much more than he'd ever thought he'd have.

For just a moment, his mind dipped into that dark

time of his childhood, where terror had merged with a loneliness so deep that he'd feared for his own life.

He'd put all that behind him, but sometimes the darkness nudged at him, reminded him that it was still there, deep inside. That whatever had caused him to be treated like an animal—worse than an animal—still lurked in his heart.

That threat was why he was going to be limited to cans of soup alone in kitchens, rather than experiencing some kind of Norman Rockwell family life.

He stirred his soup and then walked to the other window. He could see Mellie's lit-up house from there, and though the place was too far away to reveal any details, he could well imagine what was happening.

The boys would be talking a mile a minute, their mouths full, grabbing seconds, then subsiding into better manners at Mellie's quiet-but-stern order. She would be drawing them out about their school day, getting up to pour more milk, bringing in dessert.

Maybe she'd spare a thought for Ryan, the rude man with whom she'd once been close, who'd kissed her and then pushed her away. Hopefully, the thought would be a fleeting one. He wasn't worth dwelling on, and someone like Mellie had many other friends to turn to.

He poured himself a glass of milk and turned off the flame under his soup, suddenly not hungry. Mechanically, though, he poured it into a bowl and carried it to the table. He'd have dinner and then attack one of the upstairs bedrooms that Mellie and Betty hadn't cleared yet. He'd haul everything out tonight so they could do their decorating magic the next time they worked on the house together.

As he walked past the window, he lifted his glass of milk in mock salute, looking in the direction of Mellie's house. "I'm doing it for you," he said aloud. "You're better off without me, trust me on that."

And then he grabbed one of Betty's science fiction novels and propped it open at his place at the table, and forced himself to eat his soup and read the book and ignore the pain in his heart.

CHAPTER SIXTEEN

A FEW MINUTES before seven, Betty walked into the library, that wretched book and the covered plate of cookies in her hand.

She hadn't liked the book at all. Too touchy-feely, with unbelievable bursts of magic when you didn't expect them. She didn't really want to waste time hearing about how great it was, or how stupid or un-literary she was. But she'd told Linda she'd come, and the woman had actually called her to remind her about tonight's meeting. There was no way she could get out of it.

She figured she'd at least get a story for *Island Happenings* out of the meeting. The time wouldn't be entirely wasted.

She ignored the inner voice that reminded her she wasted altogether too much time wallowing around in her misery at home.

The library was officially closed, and Linda had added several wooden chairs to the small seating area by the front window of the library. Besides Linda, there was Mellie's grandmother, the postmistress, who was a big-time reader; Amaryllis Johnson, the former librarian who was pretty spry for ninety; two teenagers from the church youth group; and Mellie's friend Taylor. Sitting on a table at one end of the circle was Pastor David. Linda had explained that he was leading the discussion tonight, because the book had religious overtones. Creepy ones, in Betty's opinion, but she wasn't going to make people mad by saying that.

As she found a hard chair farthest from the pastor, a couple of young mothers hurried in, chattering together, each holding a copy of the book.

Most of the group was dressed casually but nice, and Betty was glad she'd at least put on a pretty shirt and decent jeans. She'd been doing that for work, too. No more ragged, holey clothes. It was a step. She remembered again that book about beauty and style for older women. She hadn't dug into it deeply yet, but maybe she should.

She carried the snickerdoodles to a table set off to the side and removed the plastic wrap. "Is this okay in the library?" she asked Linda.

"Absolutely. We welcome your cookies. Mmm. Those smell good."

The teenagers approached, and then Taylor, and then the pastor. "You should come every time," the teen boy said, reaching out and grabbing two cookies.

The girl slapped his hand. "Don't be a pig."

"Remember," Amaryllis said, "she's probably writing us up for *Island Happenings*. Don't say anything you don't want reported."

Pleased that everyone liked the cookies, Betty

grabbed a bottle of water from a small cooler and took her seat.

Pastor David gave a little introduction to the book and then started throwing out questions. Betty listened, not planning to contribute. She figured everyone else had liked the book, and she didn't want to be a killjoy.

Pretty soon, though, she discovered that half the people in the group hadn't liked it, some for similar reasons to hers, some for other reasons. Others had loved it, which made for a lively discussion. To her own surprise, Betty found herself contributing. She actually forgot to take notes for *Island Happenings*.

The hour-and-a-half meeting went quickly, and when it was over, people were reluctant to leave. Betty stuck around, too, since people were clustered around the cookie plate she'd brought, now almost empty. She noticed the teenage boy eyeing the last few cookies and urged him to go for it.

"Thanks," he said, taking a couple. "These are great."

"Yes, thanks for bringing them," Taylor said. "It's fun to taste someone else's baked goods."

"Oh, well, they can't compare to your fancy treats."

Taylor snagged the last cookie. "Different type of baking, and you're the best at the homey treats."

It was a nice description and Taylor was being sincere. Besides, Betty knew her baking was popular with everyone.

"Good-size group tonight," Taylor said to Linda, who was moving chairs back to their usual places.

"It was." Linda smiled.

"That new fella who's moving here, Charlie something or other, asked me about a book club," Mellie's grandmother said. "So we might get more men."

Oh, great. That bothersome man.

Amaryllis tugged at Betty's sleeve. "I haven't seen you since before your husband passed," she said. "I'm so sorry I missed his funeral." She leaned on her cane, her face crinkled into an expression of sympathy. She wore black lace-up shoes and a dark dress and looked every inch the sweet old lady, but she was sharp as any investigative reporter on TV. "I'm sorry for your loss, dear."

Thoughts of Wayne pushed in, and Betty realized, ashamed, that she hadn't thought of him once during the discussion.

Instead, she'd enjoyed herself, and how was that right? She was the one who kept wishing they'd have forever. So what was she doing, moving on like this?

He wouldn't have liked her coming to book club, unless he was away on one of his church business trips to the mainland. He'd liked her to be at home when he was home.

"Yes, Wayne was quite a regular here at the library, back when I was in charge of it."

Betty frowned. "He was?" She'd never known Wayne to do recreational reading, and he'd never mentioned setting foot in the library. On the other hand, he'd had to read and research, writing his sermons. And she'd been busy running the market. He must have started going to the library and forgotten to tell her about it.

"I'm trying to remember what type of books he liked," Amaryllis said.

Linda frowned and shook her head, putting a finger to her lips.

"What?" Amaryllis asked.

"Patrons' borrowing choices are confidential," Linda said, her voice gentle.

"Oh, well, of course. I suppose." Amaryllis patted Betty's arm. "I'm sure you know everything there is to know about your husband, anyway."

As everyone left, Betty followed along behind, thinking.

She wrote and edited the island's newspaper, such as it was. In theory, she knew most of what went on around here.

She was Wayne's wife.

And yet, here was another thing she hadn't known about Wayne.

"C'MON, MR. RYAN, this is the fun part of Oktoberfest!" Alfie grabbed Ryan's hand and tugged him toward the little park in the center of town. It was Saturday afternoon, and they'd spent most of the day together. Ryan found he didn't mind hanging out longer with the boy, not in the least.

Ryan had vague memories of a harvest festival on Teaberry Island, but what he saw in the park was on a larger scale. On one side they'd set up a temporary beer garden, complete with German-clad wenches and lads sitting around a table, looking tired. The market, being so close, wasn't represented—people could just cross the street and visit—but the bakery had a stand, as did the library and several other businesses. There was an area for kids to make crafts and one of those bright colored bouncy houses for them to play in.

He could see why Alfie—any kid, really—would be gung ho.

Alfie was pretty gung ho about everything these days. They'd spent the afternoon together, first with a little tutoring at the library. And then, as they'd walked back through town toward home and Ryan had seen how many tourists were around and how busy the market was, he'd texted Mellie, who was working. He'd offered to take Ryan with him to collect water samples on the beach end of the island.

He'd hoped to connect with her a little bit, do her a favor. That pain he'd felt since he'd pushed her away at the library door had only intensified. He missed her, plain and simple.

Not only that, but he felt terrible that he'd hurt her again. True, the hurting had been in service of her greater good, but maybe there was a kinder way to let her know that he couldn't be the man he'd acted like he could be, that night when they'd kissed.

He'd hoped the offer to take Alfie along, give the boy some extra enrichment and give Mellie a little free time, or at least undistracted work time at the market, would warm her feelings toward him. But she'd texted back a curt, Sure. Thanks.

He wasn't giving up, though, not yet.

As they walked into the park, Alfie practically jumping up and down ahead of him, Ryan smelled cinnamon and pumpkin baked goods. Hector and Taylor were setting things out on picnic tables. Linda the librarian was packing up her book display, assisted by an older woman he'd seen a few times at the library before.

Off to the side, the German music stopped abruptly. "Now we'll listen to the good stuff, folks," called Jimmy the junkman, who was playing DJ. He put on a classic disco celebration song, and people cheered and sang along. A couple of the ladies even danced.

Ryan gestured for Alfie to run ahead and stopped by the library booth. "Need a hand carrying those?" he asked, indicating the boxes of used books.

"We would love that. My van's right over there." Linda gestured to a small lot beside the park. As they walked back and forth, carrying boxes, she explained what was going on. "The last boat left," she explained, "so most of the tourists are gone. We always make our own party on Saturday night."

"Nice idea," Ryan said. He was really starting to appreciate this town. Not that he fit in exactly, because he wasn't a big, social talker. But there were people with whom he felt a kinship, like Linda. Taylor was always nice when he went into the bakery for a morning pastry—she'd started to know his preferences—and old Ms. Tanner, Mellie's grandmother, texted him when anything came to the post office for him, and chatted with him in a friendly way when he came in to pick up mail or packages.

"Go ahead and sit down," Linda urged him. "Or better yet, keep Alfie from eating all the desserts before dinner."

"Oh! Right." He guessed he was still in charge of Alfie, since Mellie wasn't around. He corralled the boy and urged him and Junior to get one plate each and sit down. Then he loaded up on food, bought a mug of pumpkin ale for himself and, on impulse, one for Mellie, and hauled it all over to the table where Alfie and Junior sat.

After just a few minutes—during which Alfie and Junior scarfed down every bite of their food—Alfie stood up and started yelling and gesturing. "Over here, Mom!"

Ryan stood when Mellie and Taylor approached.

Taylor said something to Mellie, waved and left.

He waited until Mellie had sat down—on the other side of Alfie, sadly, not beside Ryan. She gave him an impersonal smile. "Thanks for looking out for Alfie," she said, and then turned immediately to her son. "I hope you helped Mr. Ryan and didn't give him any trouble."

"I helped!"

"He did," Ryan said. "He's very careful. He'll be good in the lab."

Alfie flushed and smiled, and Mellie's smile got a little warmer, too. Alfie started talking about the day they'd had, making it unnecessary, impossible, really, for anyone else to speak. "Hey, can Junior and me go help his dad?" he asked breathlessly, pointing toward the DJ station.

"Sure, as long as you don't push any buttons without permission."

"I won't, Mom."

"Then go."

"That sounds like the voice of experience," Ryan said.

Mellie nodded, chuckling. "Once when we were visiting my sister in Annapolis, Alfie decided to push a button near the door. Turns out it was an old alarm system that hadn't been used in years, but still worked. Well, it worked except it couldn't be turned off." She shook her head. "It was blaring, and flashing… The police came, and all the neighbors…yeah. All from one little button."

"Sounds like something I would've done," Ryan admitted. "I always wonder how things work, and I didn't used to have a lot of restraint."

"I remember."

The words seemed to take on a double meaning, flashing him back to their high school days when he'd been overwhelmed with wanting Mellie. He met her eyes and suspected that she was remembering, too.

Was it a bad memory for her? He couldn't tell. "Look," he said, and cleared his throat. "I'm sorry I was rude to you, that day I started helping Alfie. I hope we can be friends at least."

She pressed her lips together and studied him without speaking.

"I miss you, Mellie."

Still with the intense eye contact, something that made him uncomfortable with almost everyone, but not with Mellie. "We can't…" she said finally.

"I know."

The words didn't need to be said aloud. They couldn't kiss again, and they definitely couldn't make love. They couldn't have a relationship.

The silence stretched on. Meaning and feelings and sparks seemed to dance between them. "Do you think we could try being friends? And I'll do my best not to be cold and rude to you."

She laughed a little. "You're not cold and rude, not exactly."

"I'm confused, is what I am. But it shows up differently sometimes."

Around them, people were eating and talking and drinking, but in their little bubble at the end of one of the long tables, it felt like they were in their own world.

Ryan was talking about being friends, agreeing that they couldn't be more, but that was on the outside. Inside, his heart reached out for her, longing for closeness. Longing to touch her hand, brush back her hair, stand up and walk around the table and pull her into his arms.

She looked away, then down at the table. She wiped up a circle of condensation with her napkin. She'd barely touched the beer he'd bought her. "I guess…I mean, for Alfie's sake, we can give friendship a try." She sounded like she was certain that it wasn't going to work.

He opened his mouth to argue and then closed it again. More talk wasn't going to help. She'd said they could give friendship a try, and if that was all he was going to get, he'd take it.

Alfie ran back over, sat next to Mellie and leaned against her, and she put her arm around him. Their easy warmth with each other made him smile. It was sweet that Alfie was still able to be affectionate with his mother.

She rubbed Alfie's back and they talked about more general things, then chatted with people who stopped by their table, watched a few more people dance on the lawn to Jimmy's country-rock playlist.

Ryan didn't want their time together to end. He'd have sat there the whole evening, just chatting a little and watching Mellie's face.

As people started to wander off toward home, Mellie patted a barely awake Alfie's back. "Come on, buddy. We've got to get home before we both fall asleep."

"Okay," he said. He sat up straighter, yawned and stretched. He looked across the table at Ryan. "I wish you were my dad," he said sleepily.

The words flattered Ryan so much that he reached out and patted Alfie's hand, clumsily. "Me, too, buddy."

And then he saw Mellie's stricken face. Obviously, she didn't feel the same as him and Alfie.

CHAPTER SEVENTEEN

MELLIE HAD TO tell Ryan the truth. Today was as good a time as ever.

She'd put Alfie on the school boat this morning. Now that Betty was working more, Mellie was able to take a day off from the market. And she'd been dithering around in her flower beds, but it wasn't a comfort.

Ever since Alfie had made his bombshell announcement that he wished Ryan were his father—and Ryan had *agreed*—she'd been a mess.

She had all the reasons she hadn't told the truth at the time: Ryan's statement that he didn't want to be involved, Wayne's worrisome advice, her fears for Alfie's well-being.

But Ryan now seemed to want to be involved. Would he have said he wished he were Alfie's father if it weren't true?

As for Wayne's advice, after spending almost two months around Ryan, after their conversation about his past, after he'd been so tender with her, she had to believe Wayne had been wrong. Ryan was so gentle and kind. The idea of him hurting anyone, physically, was ludicrous.

He *had* hurt her feelings when he'd rebuffed her participation in Alfie's lessons, but he'd apologized for it. That wasn't abusive cruelty; that was a human mistake, and a minor one at that. He'd warmed up to her again, asked if she was willing to be friends. Things were good between them, these last few days.

Telling Ryan the truth was going to ruin that, she was pretty sure. But keeping the secret wasn't fair to any of them.

A door opened and closed at Betty's house, and she turned from her work to see Ryan striding down the road. He must be headed to collect his water samples.

The clouds loomed low and the wind blew his hair, but he strode forward as if he didn't feel the fall chill.

She could go after him and tell him outside, where he was happiest. Maybe that would give him a bigger perspective.

She ran inside, grabbed a jacket and followed after him.

At first, Mellie had to jog to catch up. But once she was in sight of Ryan again, she slowed down, trying to figure out how to frame what she was about to tell him.

Should she state the bald reality first and then expand on it, explain it? Or should she lead up slowly, with "remember when" and how she'd found out and why she hadn't told him? Should she reveal Wayne's fears about him, or would that lack of confidence in his basic goodness—from both Wayne and her—crush him?

The truth was, there was no easy way to tell a man you'd borne his child and kept it from him.

Ryan turned left instead of right on High Street, heading away from town. He crossed the bridge that everyone called the kissing bridge, because it was a good spot for romantic prom and wedding photos, and headed toward the beach. His pace was fast, his head bent against the increasingly strong breeze.

She wrapped her sweater more tightly around herself, said a prayer and broke into a jog, calling his name.

He stopped, turned and waited. She slowed to a walk so she could enjoy this last moment of looking at him without him hating her for what she'd done. She was about to ruin everything between them, and she ached already at the loss of his regard and affection.

When she got closer, she saw his tight, drawn face and her plans rushed out of her mind. "What happened?"

He turned and started walking toward the beach again, gesturing for her to join him. "It's the grant. I'm not going to get it."

"I didn't think you'd sent in the proposal yet."

"No. I'm nearly done. Deadline's in two weeks." He blew out a breath. "I've counted on support from the university where I got my doctorate, but I just learned they'll only throw their support behind one person and...it's not me."

"Oh, no." She put an arm around his waist, the only way she could address the complete misery in his voice. "That doesn't seem fair."

He blew out a breath. "It's nothing formal. It's just that, behind the scenes, people make phone calls, write letters, talk with colleagues. That kind of insider stuff makes all the difference, and I'm terrible at it."

She could argue, but he knew the field and she didn't. "Can you still apply?"

He nodded. "Sure. But the lack of behind-the-scenes support cuts my chances way down. I'm not going to get it."

They'd reached the beach, deserted, and stared out at the churning, gray Chesapeake. The wind was colder here, and she tightened her arm around his waist, wanting to warm him, wanting his warmth.

"I was hoping to help the island," he said, barely audible over the wind and water. "To help save the bay. In some small way, this project was going to do that."

"I know." She wrapped both arms around him and just held him for a minute, not a romantic hug, but one meant to give comfort.

Resignation warred with relief in her chest. She couldn't tell him about Alfie now. Couldn't kick him when he was down.

They stood for a long time, looking out at the water. She couldn't think of anything to say, because there was nothing to say. She didn't know the world of science, but he did. And he wasn't given to hand-wringing and drama. If he said his chances were cut to near zero, they were.

Finally they turned back toward town and home and walked, slowly. "What will you do? You'll still send in your proposal, won't you?"

"Of course." The wind was dying down a little, making it easier to hear him. "I want to do the research. But I'll have to try to find other sources of funding. I won't have the jump-start of a big grant."

They walked back over the bridge, stopping by mutual agreement at the top to lean on the railing and look out over the marshy river. Grasses poked up out of the water, brown and green. An egret landed on the top of a withered tree, then swooped down to wade in the water, on the hunt for its next meal.

It was a natural world she'd taken for granted all her life. She rarely thought about the predictions: that the water would continue to rise and erode the land; that the island would shrink smaller and smaller, eventually disappearing into the bay; that her family's heritage and way of life would erode and disappear, too.

Sometime in Alfie's lifetime, the island might well become uninhabitable.

"Thank you for caring about our island and trying to save it," she said softly, putting an arm around him, offering comfort.

He nodded, looking out over the water.

And then he turned to her and pulled her into his arms.

They stood together for quiet moments, the

sounds of the marsh rising up around them, frogs and birds, the lap of water against the bridge's base.

Her desire to comfort him overrode her natural caution about being in his arms. This wasn't like when they'd embraced and kissed before. This was the feeling she had for Alfie when he'd been hurt by others: the ache inside, the desire to take the pain away, the intense need to let him know he wasn't alone.

She shouldn't feel this way, she thought dimly. Shouldn't feel this kind of caring for Ryan, because their relationship was doomed. A better person, knowing that, would gently disengage from him, pat his arm, spout some platitudes about how tomorrow would be another day and he'd get back on his feet.

But this was Ryan, whom she'd once loved with all of her teenage heart. This was a man who'd suffered terribly in his life and gotten back up, again and again and again.

She looked up and their eyes met, and a little of the bleakness left his. "Thank you for being here, Mellie," he said. He bent his head and kissed her.

It would have been a quick brush of the lips, only that had never been possible between the two of them. So the kiss went deeper. Mellie still wanted to give comfort, and then she couldn't think about that, or anything; she could only feel. Could only try to pull him closer and closer until their bodies were melded together. She couldn't solve his problems, but she could take a part of them off of him and into her.

When they both started breathing harder, he lifted his head, brushed back her hair and smiled a little. "Thank you," he said again.

And as they walked back toward home, holding hands, as the world and her problems and her plans came back to her, Mellie realized that everything had just gotten a lot worse. After experiencing even more closeness, it would be harder than ever to tell him the truth.

BETTY HAD BEEN up most of the night, working in Wayne's study, and she wasn't stopping now that morning had come. Boxes and garbage bags full of mostly junk were piled high outside the door, waiting for Ryan to carry them out to the truck. The office was starting to look like a regular room, with surfaces visible and much of the floor space clear. Early-morning sun slanted through the windows, making the dust motes sparkle and dance.

So far, she hadn't found out what had caused Wayne to be so secretive over the years. But she was about to tackle his big rolltop desk, and that, she suspected, was where answers would lie if they were anywhere.

Ever since Amaryllis had mentioned that Wayne did research in the library, Betty had been on fire to figure out what had been going on with him. Not upset, not angry...on fire. She'd tried to get Linda to look up old library records, had visited Amaryllis and asked her flat out what kinds of books Wayne had read at the library, but neither would budge from their position of librarian confidentiality.

So she'd finally opened the door to his study and gotten to work.

There was a tap on the doorjamb. "How are you doing?" Ryan asked, yawning, carrying two steaming coffee cups. He pulled up a now-cleared wooden chair and sat across the desk from her.

"Thanks." She took the coffee, sipped it. "I'm okay. Energized to finally get this done." She studied him. "How are *you*?" Ryan had told her about a setback with his grant, but he'd also been seen walking through town with Mellie, holding hands.

"I'm…okay. I need to see the grant proposal process through, even if…" He shrugged.

"You can't give up. Sometimes the Lord comes through at the last minute, or in a way we don't expect." Like the little hints He kept showing her about Wayne. She hoped the Lord wasn't going to reveal that their marriage had been a sham, but that remained to be seen.

"True." Ryan guzzled some coffee and looked around. "Want me to stay with you in here and work, or should I start carrying boxes downstairs?"

"Boxes," Betty decided. Truthfully, she didn't want Ryan around if she discovered something awful or embarrassing about Wayne.

"On it." Ryan stood, drained the rest of his coffee and headed out, grabbing a couple of garbage bags as he passed the stack.

She looked after him, her heart warming. Ryan

had always been her special child, the child of her heart. Oh, she loved all the boys in different ways, but Ryan...just look how he'd come back here and stayed with her and was helping her. That wasn't something most men would be able to do.

Some people said foster children weren't grateful, weren't really your children. But with Ryan, Cody and Luis, that wasn't true. Maybe because they'd been long-term fosters and had come from such tough situations, they were her kids, through and through.

She slid open the first desk drawer gingerly, afraid of what she might find.

And caught her breath.

Inside was a paperweight they'd gotten as a wedding present. Dream Big, it said on the base, and the top was a picture frame where you were supposed to put your dream.

He'd put a picture of the two of them on one side and the Eiffel Tower on the other.

Tears sprung to her eyes as she remembered the early days of their courtship and marriage. They'd discovered that they'd both studied French in school and had both cherished a dream of going to Paris. It had bonded them together, that dream, and they'd spoken of it often in the early years, had pored over guidebooks, had watched French films.

As time had gone by, the dream had faded. A small-town minister didn't make much money, and neither did the owner of a little grocery store. They'd fostered kids, but contrary to popular belief, foster parents didn't get rich; despite the payments from the state, they usually ended up spending a fair amount of their own money on their kids. That had been the case for Wayne and Betty, and they'd quietly set their dream aside.

Now, she studied the photo. It wasn't of their youngest days, and she eased it out of the frame to realize that there was another behind it, and another, and another. Mostly Christmas photos of the two of them, and she realized that he must have replaced the picture every few years with a new one.

Why didn't you tell me you still had the dream?

She looked heavenward, tears pooling in her eyes. "I wish we could have gone," she murmured to him.

Carefully, she wiped the paperweight off and set it on the desk. And then, eyes still leaking tears, she kept going through the drawers.

All the stacks of papers, old bills, canceled checks... Had the man thrown anything away? She thought of it with a little more fondness, though, now. She didn't want to just empty drawers into trash bags, because what if she found something that meant something? What if she missed another sweet item like the paperweight?

Ryan was in and out, checking on her, carrying things, and progress was slow, but she continued sorting. Mostly, it was throwaway stuff, though she did find an envelope with three twenty-dollar bills in it and a note on the front: Christmas. Hmm. Wonder which Christmas that had been targeted toward? She set it aside. She'd give a twenty each to Ryan, Luis and Cody, something symbolic since they hadn't inherited anything from their foster father.

She found a few old checkbooks filed with duplicate checks and flipped through them, then tossed them into the garbage bags. Until one familiar name caught her eye.

Melanie Anderson.

Huh. She didn't remember Wayne hiring Mellie to do anything or buying something from her, but then again, there were a lot of life details she didn't remember.

She looked through the duplicate check carbons more slowly.

There were more: Melanie Anderson, Melanie Anderson, Melanie Anderson. Check after check, all of them for five hundred dollars.

Why had Wayne been giving money, significant money, to Mellie on a monthly basis?

The sound of Ryan coming upstairs, grabbing another bag and going out got more distant, as did the sound of birdsong coming through the open windows, someone's lawn mower. It all got drowned out by a strange buzzing in her head.

She looked at the dates on the checks. First of every month. At least twenty checks, the only ones in the checkbook.

She looked at the years involved and froze.

Ryan was saying something to her but she couldn't

hear it, because a horrified realization was dawning on her.

Wayne had been paying Mellie, monthly, right after Alfie was born.

She could hardly breathe, even though her heart was pounding way too fast. Was she having a heart attack?

Betty had always suspected that Georgie wasn't Alfie's father, based on something his mother had once told her. There'd been a shortage of the MMR vaccine when Georgie was small, and he'd never been vaccinated. Hadn't seemed like a big deal, but he'd caught mumps as a teenager. She'd wondered if his fertility would be affected and had been thrilled when he'd produced a grandchild, Alfie.

However, Georgie's mom had never gotten very close to Alfie, and after Georgie had passed away, neither she nor Mellie had seemed to want to continue the connection.

Not only that, but Georgie hadn't been the bookish type. Alfie's academic interests didn't come from him.

She and Peg had speculated a few times: Who was Alfie's real father? But idly. Georgie had been his father in every important way; the biology didn't really matter.

Unless… She fingered through the checks again and thought back. When had Wayne become distant and secretive? Had it been right around the time Alfie had been born?

And Wayne, unlike Georgie, had been an intellectual. A bit of a nerd. Just like Alfie.

She let the checkbook fall to the floor and put her head in her hands. She'd discovered Wayne's big secret.

He was Alfie's father.

CHAPTER EIGHTEEN

RYAN WAS JUST lifting the last two garbage bags in the hallway when he heard something from Wayne's office that didn't sound right. Partway between a hiccup, a gulp and a cry.

He dropped the bags and walked in to find Betty hunched over in a chair, breathing audibly. "Betty! Are you okay? What's wrong?"

He knelt beside her and saw that she was conscious, but her face was pale and sweaty. "I'll call the clinic."

"No." She barked out the word and then buried her face in her hands again.

"Come on, sit up, and I'll get you some water." He hurried out and filled a tall glass, hurried it back in, his heart pounding.

Nothing could happen to Betty. He was here to take care of her and he was going to do it. The woman had lived a hard life and was about to enjoy the fruits of her labors.

Besides, *he* couldn't lose her, the only mother remaining in his life.

He eased her upright and held the water to her

lips, and she took a sip, then grasped the glass and drank deeply. She shook her head a little, like a dog.

"Let me drive you to the clinic," he said. She just didn't look right.

"No, no, I'll be okay, I just…I've had a shock."

He pulled up a wooden chair and sat beside her, patting her arm, wishing he knew what to do. "What happened?"

She held out a small booklet to him, an old-fashioned checkbook he saw, and he looked through it.

Check receipts, made out to Mellie.

He frowned. "You didn't know about these?"

"No. Look at the dates."

He did, but could see nothing upsetting in them. "I don't get it. What do you make of them?"

"Wayne was…" She drew in a breath. "He must have been paying Mellie child support. He must be Alfie's father."

"No way." Ryan reeled back, holding up a hand. Every atom in his body rejected the idea. "He was thirty years older than her. And he was your husband! Mellie wouldn't do that, and Wayne wouldn't, either."

She pointed at the checkbook and then looked at him.

"There must be some other explanation." Disparate jigsaw puzzle pieces assembled and reassembled in his head.

He'd already surmised that he and Georgie must have been with Mellie at nearly the same time. Now Betty was wanting to add Wayne to the mix?

He couldn't, wouldn't, believe it of Mellie. But even as he had that thought, doubts sent their little prickling needles into his head.

She hadn't cared for Ryan like she'd said she did. She'd been with Georgie before and after. Yet she'd never seemed madly in love with the man.

Could she have been vulnerable to advances from her much older, married next-door neighbor? Could Wayne have made such advances? Had money been a factor?

And, the scientist in him marveled, was he the only one who understood birth control?

"All those years I've helped her with Alfie," Betty said, her voice bitter.

"Betty, don't go there," Ryan said. "There must be some other explanation."

"For a man to start giving a woman monthly payments just after she has a child?" Her voice rose to a high-pitched croak. "He always did like Mellie. He always did look at younger women."

"No, no, wait." Ryan couldn't stand to hear the pain in her voice, and he worried about her getting this hysterical. "Wayne was loyal to you. I know he was."

"Stop it," she snapped. "Don't placate me."

He supposed it was a good sign, health-wise, that she was getting red-faced and energetic instead of pale and sweaty and broken-looking, but he couldn't let her continue in what had to be a misperception. "Come on," he said. "We're going to see Mellie."

On the way out, Betty wrenched the Forever sign

from beside the door and hurled it across the yard, harder than Ryan had known she could throw.

MELLIE WAS KNEELING in her garden when Betty and Ryan came across the yard. "Mellie! Mellie Anderson!" Betty's voice sounded strange.

She got up and brushed her hands on the sides of her jeans. "Hey, what's up?"

She'd been working out here to try to think. She was worried about Ryan and didn't want to hurt him. But she was also worried about Alfie, about his comment that he wished Ryan was his father. What would it do to him to go forward not knowing the truth? What would it do to any potential relationship he could have with Ryan?

She had to figure it out, and soon, because Ryan wouldn't stay on the island much longer. His grant proposal was nearly done, and Betty had gotten through the worst of her depression.

She watched them come closer now. Something was wrong. Betty was walking fast, ahead of Ryan, who seemed to be trying to hold her back. He was looking apologetically at Mellie.

"All these years I've thought you were my friend." Betty propped her hands on her hips. "And it turns out you're just a deceptive cheating witch."

The words hit her like blows, but they made no sense. "What? Betty, what are you talking about?" Mellie stepped toward the woman, meaning to take her hand.

Betty pushed a little booklet of paper toward Mellie. "What do you have to say about *this*?"

Ryan put an arm around Betty. "Come on now, let's all sit down. I'm sure Mellie can explain."

Mellie was getting a bad feeling, but part of it was that Betty seemed on the verge of some kind of attack. "Come on, come sit on my porch," she said. "I'll get you some iced tea."

"I wouldn't take water from you if I were dying of thirst in the desert," Betty snapped.

"I think we'd all like some tea," Ryan said.

When she came back out with three glasses, Betty was perched on the edge of the porch swing with Ryan beside her. Mellie set the tea on the table and then took a seat on the rocking chair placed diagonal to the swing. "What's this all about, Betty?"

"How long were you sleeping with my husband?" Betty demanded.

Mellie's jaw dropped open. "Never! I would never do that." She studied Betty's red face, confused. She couldn't understand why Betty was insulting her this way, what it meant.

Betty narrowed her eyes. "Is Wayne Alfie's father?"

Mellie's heart thudded, hard and rhythmic, as she looked from Betty to Ryan and back again.

She had no idea why Betty would think such a thing. But she was pretty sure the real truth about Alfie's parentage was about to come out.

The heavy cloak of hiding, pretending, lying, the

cloak she'd worn for more than ten years, slid off her back.

She shouldn't feel this lightening of her load, because she was about to hurt at least one person she loved, maybe two. Having kept the secret this long, maybe she should find a way to continue.

But it had been so, so hard, all these years, to pretend that Alfie was Georgie's child. She didn't like lying, and she couldn't help but feel relieved that she could set that aside and tell the truth.

She looked out toward the bay, smooth and vast and timeless. It would long outlast the three of them, was bigger than they were, more solid. Slowly, she shook her head. "No, he isn't. Wayne's not Alfie's father."

"Then why was he giving you five hundred dollars per month?" Again, she shook the little pad of paper in Mellie's face.

Mellie took it and saw that it was a checkbook, and it all became clear.

Wayne's payments to her to help with Alfie, after she'd agreed to keep the truth from Ryan. Betty had come upon the duplicate checks and jumped to the wrong conclusion.

"Well?" Betty asked.

"I'm sure there's an explanation," Ryan said.

Oh, you bet there is. Mellie sucked in a breath and closed her eyes and shot up a wordless prayer. If ever she'd needed help, now was the time.

She felt as ashamed as a child who'd caused an accident that had bigger ramifications than she could have ever imagined. She had done wrong, been wrong. So very wrong.

She needed to step up and explain now. It would be the right thing to do.

But she'd come to care for Ryan so much. Had never really stopped caring. He looked at her with a kind of warm happiness she'd never felt before, and she wanted that to continue.

If she could just get Betty alone and explain, Ryan wouldn't have to learn the truth this way. "Maybe we could talk about it, just the two of us," she said to Betty, weakly, hating her own cowardice.

"Why, so you can manipulate me just like you've been doing all along?"

"I haven't been manipulating you. Wayne isn't Alfie's father."

"I've always suspected Georgie wasn't his father," Betty continued to rant. "Georgie had the mumps and it affected his fertility."

"You're right." Mellie stared at the ground, watched an ant crawl across the porch and up the leg of the table. "Georgie couldn't have children."

"Then…" Ryan began, and stopped. When she stole a glance at his face, she saw that he looked terribly, terribly disappointed in her. "Then you turned to Wayne?"

She shook her head rapidly. "No. No, it wasn't Wayne. Wayne never took that kind of interest in me, nor me in him. He loved you, Betty. So, so much."

Betty was starting to calm down, but she looked skeptical. "He paid you child support."

"Not exactly." Resignation flowed into her like the steady waves of the bay. It was time. She'd always known the day would come to tell the whole truth. She wished she'd been able to choose the circumstances, but she'd had opportunities, hadn't she? And she'd lost them through fear. No more.

She drew in a breath and started talking. "Wayne wanted to help me out because he knew the father and didn't want me to tell him about the pregnancy."

"Why not?" they both asked at once.

"Because he didn't think the father would be a good or safe person to parent Alfie."

"That sounds like a bunch of malarkey," Betty said, but half-heartedly. She looked at Mellie's face, eyes steady now. "You're telling the truth, aren't you?"

Mellie nodded miserably. "Yes."

A crow flew by, cawing. On the street, a couple of parents headed down toward the school boats. It was almost time to pick up Alfie.

"I see." Betty glanced over at Ryan. "Or at least, I'm starting to."

Ryan looked blank. "I don't."

Mellie looked at his handsome face, his kind eyes, and knew that this was the last minute of him not hating her. She wanted to stretch it out as long as possible.

Just tell him. You have to, now.

But it would devastate him. It might cause him to reject Alfie even as a friend and mentee.

This was all her fault.

Nonetheless, she had to do it. She gripped the arms of the rocking chair and cleared her throat. "You see, Ryan," she said, and stopped.

He tipped his head to one side. "What?"

"You see…Alfie is *your* son."

CHAPTER NINETEEN

RYAN'S THOUGHTS SPUN like an out-of-control Ferris wheel. Surely Mellie hadn't just said what he thought she'd said. "Alfie's my *son*?"

Mellie's face was flushed and tears were starting to roll down her cheeks. She nodded, biting her lip and watching him.

Dimly, he felt Betty put an arm around him.

He couldn't seem to process the words, the idea.

"Mom!" Alfie shouted from the road.

Mellie leaped to her feet, wiping the backs of her hands across her eyes. She started down the porch steps.

Alfie was coming toward her. Junior waved and continued on.

To Ryan, it all seemed to be happening in slow motion. Every sense was tuned in and vivid. He suspected he'd remember this moment for the rest of his life.

"You didn't come to meet the school boat!" Alfie sounded excited. "Because I'm big now, right?"

Mellie nodded and put an arm around him and they came toward the porch, slowly, Alfie chattering.

Alfie was his son. His son. At least, that was what Mellie had said.

"Don't say anything about it to the boy just now," Betty said in a low voice. "I don't think he knows, either."

Ryan couldn't speak. He just stared at Alfie.

This bright, lively little boy whom he'd come to care about…was it possible, could it be true that he was Ryan's biological son?

Ryan's mind raced in all directions, figuring it out. That one encounter he and Mellie had had. He'd used a condom, but statistically, they weren't a hundred percent effective. No doubt the failure rate was higher for a clumsy first-time user, which Ryan had been.

Alfie was ten, so the age was correct. Ryan didn't know when Alfie's birthday was, though.

He didn't know when his own son's birthday was.

He'd missed all those birthdays. Neglected his son throughout—

His stomach clenched, painfully, as Alfie trotted up the steps. "Hey, Mr. Ryan, Ms. Betty! Guess what I got on my biology test!" He threw down his backpack and started fumbling through it.

The swing jolted back as Betty stood. "You can show everyone later, hon," she said to Alfie. "Why don't you come over and help me mix up some oatmeal-teaberry cookies?"

"Here it is!" Alfie pulled out a page, triumphant, and held it up for Mellie to see, then rushed over to

Ryan. He perched on the swing beside him. "Look, an A-," he said excitedly. "See, this is just the process we were talking about, and I made flash cards like we talked about, and reviewed it again the morning before, and it *worked*!" His eyes shone as he looked at Ryan.

Clearly, he was waiting for a reaction. Clearly, Ryan should say something. "Good job," he croaked out.

Alfie flipped through the pages, pointing and talking. Ryan looked at the letters and numbers, the clear-cut realities of simple science that had always both calmed and excited him. He tried to concentrate on the Krebs cycle, DNA replication, blood typing.

Slowly things came into focus for him. He sat beside Alfie, close but not touching, nodding as Alfie explained his process of finding the answers, how he'd gotten stuck once, twice, but he'd pictured his flash cards and remembered. He talked through the couple of mistakes he'd made, said he'd asked the teacher and the teacher had shown him where he'd gone wrong.

He heard a choked sound from Mellie and then the screen door opened and banged shut. He looked up and only Betty stood there now, watching the two of them, a bemused expression on her face.

If only he could continue sitting here forever, focused on the science, not having to deal with Mellie. Mellie, who'd lied and betrayed him and robbed him—robbed Alfie, too—of time and experiences they should have shared. Mellie, who'd pushed Ryan into being the same kind of father his own father had been.

Ryan's eyes burned and he felt hot all over. Dimly, he was conscious of Betty leading Alfie away and off the porch with questions about the test and promises of cookies to come. As they walked away together, the moment flashed him back in time. Betty had always asked him questions about his classes and listened to the answers with the same nodding enthusiasm she was presenting to Alfie now.

Because Alfie was the same kind of kid Ryan had been.

Because Alfie was his son.

He watched them disappear into Betty's house and then his brain just turned off. He sat, nudging the porch swing into a slight rocking motion, arms crossed over his chest. Princess came trotting up the steps and over to him, nudged at his leg, and he absently reached down to pet her.

The screen door opened. "Ryan?"

His calm shattered and he jumped to his feet and advanced on Mellie. "How could you keep that from me?" he shouted. He'd never understood the expression "seeing red" before, but now, it was as if Mellie were surrounded by a bloodred, pulsing frame. "Why, Mellie? Why did you do that to me and to him?"

She backed away from him, fear flashing over her

tearstained face. Good. She should be afraid. He was angry enough to reach out and…

She took another step back, and now she was pressed against the screen door and he was inches away from her. His fists clenched.

She lifted her arms, protecting her face.

Memory blasted into him and, with it, shock and self-disgust. He'd assumed that posture many times as a child, right before Cueball had slammed a fist into him.

He backed away and forced himself to relax his hands. Automatically, he went into the box-breathing some therapist had taught him when he was an angry teenager who kept getting into fights: inhale-two-three-four, then hold four counts, exhale four, hold four. A couple rounds of that and he could speak. "I won't hurt you."

She lowered her hands and stepped away from the door, nodding. "I'd like to tell you, about what—"

"Now that I found out," he said, keeping his voice flat and calm, "you want to tell me. But that didn't occur to you for the past ten years." He looked off to the side, where a gray squirrel—*Sciurus carolinensis*—ran up a tree trunk.

"I wanted to tell you…" she started, and went on to make some excuse he couldn't even try to understand.

Staying calm wasn't possible. His mind reeled wildly and his stomach roiled. "Wayne didn't think I could take care of a child. He thought I'd hurt Alfie."

She nodded, slowly. "He had seen it happen before, in people with your background, and he didn't want me to take the risk."

"And you agreed with that." Darkness washed over him, a tidal wave.

He was worthless, doomed to darkness. And he hated the woman who'd made him think, for even a moment, that there was goodness and hope and light in the world for someone like him.

"You have to be furious and rightly so," she said. "Just please, please don't take it out on Alfie."

"What, don't beat him and lock him in a basement alone for days at a time?" The words were ugly, but they burst out of him because he didn't care if she knew that it had happened to him on a regular basis. Did. Not. Care.

Mellie's hand flew to her mouth, her eyes huge.

Ryan turned away as black memories engulfed him. Of crying out for help. Of how much his empty stomach hurt. Of wanting someone, anyone, to talk to him, to take his hand, to hug the loneliness away.

The utter emptiness he'd felt. Like what he felt now.

He was a monster, unfit for human company. He stumbled a little as he turned toward the porch steps.

"Ryan, I'd like to talk as soon as you can." Her voice was shaky.

He gripped the railing and turned. "We'll talk about Alfie later. Anything that was ever between us…that's gone. Forever."

Forever stretched out in front of him like gray fog as he made his way, half stumbling, down to the bay.

MELLIE GOT THROUGH the next few days like a robot moving mechanically through a series of tasks. She went to work. She fixed food for Alfie and listened to his constant questions and chatter. She washed dishes and did laundry.

Ryan completely avoided her, which wasn't surprising. He ignored her texts and voice mails and didn't answer the door. She'd tried to talk to Betty, but Betty had just shaken her head and frowned and shut the door in Mellie's face.

At the market, Betty avoided her, communicating by notes and working opposite shifts.

Sundays, they didn't open until noon, when the first tourist boat came over. But Mellie went in early to replenish the harvest displays and restock the shelves.

Thank heavens for Jimmy and Junior, who'd swept Alfie away to work on some complicated costume the boys were making for Halloween.

Ryan had sent her one text. Will be in touch regarding visitation and custody.

Would he try to take Alfie? Or was he just looking into the minimum obligation he could get away with?

She'd never ask him for child support, not after what she'd done, but knowing Ryan, he'd try to do that much at least. She would have expected him to do much more, especially after what he'd said about visitation and custody, but he was avoiding Alfie, working on his grant from sunup to sundown. He'd told Alfie he was too busy now for tutoring and that Alfie would do fine, just like he had on his test.

Alfie was upset. He didn't understand why Mr. Ryan wouldn't take him on his research expeditions, wouldn't hang out.

Mellie suspected that her worst nightmare was coming true: Ryan, having learned the truth, was rejecting Alfie, refusing to welcome him as a son. Despite his text that mentioned visitation and custody—which was worrisome enough—his actions said something else: that he was pushing Alfie away.

And it was Mellie's fault.

She swept leaves off the store's front porch and straightened the scarecrow and hay bales. She brought more pumpkins from the back of the store to liven up the display. Hopefully, she could catch Betty when she came to work and try again to talk to her.

Fall was in the air, all right, but to Mellie right now, it wasn't the fun it sometimes could be; it was a time of darkness and decay and dying.

"Hey, long time no..." Taylor froze in the act of coming onto the porch. "What happened?"

Mellie looked up at her friend and couldn't even pretend nothing was wrong. "He found out."

"Oh, no!" Taylor came the rest of the way up, a white bakery bag in her hands. "I brought teaberry scones. Tell me."

Mellie nodded, went inside to get them both coffee and came back out. With sweaters, it was still chilly, but Mellie felt better outside than in.

"I thought maybe you'd tell him before he figured it out," Taylor said.

"I was going to, but…" She sighed and told Taylor how it had all gone down.

"Oh, man. That's awful. I can't believe Betty thought you'd betray her like that."

"I betrayed *Ryan*. He's not speaking to me. Not speaking to Alfie, either."

"He's had a shock." Taylor pulled out a warm scone, broke it and handed half to Mellie. "It would take a little while for all that to sink in. Maybe he'll come around."

Mellie pressed her lips together and shook her head. "I ruined everything. I really, really screwed up. I couldn't even go to church this morning."

"That's when you need church the most."

It was true, but Mellie felt too bad about herself, too unclean.

She took a bite of the scone, but it was dry and tasteless to her.

"You had your reasons," Taylor said.

"What?"

"He was pretty mean to you, right? Broke your heart? So how were you supposed to know that he'd be okay as a father?"

Mellie shook her head. "I shouldn't have listened to Wayne. I should have listened to my own heart."

"I mean, maybe you made a mistake, especially once he came back to the island. But he hasn't been back that long. I don't blame you for waiting to tell him."

"If you're on the clock, work." The harsh com-

mand came from Betty, who'd approached from behind Mellie.

"She's been working all morning, Betty," Taylor said. "I'm sorry to have distracted her. Want a
scone?"

Betty started to say no, but when Taylor held out
the bag, she took it. "Thanks," she said gruffly.

"You two need to talk," Taylor said. "I'm out of
here."

They both watched Taylor walk away.

Mellie doubted she could ever make it up with
Ryan, but maybe, if she could talk to Betty, the older
woman would be able to help, to negotiate some sort
of peace for Alfie's sake. "Like I said when I came
over the other day, I'm really, really sorry. I was
wrong in so many ways."

Betty's mouth went tight and she looked away.

"I really screwed up. I hurt Ryan. I can see why
you're angry."

"You took money from my husband!" Betty burst
out. "You kept a secret with him. All those years,
when I thought we were friends, you never told me
the truth."

Mellie remembered she'd felt sneaky and bad, but
Wayne had told her to keep quiet about the money,
that it would upset Betty. So she'd done that, and
she'd stopped the flow of checks as soon as she and
Georgie could get a little ahead.

Those had been hard days. Between Georgie, her
younger sisters, her new baby and her difficult father,
Mellie hadn't had a moment to think.

"I should have found a way to tell you," she said. "I just... I value your friendship so much, Betty. I don't know if I can ever have it back, but I hope so."

Betty snorted, but she did sit down beside Mellie on the market's front step. A moment later, Betty put a hand over Mellie's. "I should have known you'd never sleep with Wayne or any other woman's husband," she said, "and I'm sorry I thought that of you, even for a minute."

"It's okay." She felt the balm of Betty's forgiveness, a tiny waterfall through the dryness of her soul.

"While you and Ryan work out your problems," Betty said, "someone needs to look out for that little boy."

"Thank you, Betty." Mellie hugged the older woman. "I...I can't tell you how much it means that you're speaking to me again. And I know. Alfie is the important thing." She bit her lip. "I just don't know when or how to tell him that Ryan is his father." But it couldn't be until Ryan was willing to at least acknowledge the truth—and the child.

CHAPTER TWENTY

FOR THE WEEK and a half after Mellie's stunning revelation, Ryan buried himself in his work. It paid off; the grant proposal was nearly done. One more look-over today, here in his makeshift study at Betty's house, and he would hit Send.

He needed to stick to what was important and reliable. To the way he could make a difference. People respected him for his work.

When he'd collected his last samples, Jed and Tim and a couple other fishermen he'd met had stopped to talk. Ryan had actually enjoyed it. They were knowledgeable about the water and also aware of the challenges facing the bay, and he'd ended up snapping a couple of pictures of them to add to his proposal.

It was *good* he was avoiding Mellie and Alfie; he wouldn't have connected with the fishermen otherwise, gotten those shots. They, along with his shots of Alfie, would bring his proposal to life.

Submitting it without behind-the-scenes support of his university mentors meant he was unlikely to get the grant, he knew that. Way unlikely. Still, he'd done his best and there was an outside chance his history, his skills and his passion for the island would make the committee give his proposal a second look.

He corrected a typo and forced himself to continue reading closely, to concentrate. He didn't need his application to be derailed by a misspelled word or unaligned margin.

It should be easy to concentrate here now. He looked around and tried to relish the satisfaction of a job well done. Betty's house was nearly cleaned out. Just a couple more days' work and it would be truly livable. Betty was doing much better, too.

You did well, he told himself firmly. He even tried a couple of old affirmations his therapists had taught him over the years. When you hadn't had the affirmation during childhood, you had to supply it to yourself. It wasn't as good as the kind you got from loving parents caring for and coddling you from day one, but it could work, could help you make a life.

He heard a noise out the window, a child's shout, and he was there before he even knew he was moving.

There was Alfie.

Alfie, his son.

The boy was running with Gizmo, throwing a ball and then chasing it himself, racing the dog to it. Gizmo got there inches ahead of Alfie, but the boy dived for the ball and tugged it out of the gentle dog's mouth and lay rolling and wrestling with the dog, laughing.

He was so full of joy. Ryan had watched him out

the window for hours at a time since Mellie's revelation, and that was what most struck him: Alfie's joy.

Ryan didn't think he'd had a moment of such uninhibited delight ever, but he was thrilled that his son could.

"My son." He tried the words out aloud for the hundredth time since he'd learned the truth, quietly so Betty wouldn't hear him. Still, it hardly seemed real to him.

Real enough, though, was his anger toward Mellie, who'd kept him apart from that son for the first ten years of the boy's life. He'd been right to cut her off when she'd first told him and to evade her efforts to talk with him. He should feel good about how he'd stood up for himself. He'd gotten rid of her permanently.

But when she came out the door, fuchsia pink sweater and red hair blindingly bright, his heart seemed to reach out toward her.

She betrayed you.

He pushed aside the heartbroken feeling. Or tried to, anyway. But images kept going through his mind. Her approaching him from behind that first night he'd arrived, baseball bat in hand, ready to defend her neighbor. Her friendly way at the store that made everyone want to shop at the market, even for goods they could get cheaper on the mainland. The concern and fierce maternal love she'd shown during the meeting with the principal.

He hadn't known he was attending the meeting as Alfie's father, though, and he felt like a chump. He'd sat there deferring to Mellie, grateful to be included, happy to lend a hand. When in truth he'd had every right to be there.

And the responsibility to do it. He'd never wanted to be that man who didn't assume responsibility for a child, but inadvertently, he'd become his own worst nightmare. He glared at her and then backed away from the window and returned to his computer and his task.

An hour later, he sent the proposal off.

He wandered through the house, wanting to tell Betty, but she was nowhere around. She might be at work, or with a friend, or at the book club she'd started attending.

Which was good. Great. She'd made terrific progress since he'd arrived, and he knew his presence and his company and his help with the cluttered house had played at least some part in that.

But the upshot was, he had no one to celebrate with.

He slammed a hand down on the kitchen counter, trying to push away this strange sadness with bright, sharp anger. He'd never cared about having someone to share his successes with before. He'd sent in grant proposals and research papers without even thinking to look around and high-five his lab mates. He'd gotten a couple of terrific grants without even calling anyone to tell them about it. When he'd won the Young Scientist of the Year award, he'd left the ceremony and gone home alone without a second thought. Only when his brothers had learned about the award and called to congratulate him, asked how he was celebrating, had it occurred to him that he should.

Even then, he hadn't minded his solitary success. Had he?

Now, though, it was a different story. Mellie and Alfie, Betty and the whole ambience of Teaberry Island had awakened in him a desire for connection. Why had he let them do that? Why had he started to get close to people who would perpetually disappoint him?

He'd go for a walk. The bay wouldn't let him down.

An hour later he walked by the Floating Fisherman, now docked by Tidewater Cove, and someone called out to him. It was Tim, whom he'd spoken with earlier today. "Come on, get a drink with us."

Normally, Ryan would have made an excuse, but really, where did he have to go?

He climbed aboard, accepted the offer of a beer and listened as they talked about their day's catch, the rockfish they'd already sold. He ended up telling them he'd sent in his grant application, that he didn't think he'd get it but it was worth a try.

They'd waved aside his statement, certain he would get the grant and help the island, and he didn't have the heart to disabuse them of the notion.

"Think you'll stay?" Jed asked.

He shrugged and the conversation moved in other directions.

Ryan looked around at the craggy-faced men, the orange sunball setting over the bay. He tasted the bitter, cheap beer and inhaled the briny scent of the marsh and felt the wind in his hair.

Sitting here on this boat with these men was as surprising as if he'd been invited to an exclusive party with the high school football players and cheerleaders.

He tried to rouse up his anger at Mellie, because her betrayal was what he should focus on. He'd been robbed of something that could never be replaced or replicated, so it was inappropriate for him to enjoy this impromptu party, even a little bit.

But the experience of being accepted among a group of men was so novel to him that he couldn't help but relish the experience.

"Here's to a scientist who actually helps the island," one of the men said, and they all raised their beer cans and then drank deeply.

And Ryan had a realization. Hitting Send on the grant application hadn't been the triumph today.

Celebrating with people was.

But the people who mattered most weren't here, because he'd pushed them away. His family. Mellie and Alfie.

BETTY WATCHED FROM the porch as Ryan carried out the last boxes and bags from this day's work. There was always more to do, but they'd gotten a lot done. Ryan was such a good son, helping her when she needed it most.

And now, she was going to try to help him. "Come sit down," she said, patting the front steps beside her.

"It's almost time for trick or treat, and we make a big deal of that here on the island."

At first she hadn't thought she wanted to do Halloween. She'd planned to turn off the lights and hide inside with a book.

But then she'd thought of the little children who would come by and be disappointed not to see her traditional steaming cauldron and noisemaker pumpkin, the spooky witch-on-a-broom she rigged up to raise and lower as kids walked by. Tacky, but kids didn't know that.

She'd also decorated the porch with more classy stuff from the store, leaf garlands and hay bales and pumpkins.

She had a large container of full-size chocolate bars, and another of homemade treats. She was ready.

As Ryan came toward her, Tank, a big black lug of a dog, trotted alongside him, sporting a Halloween kerchief. Good. People had taken it upon themselves to dress up the island dogs, as happened most holidays. And she was glad to see that the fabric was reflective, helping motorists see any misguided pups in the middle of the road.

A car stopped on the street in front of the house, and three little kids from the other side of the island scrambled and rolled and tumbled out. They were dressed like various types of cats—a jaguar, a tiger, a black cat—and the mom was wearing cat ears and a tail, too. "Go ahead, run up! It's Miss Betty from the market, and she always has good candy."

The youngsters came toward the house and Betty

made the witch swoop over them, earning delighted shrieks. Ryan handed each of them a large candy bar and a wrapped popcorn ball. She'd meant to let the kids choose one or the other, but, oh, well. There would be plenty. She could always go inside and gather up some more stuff to give out if needed.

Once that family was gone, the neighborhood was quiet. She caught Ryan looking over in the direction of Mellie's house, and it gave her the perfect opening. "You seeing anything of Alfie?" she asked.

"Not yet," he said, "but I will."

"Seems to me you've been ignoring him," she pointed out.

His face closed in a way she remembered from years ago. "I know, I just…I'm still processing it."

Time for some tough love. "No. Uh-uh. A father doesn't have that luxury. Think of what your distance could be doing to Alfie."

He looked stricken. "Do you think he knows? Did she tell him?"

Betty shook her head. "I doubt it, because she wouldn't want to let him know if you're not going to step up."

"I will. Soon."

"And you should make up with Mellie, too," she said. "Don't let Alfie be the reason you two are throwing away your chance at love and a family."

There was some rustling from the side yard, and a couple of kids jumped out and yelled, "Boo!" So she didn't get the chance to see how her words had affected Ryan right away.

But after the kids had showed off their scary costumes and gotten their treats and left, she saw that Ryan was frowning in that thoughtful way of his. He dived right back into the conversation. "She lied to me for ten years, Betty. Stole that time with Alfie away from me. How am I supposed to forgive her?"

She reached out and rubbed his arm. "I know, and it was wrong. I won't deny that, and I'm still mad at her. But think about why she might have done that."

He nodded. "I was a jerk to her. And Wayne—" He broke off.

Betty sighed. Talk about mistakes.

"He told her I wouldn't be a safe father. That I might..." He trailed off.

"That you might what?" She knew, but she wanted to hear Ryan's interpretation.

"Abuse the child she was carrying the way I was abused." He met her eyes, his own full of pain. "Do you think I will?"

"No!" She wished Wayne were here so she could strangle him. What right did he have to make the kind of blanket statement that could push a young family apart forever?

A better wife would have stayed more connected with Wayne, found out his secrets, done damage control. *She* had known Ryan would never hurt anyone.

She took his hand now, shaking her head back and forth rapidly. "No way. He was wrong about that, completely wrong. You're one of the gentlest men I know."

She paused, wondering how to drill enough sense

into him to force him to reconcile with Mellie, for Alfie's sake if not for his own.

"I think I know why Wayne was so concerned," she said, speaking aloud as it came to her. "When he was a younger man, he counseled a woman to stay with her husband, who was showing signs of becoming abusive. She ended up being badly hurt, and their baby…" She shook her head. "He didn't make it. Wayne always blamed himself for counseling her to stay involved with the man. I'm sure that's part of what he told Mellie."

"Mellie believed him! And if she thought that badly of me—"

She was still holding his hand, and now she squeezed it. "I've never been pregnant," she said slowly, "but I've heard what an emotional time it can be. Your hormones can do a number on you."

He didn't look convinced.

"Put that together with her being barely eighteen and under all kinds of home pressure," she said. "And you just admitted you were a jerk to her. As I recall it, the two of you were starting to look at each other like lovebirds, and then you were gone without a trace."

"Yeah." He pulled his hand away and propped his cheek on it. "I panicked."

"If you could panic from what happened, even without knowing you'd made a baby, imagine her feelings."

"I get that, sort of. But then she married Georgie."

"Right. That has to hurt." But she'd been thinking that through, and she was pretty sure she understood

Mellie's reasoning. "Women do all kinds of things for their kids," she said. "You were gone, and she had two younger sisters still to care for and a father who would probably disown her for being pregnant without benefit of marriage. And there was Georgie, ready and willing to take her back and marry her." She shrugged. "Rich women with a lot of options can decide to raise a child on their own. Mellie was in a different situation."

Another little crowd of kids came then, and they passed out candy and oohed and aahed over their costumes, and the moment for deep conversation was past. But she could tell from his expression that Ryan was still thinking about it.

Good. Maybe she'd gotten through to him.

Suddenly there was a shout from next door. "Alfie! Alfie, where are you?"

Mellie sounded panicky. They both stood and looked toward her house.

Mellie shouted again, closer now. "Alfie!"

They started down the stairs as Mellie came into sight.

"What's wrong?" Betty asked, hurrying to Mellie.

"I can't find him," she said, her voice on the edge of panic. "Alfie is gone."

CHAPTER TWENTY-ONE

MELLIE'S HEART POUNDED like a powerboat's motor. Where was her son?

Even as Ryan and Betty questioned her, she was hunting through the bushes around Betty's porch. "Alfie! Come on home!"

Betty flicked on all her outdoor lights, ridding the place of its Halloween ambience and making it bright as day, and Mellie's hopes rose. But a few minutes' search didn't reveal Alfie.

"I'll run down to the bay and look around," Ryan said, his voice conveying the same fear that was gripping Mellie.

"The bay!" Mellie started to run after Ryan. Why, oh, why had she let him out of her sight? What kind of mother lost her own child?

"Wait, honey," Betty called after her. "Come on back. He'll look, and we can think."

Mellie stopped running and turned back toward Betty. "But if he's—" She broke off and pressed her hands to her mouth.

"He's known the bay all his life. He's not going to take any risks." Betty's voice was matter-of-fact.

Mellie clung to that calmness and took a few steps back toward Betty.

"Come on, let's search around your house one more time."

"I looked everywhere. He's not there." Mellie was breathing hard.

"Okay. He couldn't be inside my place. Ryan and I have been sitting on the porch for an hour. But maybe my shed?"

"He loves it. Let's look." Mellie's hopes rose as she envisioned finding him there, goofing around or hiding. She was going to give him such a lecture.

But he wasn't there, and a moment later, Ryan came back from the bay, his forehead wrinkled. "No sign of him."

Panic rose in Mellie again. She spun around, ready to take off running in any direction, just to be moving, trying to find him rather than doing nothing.

Ryan put a hand on her arm, stopping her.

"Let's be logical," Betty said. "Mellie. Where did you see him last?"

"He said he was headed over here." Mellie re-created their last conversation in her mind, trying to figure out if she'd missed a clue. "I was cleaning up from dinner, and he wanted to come over here before going off with some kids from school. We were arguing, in fact, because I wanted to go with him all evening and he said he was too old for that." Her stomach roiled at the memory of how they'd yelled at each other. "I…I got upset. I'll admit it, I have trouble with letting him be independent sometimes."

And if only she'd stuck to her guns, he wouldn't be missing now.

"It's normal." Betty rubbed a hand over the back of her shoulders, a gesture of comfort. "How did you leave it with him?"

"He said okay, I could go with him, but he just wanted to come over here by himself. That was a compromise I could accept." She bit her lip. "I shouldn't have." Fear pushed against her like repetitive waves. She needed to think, not give in to it. Needed to be strong, but Alfie was her baby, her son, her world.

Betty looked at Ryan. "I wonder if he overheard us talking."

Ryan winced.

Mellie's senses went on high alert. "What were you talking about?"

"Him," Ryan said slowly. "We were talking about him being my son."

Mellie clapped a hand over her mouth. "Oh, no. Do you think he overheard?"

"It's…definitely possible." He frowned, thinking. "There were kids running around some of the time we were talking." He pounded his fist into his opposite palm. "Why didn't I think of the fact that he could be around and could overhear?"

"What's done is done." Betty's voice was calm, but not quite as even as before, and her brows had drawn together.

"At least, if he overheard something and got

upset," Ryan said, "we know he ran off. He wasn't abducted."

Mellie stared at Ryan. "It's the island," she said.

"We know everyone who lives here. He wasn't abducted," Betty said firmly. "Let's think. Where are some places he could've gone?"

"Maybe Junior's house?" Ryan suggested. "Or the junkyard itself?"

"Could be," Mellie said. She pulled out her phone to call. "Or the market. He knows the code to get in." She scrolled to find Jimmy's number and then realized she didn't have service.

"Taylor's keeping the bakery open," Betty said. "A couple of other businesses are open, too. Lots of kids are going through downtown, trick-or-treating."

"Could he have gone off with the other kids without you?" Ryan asked.

Mellie shook her head. "I thought of that. But his friends came by looking for him. That's when I realized he wasn't back from here yet." She spun around, squinting through the darkness, praying that he'd show up.

"How was he dressed?" Ryan was getting methodical, and she felt a flash of gratitude that he was on board.

"He dressed up as a scientist," she said. "White lab coat, goggles, a clipboard. He wanted..." She bit her lip, looking at Ryan. "He wanted to look like you."

Ryan sucked in a quick breath. The muscles worked in his jaw.

This stunt of Alfie's—Mellie fervently hoped it was just a stunt—had to be throwing him into more confusion about the fact that he was Alfie's father.

But she couldn't worry about Ryan's emotions now, and she couldn't stand here one moment longer just discussing the situation. "Betty, can you stay here and coordinate and watch for him? He's most likely to show up here rather than anywhere else. Keep trying to call Junior and Jimmy. And call Taylor at the bakery, tell her to keep a lookout for him."

"Will do." Betty went to the porch, grabbed her phone and started scrolling.

"We'll start downtown," she said to Ryan. He probably didn't want to search with her, but too bad. Alfie was more important.

"Car?" Ryan asked.

Betty looked up and shook her head. "Go down to the diner. They'll lend you their golf cart. You can make good time and still see and hear everything."

"Good idea." They both turned toward the diner.

"Cell reception's still spotty. If you don't hear from me that's why," Betty called after them. "I should never have given up my landline."

They jogged toward the diner. A cluster of young kids passed them en route to Betty's place, their parents in the car waiting for them, but most trick-or-treaters were surely in the more densely populated part of the island.

"I should have realized he might be nearby and hear." Ryan was barely out of breath.

Mellie, on the other hand, was gasping, slowing

down to a fast walk because she couldn't run anymore. "I shouldn't have let him out of my sight."

"Done is done. We'll find him." Ryan put a hand
on her upper arm and gave a quick squeeze.

It gave Mellie a tiny measure of comfort. She was
glad to have him at her side.

As they approached the diner, a spotlight turned
on and the owner came toward them, holding out
a set of keys. "Betty called me. Take the cart. I'll
spread the word to all my diners and staff."

"Thank you." They climbed in, Ryan taking the
wheel, and were soon buzzing toward downtown,
both of them looking back and forth, back and forth.
Aside from a few house lights, the night was dark.

As they got closer to downtown, a new problem
became apparent. There were clusters of kids everywhere.

"Hard to recognize Alfie," Ryan said.

Mellie squinted through the darkness, studying
each group of kids, thankful that at least Alfie had
worn a white costume. If he'd kept it on. "Go slow
and pray," she said, because that was what they'd
need.

*Oh, Alfie, what did you overhear? How could you
run off?*

RYAN DROVE THE golf cart slowly down High Street.
They'd been delayed by speaking with various clusters of kids, all of whom knew Alfie, but none of
whom had seen him.

Worry hammered at him, worse than any he'd ever

felt before—the worry of a parent. This was what Mellie must feel all the time, but he'd gone blithely through the past ten years never knowing all the things that could be happening to his son, because he didn't know he *had* a son. Surely a better person would have sensed it, intuited it?

But Ryan wasn't good at relationships, sensing nuances, figuring out the people side of life. It was his failing, one of many. Now he'd allowed a talk to happen that might have driven Alfie off.

Off, and into danger.

Mellie jumped off the cart and ran into the bakery, and Ryan saw Taylor's face change from a smile to a frown, like she was hearing the news for the first time. So Betty hadn't been able to get through. He checked his own cell phone: no messages. Again, that was probably the poor cell reception.

Like Betty, a lot of the islanders had given up their landlines as the price had gone up. Now, they could only rely on in-person messages. He'd seen some of the kids they'd interrogated running up to other kids and houses, hopefully spreading the news as requested.

Surely, someone would be able to shed some light on where Alfie had gone.

He asked Hector, who was giving out small packets of hard candy and pressed a couple into Ryan's hands. The older man hadn't seen Alfie, but he took Ryan's phone number and promised to ask everyone who came through to spread the word.

Ryan gunned the golf cart down to the library

where Linda was handing out bookmarks and candy from the open front door. She, too, promised to keep her eyes open and spread the word.

Mellie came out of the bakery and spoke to her grandmother, the postmistress.

Ryan looked around, dismayed. They'd spoken to everyone they'd seen and learned nothing.

Alfie must not have come through downtown. If he had, someone would have seen him.

And then it came to him.

According to Mellie, Alfie wanted to be a scientist like Ryan and had dressed up in scientist clothing as a costume.

But Ryan, the main scientist Alfie knew, didn't work in town. Ryan worked out on the coastline and in the marshes, and there were several spots where Alfie had helped him.

Ryan would bet money that Alfie had headed out that way.

He waved Mellie down and told her his theory, and she nodded, frowning. "It could be. I don't think he'd go out there alone, but maybe he would."

Beside Mellie, Taylor shook her head. "I don't think he'd go out into the marshes alone. I'm guessing he's in town. I'll take charge of looking here, and you guys go out to the marshes. Together. No one should be there alone in this dark."

Mellie bit her lip and looked at Ryan, and he knew exactly what she was thinking: *Alfie* could be out there alone in the dark.

"Come on," he said, helping Mellie into the cart

and running around to the driver's seat. "I have an idea of some people who'll help us."

Moments later, they were at the bay beside the grand marsh.

And sure enough, there was the Floating Fisherman. Ryan called out a warning and jumped aboard, then held out a hand to help Mellie follow.

Jed, Tim and two other fishermen were in the midst of a card game, glasses of beer or soda beside them.

"Alfie Anderson is missing," Ryan said. "We think he's somewhere along the shore or in the marshes."

Instantly, they started barraging the two of them with questions, grabbing coats, locking up the Floating Fisherman. Mellie explained the costume Alfie was wearing. One of the men gave a piercing whistle, and a minute later two dogs, Tank and Spotty, trotted up.

"We'll find the child," Jed assured them, confidence in his voice. "Kids run off. They don't get far."

"Stay in pairs," Mellie urged.

"Goes without saying. And you, too." The fishermen started climbing into boats, one a commercial fishing boat and one a rowboat, talking among themselves about directions and likely hiding places.

"If the phones don't work, use a signal beacon." Tim tossed one to Mellie, and she grabbed it and climbed into the golf cart.

"We'll head to the spot where I did most of my sampling." Ryan got in beside her and started it up.

As he drove, Mellie peered out into the darkness,

calling Alfie's name. Spotty had hopped into the back of the cart and was sniffing the air. Did the dog know that they were searching for Alfie? Ryan reached back, and the dog licked his hand.

Talk about darkness: no place was as dark as Teaberry Island once you got away from houses and shops. The moon, waning crescent, shed little light even when it peeked out from behind clouds.

Ryan slowed, because it was too dark to see well and he had to be careful to stay on the path.

As he drove, slowly and carefully now, punishing thoughts pushed at him. Alfie had been put at risk by Ryan's actions and words. Ryan was destructive just like his stepfather.

Stop. Focus on Alfie.

They reached the area where he'd done most of his work, got out of the cart and started searching. Fortunately, he'd grabbed a flashlight and Jed had given Mellie one, too. "Stick together," he said as they walked the perimeter of the little cove area, calling for Alfie. "It won't help anything if one of us gets lost."

There was no sign of the child.

Mellie shivered, and Ryan took off his coat and wrapped it around her, ignoring her protests. "I'm fine. We've got to keep you safe because Alfie will need you when we find him."

She looked up at him, her eyes teary. "Thank you. I'm so scared."

"Don't be," he said firmly. "Alfie knows this island the same way I did when I was a kid. No way will he get into trouble." The need to be strong for Mellie pushed steel into his backbone. "We'll find him."

"Alfie, Alfie!"

The tenth, or was it the twentieth, time they called, there was a thready voice in response, and Spotty ran toward a metal structure that had once been on land, but was now several feet out in the bay. It was the size of a small garage, on short stilts, and was unused now that the shoreline was eroding away.

"Mom?" The voice was faint.

"Alfie! We're coming, baby!"

They both waded out to the shack. Ryan pried open the door.

Mellie shone her flashlight around.

And there, in the back of the structure, was Alfie. "Oh, you're safe!" Mellie's voice was ecstatic. "You scared us so much! Come on out." She started to climb in, and the little shack wobbled.

Ryan put a restraining hand on her arm. "Careful," he warned.

"I can't come out, I'm scared." Alfie's voice trembled, and he was shaking violently. No wonder. The water was cold, and several inches deep on the shack's floor. If Alfie had been there awhile, he had to be close to hypothermia.

Ryan started in to get him and then stopped as the darkness closed around him.

The air seemed to go thin, making it hard to breathe. Dark speckles crossed his vision and sweat dripped down his back. He couldn't make himself go farther into the darkness.

Mellie pushed past him and crawled to Alfie. "Oh, my baby, my baby."

"I'm cold." Alfie's teeth were chattering.

Shamed by his weakness, Ryan backed out of the tin house and called Jed. "He's found and he needs a blanket," he said, giving the details of where they were. Then he sent texts to Betty and Taylor, saying the boy was safe. God willing, they would go through, but if not, the fishermen would spread the word.

Mellie and Alfie weren't emerging from the shack. Ryan sucked in a couple of big breaths, waded back to it and shone his flashlight inside.

Mellie was struggling to half carry, half drag Alfie, but clearly, the boy's weight was too much for her. Alfie was shaking and crying, obviously unable to help himself.

All of a sudden Ryan's panic attack was gone. "I'm coming," he said, and crawled toward them, focusing on his son. He swept the boy into his arms, ordered Mellie to go out first and then scooted toward the door himself, arms wrapped around Alfie.

The building was swaying. It was too much weight and movement.

If they got stuck in here…if the water closed over their heads… Ryan pushed away the image of terrifying blackness, ignored the racing of his heart, and with superhuman effort he scooted and pulled

Alfie to the doorway where Mellie was waiting to pull him into her arms.

The building swayed more.

Ryan pushed himself out just as it toppled sideways, creaking and clanking as it fell into the bay.

Ryan staggered to the beach and sat down beside Mellie and Alfie. She'd wrapped Ryan's coat around the shivering boy. Spotty came up and plopped down into Alfie's lap, and he wrapped his arms around the dog.

Mellie and Ryan looked at each other over his head, and in her eyes, Ryan could feel the relief that he felt himself. In this, at least, they were as one.

After a few minutes of catching their breaths and comforting Alfie, they started messaging the rest of the searchers.

"We should go back," Mellie said, "but…wow. I can barely move."

"Aftereffects of adrenaline." Ryan was feeling it, too. "Let's just rest here until Jed comes." He paused, then added, "I'm sorry I couldn't go in after him at first. That was a claustrophobic's worst nightmare."

She smiled a little, fist-bumped him. "Teamwork. I never would have found him without you."

Alfie lifted his head and looked from Mellie to Alfie. "I'm sorry I broke you apart," he said.

"What?" Mellie asked. She was rubbing Alfie's back in slow circles.

"What do you mean, buddy?" Ryan asked.

"Miss Betty said not to let me get in between

you, so I left. Only I got cold and scared and I made a bad decision."

Ryan rewound his conversation with Betty as he wrapped an arm around Alfie's shoulders. She'd said something about not letting Alfie keep them from getting together. "You didn't break us apart at all," he said, squeezing Alfie gently. "You brought us closer."

"What exactly did you overhear?" Mellie asked. "Because I'm pretty sure it didn't mean what you thought it meant."

"I know he's my dad," Alfie said. "But I kind of knew it all along."

Ryan felt like all the breath had been sucked out of him. All he could do was to stare at his brilliant, lovable, intuitive son as tears came to his eyes.

"Oh, honey." Mellie hugged Alfie. "We'll talk about all of it. A lot. But for now, just know how much we both love you."

Alfie nodded. "I know," he said with complete confidence.

Ryan blessed Mellie for nurturing their son so well that he could easily take in their love, accept it, believe it.

And then he did the only thing he could think to do: he pulled Alfie and Mellie and the dog close and held on.

CHAPTER TWENTY-TWO

RYAN DIDN'T SLEEP that night.

What if he'd lost Alfie? What if that bright light had been snuffed out? If the structure had collapsed and he'd gone into the bay... Ryan's mind rebelled against the thought, but it kept sneaking back in to torment him. He'd heard it said that having a child was having your heart forever outside your body, and he'd paid little attention aside from noting that the concept was unscientific.

Now, he knew exactly what it meant.

Last night, they'd brought Alfie home and Mellie had given him a hot bath and some cocoa while Ryan paced the living room. Eventually, Mellie had come downstairs. She'd looked surprised to see Ryan still at her house and had reassured him that Alfie was fine; he'd already gone to sleep. Ryan had seen Mellie's exhaustion and felt his own, recognized that there was nothing to be gained by staying and left.

He blamed himself that Alfie had overheard his conversation with Betty, even though Betty had assumed more than half of the blame for the mistake. And he felt sick inside that he'd struggled with his claustrophobia before managing to go into the en-closed space to get Alfie out of there.

In the night, everything had crystallized: he wanted to have a connection with Alfie, wanted to help raise him. No more dwelling on his issues with Mellie. No more delaying, even though he feared he'd be inadequate to the task. He would work at it. He would try. He'd succeed, because he had to.

What if he'd lost Alfie just when he'd found him? What if he'd never gotten the chance to tell Alfie he was proud of him?

In the morning, he'd showered and taken coffee out onto the porch, looking toward Mellie's place and trying to resist going over there again. After the night they'd had, Mellie and Alfie would sleep in, he figured. He didn't want to bother them.

But in the early-morning semidarkness, they'd come out, fully dressed, Alfie carrying his back-pack. As they headed toward the docks, Ryan didn't hesitate. No more of that. He speed-walked to catch up with them.

He fell into step beside them feeling self-conscious. What were his rights here, his responsi-bilities? "I'm surprised you're not taking a day off from school," was all he could find to say.

Alfie glanced at him and shrugged, seeming to take his presence for granted. Which was wonderful and more than Ryan had dared to expect.

Mellie looked over at him, and he read confusion and concern in her eyes. "Alfie's a little sleepy, but he wanted to come to school," she said.

"I gotta tell my friends about my adventure!" Alfie sped up, hurrying ahead. In the distance, the lights of the school boat came into view as it chugged toward shore.

Mellie watched him, a mixture of pride and concern and love in her eyes, and Ryan caught a glimpse of how challenging her life had been as a single parent of this boy. Challenging, and rewarding. She'd done it alone. And he was still angry about that, but mixed with the anger was a sense of shame that she hadn't felt able to tell him so that he could help her, that she'd thought raising Alfie alone was preferable to getting Ryan involved.

Alfie was greeted with exclamations from the other kids, hugs from the girls and mock-punches from the boys, everyone talking to him at once. His smile broadened as he started to tell the tale of his disappearance. He didn't even hint that he'd been scared, though he played up the risk of the collapsing tin structure. His shoulders squared, his back straightened, and Ryan could only admire his showmanship.

His *son's* showmanship.

The boat docked, the ramp was adjusted and the kids started to go aboard. The damp, cool morning air made Ryan shiver.

"Alfie." Mellie's voice was low but stern.

Alfie turned back, looked at Mellie and came over.

"Even though you're proud of your adventure," she said, "you know it was dangerous."

"I know."

Ryan felt like he had to chime in, play the role he'd only just learned about. "You can never, ever do anything like that again."

"I won't. I was scared," Alfie admitted. He looked up at Ryan. "Mom said you were scared, too."

Ryan nodded. "I was. I don't like small, enclosed spaces."

"But you came in, anyway."

"Yeah. I was worried about you."

"You saved me." Alfie said it in a matter-of-fact way, not surprised.

Ryan loved that Alfie could take that for granted, that his parents would help him when he got into trouble. "We both saved you."

"Come on, Alfie!" a couple of the kids yelled, and Alfie turned and ran toward the boat ramp.

Ryan watched him go, his heart outside his chest again. Man. Parenting was *all* about the feelings.

"You okay?" Mellie didn't look at him; she was watching Alfie.

"Yeah. Or I will be. You?"

"I will be." She gave him a brief smile.

Halfway up the ramp, Alfie turned. "Bye, Mom," he yelled. And then, "Bye, Dad."

And then Alfie was engulfed in the crowd of kids and the boat chugged off. And Ryan's world broke apart and reconfigured, and he knew that life would never be the same.

MELLIE TURNED AWAY from the boat, blinking back tears.

Her son was amazing. Not least because he'd accepted Ryan as his father, no questions asked.

Of course, he would eventually have questions, dozens of them. They'd have to figure out how to answer, how to explain.

But for now, Mellie was reeling with relief that Alfie had been found, saved and seemed none the worse for his adventure.

She stole a glance over at Ryan. He was collecting himself, too; this must be doubly emotional for him. He'd never been called Dad before.

Once she'd looked at him, it was hard to look away. She wanted to feast her eyes on his unshaven, strong-boned face and muscular shoulders.

He was really handsome, but that was just the beginning of his appeal. Last night he'd stepped right in, helped take charge of the search, figured out where Alfie was. And then he'd overcome his claustrophobia to save his son.

Why had she ever thought he'd be a bad father?

He glanced over at her. "We should talk. Do you have time for breakfast at the diner?"

"Uh, sure?" The thought filled her with a mixture of trepidation and eagerness, both of which she tried to conceal. "I don't have to open the market for another hour."

So they walked into the Dockside Diner. The fragrance of bacon and fried potatoes filled the air, and most of the tables and booths were full of chattering people.

"Looks like there's a table in the corner," Ryan said, gesturing. "Let's grab that one."

He pulled out her chair for her, melting her with his ingrained gentlemanly manners.

But if they'd thought the corner table would afford them some privacy, they were wrong. As soon as they were both seated, people started coming over to ask about Alfie. Fair enough, since the whole community had gotten involved in the search for him.

As she and Ryan took turns answering questions and explaining where they'd found Alfie, Mellie noticed a few speculative glances at her and Ryan. Mellie had to think people were curious about the two of them being together at breakfast time. This was confirmed when Amaryllis Johnson asked her friend, "Are they dating?" in a voice she probably thought was a whisper, but that carried across the diner.

Mellie hoped that was people's only speculation. They would learn soon enough that Ryan was Alfie's father, but she wanted to talk to Alfie first, figure out what to say.

If he kept calling Ryan "Dad" in public, though, the word would spread fast.

Once they'd placed their orders—the special for him, eggs and toast for her—and everyone else had gone back to their own tables and breakfasts, Ryan leaned forward, shining the light of his intense focus on her. "How do you want to explain all of this to

Alfie, if you haven't already? Doesn't he see Georgie as his father?"

She'd been mulling that over for weeks as she'd thought about telling Alfie and Ryan the truth. "I'll tell him I was pregnant before Georgie and I married, and that Georgie agreed to be a father to him." She was pretty sure it wouldn't upset Alfie. He'd grieved Georgie's death, but like all kids, his focus was primarily in the here and now.

He nodded thoughtfully. "All true, which is good," he said. "But how do you want to explain my role?"

They waited while the waitress filled their coffee cups, a welcome interruption that gave Mellie time to think. "I'm considering what to say. Do you have an opinion?"

"First off," he said, "I'm assuming Alfie knows the facts of life."

"Since he was three," she said, smiling to remember how he'd peppered her with questions after seeing two dogs mating.

Ryan didn't smile. Of course he didn't. It was yet another milestone that he'd missed.

"I don't want him to put any blame on you," she said. "I'll tell him I was young and scared, and you left without knowing you'd made a baby."

He nodded. "I guess that makes sense."

Their food arrived. Ryan dug in and Mellie picked, too overwhelmed and emotional to have much of an appetite.

Ryan pushed his plate away half-eaten. "I want to help raise him. Partial custody."

Mellie's heart sank. She looked at the table. Ryan was entitled to do that, of course, but for Alfie to go off-island to stay with Ryan…that would be hard.

"You have every right," she said. "I won't lie, it'll be hard on me to lose control and to have him stay overnight away from home. But I will make it happen."

"I haven't quite figured out how to manage it. But are you willing to work with me on a custody agreement that's fair?"

"Of course." She pushed her own plate away. "And, Ryan, I know it's not enough, but I am truly sorry for keeping him a secret from you."

He nodded. "I know you are."

It wasn't forgiveness, but at least he didn't hate her. "For Alfie's sake, we need to be cordial and get along."

"Yes, we do." He studied her, eyes intense. "Do you trust me to have some custody? You don't still think Wayne was right about me?"

"Not anymore. If I had any remaining doubts, you proved yourself last night."

He shook his head. "I was slow to help him."

"But you did. In the end, you saved him. If that structure had tipped with him alone in it…" She shivered and pushed the horrible images away.

"We both saved him. And that's how we need to work together from here on out."

"Yes." She felt awful at the thought of losing some control as his mother, but she had to be fair. "It'll be a huge benefit to him, having you in his life on a regular basis."

"Thanks. I'll draft a custody schedule and send it to you, just to get us started." He seemed about to say something more, but didn't. And then a couple other people came up to talk about Alfie before it was time to go.

They parted in front of the diner formally, with a handshake.

And Mellie walked to the store with her heart in her shoes. She shouldn't feel that way, because things were better between her and Ryan now. Alfie was safe, and he'd have his father in his life regularly.

She felt so empty, and why?

But she knew why: she'd let herself hope for something not just for Alfie, but for herself.

She'd never been much for fairy tales, but she'd let herself dream a little about Ryan. The glass slipper had broken when he'd found out about her lies, of course, but she'd half hoped it would be put back together last night.

Obviously, it hadn't. Ryan was willing to be a dad, but not a prince.

She couldn't blame him. Couldn't be surprised, either, not really.

Girls like her never got the prince.

CHAPTER TWENTY-THREE

IN THE END, Ryan couldn't wait until a custody schedule was drafted and approved. He'd already missed so much time with Alfie, and he wouldn't be on the island much longer. He wanted to learn to interact with Alfie as a father.

So he texted Mellie a couple of hours after their talk in the diner to ask if he could spend time with Alfie after school, and Mellie agreed.

Once Alfie had dropped off his books at home and grabbed a snack, they headed downtown.

On the way, Ryan explained what he wanted them to do, wondering how Alfie would react. "A lot of people dropped what they were doing to search for you last night," he said. "They were glad to do it. That's the blessing of a place like Teaberry Island."

Alfie nodded and kicked at a rock as they walked.

"But since we took up people's time and energy, it would be nice if we offered to give them a hand today. Are you...are you game for that?" Ryan didn't know how to be with Alfie now. Should he act tough, like this was a punishment, or try to explain and get Alfie on board?

Ryan had mostly known negative father figures

himself, from his violent stepfather to a couple of foster fathers who'd left the parenting to their wives.

Wayne had been the exception. He'd taken the time to explain to Ryan, Cody and Luis what they'd done wrong and how they might repair it. It was from Wayne's parenting that Ryan had gotten the idea to do this activity with Alfie.

And it worked. "Sure," Alfie said. "We can help."

Sun slanted down, warm on their backs, as they approached the market. The smell of fall leaves and someone's wood fire mingled in the air. They walked up the steps, lined with carved pumpkins on one side and pots of flowers on the other. Before they could walk in the door, Betty came out with a broom in hand.

"There's my favorite Halloween scientist," Betty said, putting an arm around Alfie and squeezing him to her side. "How are you feeling today, honey?"

"Good." Alfie put up with the affection for a few seconds before pulling away. "Me and…and Dad are going to help everyone take down their Halloween decorations. Do you need help?"

"Bless your heart," Betty said, ruffling Alfie's hair and smiling at both of them. "You go help other folks, and come back here if you have time and energy. I'm not so old that I can't dispose of a few jack-o'-lanterns on my own."

Ryan studied Betty. He was glad to see that she looked healthy and strong. She'd come a long way in the two months he'd been on the island. "If you're sure," he said.

"Pretty sure Taylor could use some help, over at the bakery," she said. "I expect she has some leftover sugar cookies from last night, too."

"Let's go!" Alfie said, and took off for the bakery.

"I'll be right over." Ryan wasn't passing up a chance for one—or several—of Taylor's big sugar cookies. But before he followed Alfie toward the bakery, he put an arm around Betty. "You're none the worse after last night?"

"No, except that I'm still kicking myself for blabbing something upsetting that Alfie overheard." She leaned against him for a second. "How's Alfie doing?"

"He seems just fine." Ryan smiled at her. "Better than me, to be honest. Last night gave me a few gray hairs."

"Welcome to parenthood." She patted his back. "Now go be a daddy. I've got a porch to sweep."

Would he ever get used to the idea of being a daddy?

At the bakery, Taylor accepted their help at taking down a window display of cut-out black cats and witches on broomsticks, then sent them on their way with giant, orange-frosted sugar cookies in the shape of pumpkins. They hit the library next, where Linda had already taken down the Halloween decorations, but got them busy putting together a display of Thanksgiving books.

All the while, they talked.

"I want to spend time with you, going forward,"

Ryan said. "Your mom and I are going to work out a custody agreement."

Alfie frowned briefly when Ryan said the word *custody*, then nodded. "Okay."

"I'll probably be working off the island, back in Baltimore," Ryan continued.

"How come?" Alfie pulled out a kids' Thanksgiving book and crossed it off the list Linda had given them. "Can't you stay on the island and work, like you have been?"

Ryan explained about the grant he didn't expect to get. "I've applied for one other, but it's smaller and I'd still need to teach some," he said. "And if I don't get that, I'll be teaching full-time at the university."

Alfie looked thoughtful. "I *guess* I could come spend time at your university. Colleges are cool. Could Mom come?"

Ryan hesitated.

"Or is it like my friend Brenden? His parents don't get along, so he goes to his mom one week and his dad the next week. They're both on the island, though."

"Your mom and I will get along," Ryan hastened to assure him.

Alfie frowned, looking worried.

With his new insight, Ryan understood why. "You didn't come between us, and you never would," he said. "What you overheard… Betty was concerned that your mom and I would have trouble getting along, kind of like your friend's parents, but that's not your fault and it's not going to happen."

Alfie pulled out another book and crossed it off his list. He didn't look at Ryan.

"We're closer together because of you," he said. "We both want to help you."

"Could you live with us?" Alfie asked in a small voice.

"I don't think so." But the idea lit a fire in Ryan. And as they finished their task at the library and walked outside into the cooling November dusk, images played in his mind.

He, Mellie and Alfie at the dinner table. The three of them settling in to watch a movie. Taking a walk by the bay.

It was probably what Alfie was imagining. Just a kid's fantasy, he reminded himself.

There was no chance it could actually happen, not after all that had gone on between him and Mellie. He wasn't a person who could have close, loving relationships.

Was he?

AFTER ALFIE HAD left with Ryan, Mellie browned beef for stew and got a pot simmering. Then she did what she always did when she was at loose ends: she headed for her garden.

Some of her marigolds were, improbably, still blooming, but another set of them had died, so she set to pulling them out of the ground, debating whether to add them to the compost heap. She'd already tossed a pumpkin there, knowing its seeds might germinate and grow into a new plant, so why not add marigolds to the mix? She could end up with the prettiest compost heap on the island afterward.

A thought crossed her mind—something about making beauty out of garbage, which she pretty much specialized in—but she let the fancy pass. No need to be melodramatic. Her real life right now had drama enough.

Plenty of uncertainty, too. She hated the thought of Alfie going off-island to spend time with Ryan, and yet she knew it was right. She had to examine her conscience to figure out if, somewhere inside, she'd wanted to have full control of her son's life.

She didn't *think* that had been a motivation, not at first. But after ten years of raising him alone, it would be hard to share the reins of his life with someone else.

Just as well, though. Alfie would all too soon assume control of his own life, and she'd be cheering from the sidelines. That happened to all parents as their kids grew up, provided the kids had been raised well and were able to live on their own.

She was staring gloomily at some late-season blue-star asters when she heard a golf cart putter up her driveway and stop. Her grandmother emerged.

Mellie got up and hurried over. "Gram! Everything okay?" She started to offer her arm and then thought better of it. At eighty, Gram was steadier on her feet than most people ten years younger. "Want some sweet tea?"

"No, I've got my DP." Gram fumbled in her giant purse and pulled out a large plastic bottle of Diet

Pepsi, half-empty. "I'll sit out here while you work and maybe help you out a bit."

"Um, sure." Mellie pulled a sturdy lawn chair over toward the flower bed and put her gardening gloves back on. Gram didn't drop in for no reason, but she also didn't get to the point of the visit on anyone's schedule but her own. And she didn't like a fuss being made over her. "How's the PO?" she asked as she pulled a couple of weeds.

"Fine. Same as always." Gram opened her completely fizzless soda and took a long draw, wiping her mouth with the back of her hand. "Is Alfie all right?"

Ah. That made sense. "He's doing better than I am. He thinks he had a big adventure. Which technically he did, but I'm praying he never has another one, not like that, anyway."

Gram nodded and was silent a moment.

Mellie pulled out a few dead plants.

"Is he Ryan Hastings's son?" Gram asked abruptly.

Mellie's hands went still. She stared at the blackened plant in her hands, then tossed it into the bushel basket she'd take out to the compost heap later. "He is," she said. "But we haven't figured out how to tell people yet."

"No need to figure," Gram said. "They've already guessed."

"Really?" Mellie sighed.

"And don't you worry about Georgie's mother. I've already talked to her, and she's glad to know. Lets her off the hook."

"Wow." Mellie had never been close with Georgie's mother, and the woman hadn't exactly made a fuss when Alfie was born. Later, Mellie had realized that she probably knew Alfie wasn't Georgie's biological son.

Gram seemed to have delivered all the news she'd come to share, so Mellie went inside and came back out with a bowl of pretzels and cheese curls, Gram's favorites, along with a glass of tea for herself. She set them on the table beside Gram and pulled up a lawn chair. For several minutes they both sat, looking out at the bay.

"I've been neglectful," Gram said abruptly. "I should have been helping you all along, but I let my feelings about your father stand in my way."

Mellie looked at her in surprise. "You mean with Alfie? I never expected—"

Gram waved her to silence. "I was ashamed of what my daughter did."

Gram's daughter, Mellie's mother. Someone they never discussed. Mellie tried to keep thoughts of her mother out of her mind. It was too painful to think of the beautiful, winsome woman who'd abandoned Mellie and her sisters.

"She always was flighty," Gram continued, "and she never did have an easy time connecting with other people."

Mellie opened her mouth to speak, maybe to stop the flow of Gram's words, but Gram held up a hand. "I had bad postpartum after she was born, didn't give her quite what she needed," she went on. "And this island was too small. I just want you to know that it wasn't you, it was her."

Mellie swallowed the tightness in her throat and didn't speak. She didn't know why she felt like crying. Was it sadness for her mother? For herself? Or was it more about being touched that Gram felt the need to tell her this?

"I honestly wasn't surprised when she left," Gram said. "I was more surprised she stayed with your father long enough to give him three daughters and make a start at raising them. But I should have helped you when she left and you took on all the cooking and cleaning and mothering."

Even this long after the fact, the acknowledgment of the burden she'd taken on warmed Mellie's heart. "I know you and Dad didn't get along," she said, reaching for Gram's weathered hand and giving it a quick squeeze.

"True enough. But you're my blood and you should have been my priority. I can be stubborn."

That was such an understatement that Mellie smiled. "Well…maybe a little."

Gram waved a hand at Mellie, smiling a little herself. But to Mellie's shock, Gram's eyes were actually teary. She started to say something, but choked up and stopped.

"If you want to be more of a grandma to Alfie," Mellie said hesitantly, "I would be all in favor."

"Great-grandma," Gram said roughly.

"Great-grandma. Of course. I'd love that so much. I know he would, too."

They sat another few minutes and looked out at the bay. "You're a good person, Mellie," Gram said.

The praise was so unexpected that Mellie blinked. She didn't know what to say.

"You've taken on a lot, and with a smile. And look how forgiving you are."

Mellie waved a hand. "I've made so many mistakes myself. I haven't exactly been there for you, either." Though she'd seen Gram often at the post office, and usually stopped by her little cottage on holidays, it was so much less than most island people did for their elders.

Gram shook her head. "I should have been helping you." She pushed herself to her feet. "I'll do better. That's all I wanted to say."

Mellie stood and hugged her. "Let's help each other," she said. "And Alfie."

As Gram nodded, climbed into her golf cart and drove off, Mellie marveled. Closeness with her grandmother was something she hadn't expected. The sky seemed brighter, the bay bluer.

And more than that, Mellie felt affirmed. If *Gram* thought she'd done a decent job, thought she was a good person…maybe, just maybe, she was.

CHAPTER TWENTY-FOUR

ON WEDNESDAY, RYAN sat in his bedroom at Betty's house, reading a sports magazine. He ought to start preparing for his departure from the island. Not packing, not yet; he had a little under two more weeks here. But he needed to reconnect with the faculty from his graduate program, see about extending his postdoc locally, maybe even apply for other jobs for next year.

He wasn't going to get the grant; he'd resigned himself to that. Chances were slim he'd even get the much smaller grant focused on creating "living shorelines." He had to get going.

But the last few days' events had sapped all of his energy. At least, they'd sapped his enthusiasm for leaving the island.

How could he leave when his newly discovered son was here? When Mellie was here?

But given that he had to earn a living and that his relationship with Mellie seemed doomed to be cordial but distant, how could he stay?

There was a pounding on his bedroom door, way too loud to be Betty.

"Get out here and show us you're a man!"

"We are *set up* to *set you down*!"

Cody and Luis?

By the time he opened his door, he heard them thundering down the stairs, and then they were gone. Bemused, he threw on a sweatshirt and headed down.

The kitchen smelled fantastic—something good was baking—and Betty was at the stove.

"Was that…?" he asked as he came into the room.

"Your brothers. You'd better get out there."

"But how…?" Cody had been overseas, and Luis was occupied with his business. "Did you call them?"

"I did."

"But how…they couldn't—"

"You've had a shock about Alfie," Betty said firmly. "And bad news about your grant application. I thought you could use some support."

He looked out the window at his foster brothers, the only two men who truly understood his background because theirs was similar. Seeing them joking and laughing as they pulled the old cornhole boards out of the shed, he felt his mouth curve into a smile.

Betty came to stand beside him, and he put an arm around her. "Thanks, Betty."

She hugged him back. "We're family. We help each other. Now, get on out there. I'm making cornbread and greens, and we'll grill up some rockfish. Dessert's a surprise."

So he went outside, side-hugged and fist-bumped his brothers. "How'd you get away?" he asked them.

"Finished one deal and can't start another for a

few days," Luis said. "I had to get out of there before I went insane."

"And I'm stateside for a while." Cody's voice was casual, too casual. "Reason isn't important."

Ryan had the feeling that it was, but before he could question Cody about it, Cody started busting on him about his inability to win at cornhole.

Two matches later, Ryan had to admit Cody was right. He'd never been anywhere near as athletic as his brothers.

Luis went into the kitchen and brought back three beers, and they sat down at the picnic table to take a break. A cool breeze blew in from the bay. Along with the smell of fall leaves, it warned of a change coming in the weather.

"So," Cody said, "you have a son you didn't know about."

"Yeah, what the *what*? You were with Mellie?" Luis took a long draw on his beer and looked at Ryan, clearly waiting for an explanation.

"Briefly." Ryan looked out over the bay, where a couple of fishing boats bobbed in the distance. The sun warmed his face.

"And you left her in the lurch?"

"Yeah." Ryan didn't look at either of them. "I'm not proud of it, but I ran when I saw how close we were getting. I'm no good at that stuff."

"You ran. From a woman who was carrying your child."

"I didn't know that part," Ryan said. He stared

down at his hands. "She didn't feel like she could tell me. And Wayne…" He broke off.

"Wayne what?" Luis asked sharply.

"Wayne told Mellie I was likely to abuse a child," he said, heat rising into his face and neck. "She was afraid to tell me she was pregnant after hearing that."

"Whoa." Luis blew out a breath. "Wayne was a smart guy, but in that, he was dead wrong."

"People can change." Cody looked out over the bay. "We're all examples of that."

"Yeah, but how much? Anyway, I just found out about Alfie, and now…"

"You're going to stay and help raise him." Luis said it flatly, as if there were no other choice.

Ryan shook his head. "No. No, I can't do that."

"Why not?"

He shrugged. "My life, my work, is on the mainland." He told them about the grant, and the postdoc and job possibilities he had.

Cody leaned forward, elbows on his knees. "Don't people like you, college faculty, don't they get away with just teaching a class or two? So you could do that and live out here most of the time."

"Only if I got a position at a Research One university. Which, yes, I'm applying for everything, but given that I can't even get a grant, it isn't likely."

"Your son's here." Luis stood and retrieved the beanbags, then turned back, frowning. "You thinking about a DNA test?"

"What?" Ryan asked. "No. No, Alfie's mine. One hundred percent." Truthfully, the idea of Mellie lying about Ryan being Alfie's biological father had never occurred to him. She wouldn't do that.

And he saw too much of himself in Alfie to have any doubts that Alfie was his son.

"Then you have to try to make it work," Luis said. "At least to where you can be close by and help raise him. Come on, my turn to whip your sorry self."

So Ryan played Luis, did a little better, but still lost. "It's okay, man," Luis said as they went back to the picnic table where Cody was watching the bay, dreaming. "You're distracted."

"I am." He sat down beside Cody.

The breeze cooled his face and he was glad, so glad, that his brothers were here.

"So you don't think you can get that grant?" Cody asked.

Ryan shook his head. "Chances are almost nil."

"Stinks."

They chatted a few minutes about what was going on in the other two's lives.

Movement next door caught his eye. Mellie had come out and stood on her porch, wearing a bright turquoise sweater. Alfie approached from the street and they both went inside.

"Mellie, huh?" Luis stood and cupped his hands around his mouth and yelled. "Mellie Anderson, get your pretty self out here!"

"Yeah, Mellie!" Cody added his voice.

Mellie came back to the door, looked out and then let out a shriek and came running over. Cody and Luis took turns hugging her. Ryan watched, jealous.

"Now go get that kid of yours," Cody said. "We're his uncles and we've got to start training him up right."

Mellie's eyes filled with tears. "I will." She walked back toward her house, backhanding her eyes.

"She could've had this all along," Ryan ground out. "If she hadn't kept Alfie a secret. Hadn't pretended he belonged to Georgie Anderson."

"Yeah, that was an odd couple." Cody frowned at him. "Should never have happened. Why didn't you stop her?"

Ryan sighed. "I told you, I bolted. I didn't know about Alfie."

"I'd be mad," Cody said.

"I am," Ryan said. "At Wayne and at her."

"She made a mistake," Luis said. "People make mistakes all the time, though."

"Not telling me I had a son was a pretty big mistake."

"Just like you sleeping with her and then dumping her was a mistake?"

Cody's words pierced Ryan.

"Yeah. I guess."

Luis studied him. "You screwed up. But that doesn't mean you're like your birth family. Everybody screws up this stuff sometimes. It doesn't mean you're the same as your old man."

"Yeah," Cody said. "You screwed up, and Mellie did. But man, if you have a chance with her…"

Betty came out then and gave orders about heating the grill. So Cody did that, and Luis went over to tell Mellie that she and Alfie were invited for dinner.

Ryan's phone buzzed, and when he saw that the call was from Charlie, he took it.

"Hey," Charlie said. "I'm here on the island. Wondered if you wanted to grab a drink."

He looked at the spread that was starting to appear on the picnic table. "My brothers are visiting and we're cooking out. Come on over."

"Betty won't mind?"

"No way. She's always got enough for one more."

"You don't have to ask twice. I'll be there."

"Good thing I'm used to cooking for an army," Betty said. "Who else is coming?"

"Charlie."

"What?" Betty looked distressed.

"He's on the island and wants to get together. Who knows, he may have some news about the grant." And he'd be another layer of buffer between Ryan and Mellie.

Which, Ryan thought gloomily as he watched Mellie and Alfie approach, arms loaded down with dishes and baskets to contribute to the feast, was something he sorely needed.

BETTY SAT BACK on the picnic table bench after everyone had eaten their fill.

Having all three boys together, cooking them a meal, watching them talk, advise each other and joke around—it just plain made her happy. She and Wayne had fostered a few other boys throughout the years, but these three were closest to her heart. It was true, what people said: the difficult kids were the ones you ended up feeling the proudest of, because they'd overcome so much.

She wasn't so arrogant as to take a lot of credit for how they'd turned out; they'd helped each other, understood each other. Coming from similarly awful backgrounds, they'd known when to offer sympathy and when to give a kick in the pants. Sometimes literally, she thought with a smile, remembering the fights they'd gotten into.

Inviting Ryan's brothers to come for a few days had been a genius move on her part, if she did say so herself.

Not so good had been Ryan's invitation to Charlie. The man was staying on the island for a week, finalizing his purchase of a house here and getting to know people.

And bothering *her*.

Why was he hanging around her, getting into her business, asking questions? Did it mean he *like* liked her, as she and Peg used to say when they were preteens?

What a fool she was to even ask that question, at her age and in her situation. A better woman would tell him firmly that Wayne had been her one and only and that the way he looked at her made her uncomfortable. She needed to take a page from a younger woman's playbook and speak up.

The trouble was, she didn't know how she felt, wasn't one hundred percent sure that the attention

was unwanted. All the years she'd been married to
Wayne, she'd blocked any kind of attraction to his
good friend Charlie. She'd been crazy about Wayne,
loyal to Wayne.

Now that Wayne was gone, though…

She pushed Charlie out of her mind, stood and
started stacking up dirty plates, watching Alfie stare
at his new uncles with open hero worship.

"Should we back off and let them get to know
each other?" Charlie had come over and now stood
beside her, too close.

She didn't like agreeing with him, but he was
right. Ryan and his brothers were building a bonfire.
Mellie sat on the edge of one of the wooden chairs,
now painted red by Ryan. Alfie leaned against her
chair, watching the men.

Betty had intervened as much as she thought
right, telling Mellie and Ryan to forgive each other
and focus on Alfie. And then the big intervention for
Ryan: inviting his brothers here and telling them it
was important, really important.

Now she needed to back away.

She watched Luis laugh at Ryan for his fire-
making abilities, or lack thereof, saw Ryan toss the
long fireplace lighter to Luis. Cody came over with
a small stack of sticks and started arranging them,
at which point the other two joined together in what
looked like ridiculing of his skills.

They were acting like brothers, and Alfie was
taking it all in.

How must he feel to have gotten a family, a pretty intense one, so suddenly?

She knelt to look under the picnic table, untying the strings that held the plastic tablecloth down.

When she stood up, Charlie was there, so close she nearly bumped into him. "Let me help you with that," he said.

"I've got this one just fine. If you want to untie the other end, that would help." And it would give her a little space. She pointed to the garden hose on the side of the house. "You can wash it off, too." A picnic with a bunch of men was a messy business.

"Sure thing." He did what she'd said while she carried dishes inside. She put the extra food into plastic containers in the refrigerator. No doubt it would get eaten with all three boys staying here.

She breathed out a sigh. As recently as two months ago, the boys had had to sleep on the downstairs couches because the spare bedrooms had been so full of junk. Now, the house was livable again.

She rinsed one soapy platter and started in on the next. Things had begun to turn around for her when Ryan had arrived. She *liked* having Ryan in the house. It was good to have a family member to fuss over a little bit. Plus she could bake more and not worry about eating too much and gaining weight. When Ryan was around, a plate of cookies didn't last long.

"Betty." Charlie's deep voice behind her made her jump.

She spun around. "Quit sneaking up on me!"

"Sorry. Sorry." He lifted both hands, palms out, and stepped backward. "I just...there's something I want to talk to you about."

Here it comes. She felt overly warm and flustered and annoyed. "Okay, talk."

"Can we sit down?"

She might as well get this over with. "Sure." She pointed at the kitchen table. "Sit. Want coffee? Or a glass of wine?"

"Wine would be good."

She got him a glass from the box in the refrigerator, deliberately ignoring the two good bottles Luis had brought her. She wasn't going to treat Charlie like he was special. She'd serve him what she usually had, and he could take it or leave it.

But she couldn't resist poking at him. "Ever have boxed wine before?" she asked as she handed him his glass and sat down across the table from him, sipping from a glass of her own. Maybe wine would make this conversation less awkward.

"You'd be surprised at all the types of wine I've had over the years." He took a sip. "This is just fine."

That surprised her. Charlie was a sophisticated man who'd traveled all over the world, and he had to be used to the finer things. Still, Betty had never been ashamed of how she lived, and she wasn't going to start now. She was on a budget, like most people she knew—at least, most people on the island.

He set down his glass. "Listen, Betty. Shortly after that last doctor visit, when he learned he didn't have much time left, Wayne and I had a conversation. A serious one."

That wasn't what she'd expected him to say. "A serious conversation about what?"

"He wanted me to give you something when I thought you were ready. I think you are." He reached into his pocket and pulled out an envelope. Silently he handed it to her.

Betty took it, staring at Charlie, her heart pounding fast enough that she thought she might be having a heart attack. This felt like a communication from beyond the grave.

What did Charlie know? What had Wayne done?

Was this the answer to all the little mysteries she'd been uncovering?

She'd thought she'd discovered the answer, and that it had been a bad one, when she'd come upon those duplicate checks made out to Mellie. That had been a false alarm.

Was there more?

"I'm scared to open it," she admitted. "Do you know what's inside?"

He nodded.

"Can I handle it?"

One corner of his mouth turned upward in a half smile. "Pretty sure you can handle whatever comes your way."

She looked at the envelope. "Betty" was written on the outside. In Wayne's trademark, nearly unreadable scrawl.

Funny how you never forgot someone's handwriting. Sadness mingled with the fear she felt about what was in the envelope.

She straightened her shoulders, just as she had so many times in her life when a challenge faced her, whether a fight with Wayne, a problem with one of the boys, a threat to the market's survival. She'd handled all that. She should be able to handle a simple piece of paper. She should get on with it, rip it open.

But this was from Wayne. The last message; maybe, just maybe, the key to him. What she'd been looking for, but afraid to find, in the months of not-cleaning and then cleaning out the house.

Her hands shook as she opened the envelope.

Inside was a folded sheet of paper. She opened it.

Reservation number 860112—air
One week at the Hôtel de Triomphe: www.triumphe.com
One week at the Maison Verde: www.maison.com

There was no note, no explanation. "Is this where he was taking some woman?" she asked Charlie, indignant. "Why would you even show this to me? Why would he want you to?"

"It's not for another woman, Betty," he said quietly. "It was for you two to go together."

"But these are...if these are real airline and hotel reservations, there are thousands of dollars tied up in this."

Charlie nodded. "He was saving for it in secret for several years. It took time for him to get to that point. He told me he was squirrelling away money whenever he could, putting it in locked boxes around the house, so he could treat you in style once you got there."

The boxes they'd found. "The reservations are legit?"

"Yes. The airline ones are open tickets. The hotel reservations are dated, but they can be changed." He smiled at her. "He said you always imagined going to Paris. He was going to make that dream come true this year, at Christmas."

Betty sucked in a breath, trying to take it in. "That's what he was hiding?"

"He wanted it to be a surprise."

She stared down at the piece of paper as her view of her husband reconfigured once again. He'd been hiding money things, but to make a big experience for them as a couple. To make a big surprise for her.

Her eyes filled with tears. She thought of the picture frame she'd found, the two of them, always updated, alongside the picture of the Eiffel Tower, in the Dream Big frame.

The side-by-side images merged in her mind's eye, and it was as if she were there beside him, looking up at the Eiffel Tower, hugging each other as that old, beautiful dream came true.

She hadn't known he remembered, definitely hadn't known he still wanted it. Maybe he'd been researching Paris at the library. And he'd managed to save all this money without her knowing—that had taken some major effort.

Some major love.

But he'd died too soon. "I wish we could have done it," she whispered, her heart aching. If only they'd had forever together, or something a little closer to it at least.

"I do, too." He hesitated and then leaned forward. "Betty…"

There was something in his tone. "What?"

"I'd love to take you."

What?

Betty didn't think it was possible to be more surprised than she had been, but it was. She just stared at him.

He looked back at her with a steady gaze, his eyes warm. There was no doubt about what he was saying.

Ten minutes ago, she'd worried that the envelope held evidence that she was a woman scorned by her secretive, cheating husband. But now everything had changed. Now, she was a woman beloved by her husband and desired by another man. Her head spun. She could barely take it in, any of it.

"Wayne said I could. If I could talk you into it."

"Talk me into…" When Charlie's meaning sank in, she exploded from her chair. "He told you that you could, what, *have* me?"

"Now, Betty. Sit down. I said it wrong. It wasn't like that." Charlie's voice was overly calm, the way you'd talk to a child who was upset.

She paced the kitchen as her view of her husband reconfigured once again. He'd *bequeathed* her, as if she were a piece of family jewelry?

But as she thought about it, her lips started to twitch a little. Men. So sweet and so ridiculous.

The fact that Wayne had saved up for tickets for them was so touching. He hadn't needed to do that; he could have told her so that they could save together, faster.

Except maybe not. Maybe she'd have gone all practical on him, suggested they fix up the house with any money they had to spare.

And maybe he'd even had some reason for encouraging Charlie to make a pass. Maybe, for whatever reason, he'd thought that would be welcome.

Wayne had been old-school. He'd been the head of the household, making the big decisions, keeping control of the money. When one of their foster kids needed discipline, serious discipline, he'd been the one to decide on and administer it.

Betty had always known that position of leadership was a little bit for show. Inside, she'd known she was the stronger person, just like most women were stronger than most men. In her opinion, anyway. The power behind the throne. The ones who could go through childbirth, get right back up and nurse and care for a squalling baby while managing the rest of the home and sometimes a job, as well.

She was *definitely* stronger than Charlie, and she knew it no matter how patronizing his tone of voice. He was a little fragile, just as Wayne had been, ego-wise. "Charlie. You're a good man, no doubt. And

I'm overwhelmed because I thought he was hiding something else, like another woman."

Charlie looked shocked. "Wayne wouldn't do that. He was crazy about you."

His words, so quick and definite, put a little extra balm onto the healing wound in her heart. She also remembered that Ryan had said exactly the same thing, and Mellie, too. "Thank you for telling me that. I'm glad to hear it. But in *no way* am I ready to take a trip to Paris with you or any other man."

He looked down at the floor, letting his clasped hands hang between his knees. Finally, he said, "It was worth a try." He held out his hand for the tickets. "I can help you cash those in."

She stepped back, out of his reach. "No. Uh-uh. I'll keep them."

He frowned, tilting his head to one side. "Why?"

She studied the paper, thought about the dates.

She and Peg had never done anything fun together. They'd mostly shared household duties and sat in each other's kitchens drinking coffee.

"I'll find a use for the tickets," she said, and tucked them safely into her pocket.

Maybe, just maybe, there was a girls' trip in her future. She stood to walk Charlie to the door. When she got there she reached out and straightened the Forever sign she'd rehung a few days ago. She and Wayne hadn't had forever, no one did. But what she'd learned tonight had made him feel close. Maybe that close feeling was the part that lasted, the forever part.

MELLIE PASSED CHARLIE on the way out. The man did *not* look happy.

She walked into the kitchen, carrying half-full bags of marshmallows, graham crackers and chocolate. "What did you say to your gentleman friend?"

Betty was sitting at the kitchen table, drinking wine and solving a sudoku puzzle, but at Mellie's words, she threw her hands up in the air. "He's not my gentleman friend!"

"Um, does he know that?"

"No. He just asked me to go to Paris with him. I've been widowed less than six months, for Pete's sake. I was married to his friend!"

Mellie clapped her hand to her mouth, laughing. "Did he *really*?"

"Long story," Betty said. "But yes, he did."

"Some men…" Mellie shook her head. She'd always thought of Betty as way older and wiser in the world of relationships, but right now, she sounded as confused and annoyed as Mellie and Taylor ever did. "Do you want these in the pantry?" She held up the s'more fixings.

"Sure."

When she came back out, Betty smiled at her. "Grab yourself a glass of boxed wine, if you'd like one."

"Twist my arm." She held it out for an instant, pulled it back and then went for the wine.

She sat down across from Betty, who pushed aside her puzzle book.

"How's everyone getting along out there?" the older woman asked.

"It's good. They're male-bonding with Alfie and he's loving it." She thought of Alfie's rapt face and felt a happy ache. Happy, because clearly Ryan and his brothers were going to be a wonderful part of Alfie's life. That ache, though…it was an inner acknowledgment that, although she'd tried her best to give Alfie everything he could possibly need, and she knew she'd been a good mother to him, there was something more that his father and, to a lesser extent, his uncles could give to him.

"I'm glad." Betty studied her, a speculative expression on her face. "What about you and Ryan?"

That was the million-dollar question, but Mellie didn't have the emotional chops to answer it right now. "We're going to do okay with the co-parenting, I think. We both want to make it work for Alfie."

"That's good," Betty said, "but what I meant was, how are the two of you getting along? I thought there was a spark."

Mellie blew out a sigh and leaned back in her chair. Apparently, she wasn't going to escape without responding to Betty's probing, at least a little bit. "There was. Still is, on my side. But now it just feels so awkward. I don't think he'll ever forgive me for keeping Alfie a secret from him."

"Yeah. That's significant." Betty frowned. "But even when you make mistakes, or he does, you need to keep trying. That's my advice from forty years of marriage."

Mellie sipped wine, put her glass down and sagged back against the chair. "It's hard. Exhausting."

"It is. I didn't always follow it." She pulled a piece of paper from her pocket, looked at it and then tucked it away. "Now, I regret I didn't push for answers and make him stay connected with me. Men aren't always the best at that, you know."

"True."

"Ryan's going to leave the island soon," Betty said. "Are you just going to let him go be a long-distance dad? Let go of any chance things could work out between you?"

Was she? Could she, when she thought of Alfie's joyous face as he spent time with his uncles and his father?

And yet there was even more at stake here than Alfie's happiness. There was her own happiness. Something she hadn't prioritized since the day her mother had abandoned the family.

"You're stronger than that, Mellie. You raised your sisters and kept house for your dad, and you're a fine mother to Alfie. Don't wimp out just because you'd be taking care of yourself instead of others." Betty paused. "Or should I say, taking care of yourself first, so you could take care of others? I know forming a family of you and Ryan and Alfie would benefit both of them, a lot." She paused. "And I think it just might make you happy, too."

Mellie sipped wine. "I'll think about what you said."

There was a tap on the kitchen door and then Ryan

came in, leading Alfie by the hand. "He's ready for bed."

Mellie looked at her son, and at Ryan, and assessed the state of her own heart. She loved that Ryan was taking care of Alfie, that he was stepping up to be a father.

As far as she could tell, though, he wasn't stepping up to be anything else, like a partner to Mellie.

She'd been there before, in her first marriage to a man who liked her fine, liked her a lot, but didn't feel true love for her. And it hadn't been awful. It had been tolerable, good even. Love had grown between them.

But did she want to make a push for the same kind of risky arrangement with Ryan? Could her heart bear the bruising?

"Thanks." She stood and took Alfie's hand, and Ryan let go. "Thanks for watching out for him."

"Glad to. Anytime."

"Thanks." Then they just stood looking at each other.

Awkward, awkward, awkward.

And she had the feeling that Ryan wasn't going to be the one to make it less so. That fell on her.

She could take the safe route and let it go. Ryan would still be a good father to Alfie. And her heart would be protected.

But, looking into Ryan's eyes, feeling the warm love for him that had never really left her heart, courage trickled in and grew stronger, like a creek becoming a river.

Maybe there was a way she could help Alfie have a better life, and at the same time have a life with this man she now realized she loved. Maybe Betty was right about the family of three.

Doing something about it would be risky and possibly humiliating. But for Alfie's sake, and for her own, she had to figure out a way to try.

CHAPTER TWENTY-FIVE

ON SATURDAY, A week and a half after his brothers met Alfie, Ryan walked toward Mellie's house. He was carrying a bottle of wine and a gift for Alfie and a whole bundle of nerves.

He'd seen Alfie every day since that evening with his brothers, meeting him at the school boat, taking him out exploring the marshes, playing ball in the yard. Trying to make up for lost time.

Nothing *could* make up for what he'd missed, though. And he was leaving the island on Monday, so he was about to miss more.

He'd seen Mellie only in passing, and when he'd tried to talk to her, she'd brushed him off. Not in a mean way; she'd been cordial, but distant.

They needed to figure out a plan for sharing custody of Alfie. They had to discuss it tonight.

He tapped on the screen door, and Alfie came running, yelling, "He's here!" Then he opened the door and beckoned for Ryan to come in. "What's that?" he asked, pointing to the gift bag.

"Just a little something for you." Ryan knew he couldn't buy Alfie's love, but he'd missed so many birthdays and Christmases. He wanted to make up for that, at least a little.

"Cool!" Alfie knelt on the floor and started pulling out the tissue paper as Mellie walked in. She wore a slim-fitting orange sweater and butterscotch-colored jeans and she looked...spectacular. Gorgeous. Like everything he'd ever wanted.

And yet...he couldn't push past what she'd done to him, not entirely.

He hoped this meal with Alfie and Mellie, probably his last for a few months, didn't break his heart. He took slow, deep breaths to keep his emotions in check. He didn't want to scare Alfie or worry Mellie. Didn't want to embarrass himself.

"It's a rock tumbler!" Alfie pulled out the kit and clasped it to his chest. "I always wanted one! Look, Mom!"

Mellie gave Ryan a glance he couldn't interpret and then knelt down beside Alfie. Together, they examined the box. Then Alfie jumped up and hugged Ryan. "Thanks, Dad! That's so cool!"

His son's easy acceptance of the gift, of *him*, warmed Ryan's soul.

Mellie rose and took the bottle of wine Ryan held out. "Come on in and open that," she said. "I'm going to mash the potatoes and then we can eat."

Dark was already falling outside, but the kitchen was warm, steamy. Alfie set the table and Mellie mashed potatoes and stirred gravy and Ryan opened the wine, and it was so homey and sweet that Ryan's chest almost broke open with longing. Longing for this to last.

Foolish, impossible longing. He'd have to force himself to take care of business. He'd talk to her after dinner and at least find out what she was thinking about a visitation schedule.

Since learning that he was Alfie's father, his focus had changed. He wanted to get the grant to help save the island so that future generations of kids could have the experience Ryan and his brothers, and Alfie, had had.

If he got the grant, one of the two, his time would be more flexible than if he had a full teaching schedule. But no matter how it turned out, he wanted to be successful for a different reason than ever before: so that he could be a good example to Alfie and also help support him.

The trouble was, he wanted to be able to spend time with his son, too.

Fatherhood was turning him upside down and inside out.

They sat down to dinner, and prayed, and even though Ryan was agitated inside, he couldn't not eat his favorite meal. Alfie scooped in the food, too, at an alarmingly rapid rate. They chatted about Alfie's schoolwork and Mellie's day at the market.

After Alfie had cleaned two plates in record time, he got fidgety. "Mom, can we—"

"Dessert first," she said. She went into the kitchen and returned a moment later with a lemon cake. "I know it's your favorite," she said to Ryan, "but I'm not nearly as good of a baker as Betty is, so I got her to make us one."

"You didn't have to go to all this trouble," Ryan said as she cut big slices of cake.

"I wanted to."

Why had she wanted to? Why had she made him his favorite meal? Was this a goodbye?

The cake was delicious, of course, and they all ate some, but after the first few bites, Ryan had trouble swallowing. His stomach knotted.

He didn't want to leave on Monday.

Alfie was so smart and good and perfect. Just looking at him made Ryan's throat tighten. How could he leave?

Was there any possible way he could stay?

But, staying, he didn't want it to be just what the past week and a half had held. He wanted it all: to make a home for Mellie and Alfie. To have this kind of togetherness every night.

It couldn't work, though, if Ryan held on to his anger about what Mellie had done.

"Now, can we?" Alfie was looking at Mellie, bouncing on his chair.

She pushed her plate aside and took a deep breath. She looked both nervous and incredibly appealing.

"Alfie and I have something to show you," she said in a shaky voice.

What was going on?

He started to carry plates into the kitchen, but she stopped him with a hand on his arm. "I'll get that later," she said. "Come on in here and sit down."

She led the way to the living room, colorful and full of houseplants, where Alfie was fiddling around with the TV.

"Got it," he said as an image came up on the screen.

An image of a baby. *Alfie's first ten years*, was the caption.

"We made it because you weren't here," Alfie said.

Ryan's gut twisted hard. He'd been a bad father.

"You know why he wasn't here," Mellie said.

"Because he didn't know about me. Can I start?"

"In one minute." She handed Ryan a card. "Let him read this first."

The look she gave to him seemed full of meaning. Meaning he couldn't interpret. He opened the card, blank inside but for a couple of lines in Mellie's neat handwriting.

This isn't anywhere near enough to make up for what you missed, but I hope it's a start.

He looked at her, bemused, unsure of what to say, what to feel. What was she talking about?

"I'm sorry," she said quietly. "So, so sorry. I can't keep saying it, and I won't. I just want to be sure that you know."

Ryan looked into her eyes and then inside himself, found that he believed her and nodded.

"Can I start it now?" Alfie, oblivious to the adult

communication, was kneeling in front of the TV, his hand on a remote.

"Yes, start it." Mellie's voice had a little catch in it.

Alfie started the video, and immediately there was an image of Mellie, very pregnant, unsmiling, stirring something on the stove.

"Not a great picture of me," Mellie said, "but it's the only one I have of me pregnant."

Quickly the image shifted to a newborn baby in a hospital crib. "That's me!" Alfie said. "I was real little."

Mellie glanced at Ryan and then back at Alfie. "You were premature."

"That means I was born early," Alfie explained. "I wanted *out*!" He made a sweeping gesture with his arm.

Mellie blushed and smiled. "That's what I always tell him."

The video show went on with some still baby pictures, soft music playing in the background. And Ryan started to realize what it was.

Mellie, or maybe Mellie and Alfie, had made him a video of the moments he'd missed in Alfie's past.

There was an image of Alfie sitting up, propped against an ottoman. Of him playing with a toy, eating in a high chair, standing up in his crib.

Georgie was in some of the pictures, which slayed Ryan. Was Mellie trying to torture him?

"That's my first dad." Alfie frowned. "Sometimes I miss him."

"Of course you do." Ryan's jealousy floated away

like a soap bubble headed into the sky. This video was for Ryan, but clearly, it was for Alfie, too.

Georgie was part of Alfie's past; he'd helped Mellie raise the boy. He couldn't simply be photoshopped out of their lives.

There was a picture of Alfie nursing. Wearing a scarf draped over her chest, Mellie looked down at the baby with pure love in her eyes.

Ryan had missed all that. His fists clenched.

Next came a video: Mellie holding out her hands, saying, "Walk to Mama." And Alfie let go of the couch he'd been gripping and took halting, unsteady steps toward his mother.

The video panned to Mellie's laughing, crying face as she caught Alfie in her arms.

Georgie must have been the one filming Alfie's first steps. And wow, that hurt.

But mostly, it hurt to have missed all this.

More photos followed, blending together. Mellie, holding Alfie's hand as she waved to her sister, who was standing beside a stack of luggage on the ferryboat. A minute later there was an almost exact duplicate, only with her other sister.

There was Alfie in a playpen at the market, then in some sort of walking toy, banging around the aisles while Mellie worked the register.

Alfie with spaghetti sauce all over his face, laughing. Alfie getting his first haircut, safe in Mellie's lap. Alfie in Betty's arms, laughing up at her.

It went on and on. Ryan hadn't even known there were so many firsts, so many photo opportunities, in the life of a child. Ten years of growing from a baby to a lanky, intelligent, bighearted ten-year-old boy.

Ryan's eyes burned and his throat tightened. It wasn't all frustration and sadness at having missed all this. It was happiness for Alfie, that he'd had parents who cared enough to record his milestone moments, big and small.

He was glad Georgie had been there. Jealous, but glad.

There was a close-up of Alfie's smiling mouth, with a gap where a front tooth should have been.

"Mom pretended there's a tooth fairy, but there isn't," Alfie said.

Mellie ruffled Alfie's hair. "I could never fool you," she said.

"But I still get money for my teeth!"

There were a couple of images of her sister Em with Alfie, but nothing with her dad. So he'd apparently passed without being much of a presence in Alfie's life.

More pictures. Alfie and Georgie fishing, the big man beside the small boy. A school performance. "I was a tree!" Alfie said proudly.

And the video ended with Alfie and Ryan together. He'd barely noticed Mellie taking pictures and videos, but there they were: the two of them at the shore, studying something in the sand. She'd even caught an image of Ryan and Alfie with Cody and Luis, throwing a ball and laughing.

Finally, there was a still shot of Ryan and Alfie

walking, Ryan's arm around Alfie's shoulders. And then it was over.

"Did you like it, Dad?" Alfie asked.

Ryan nodded. He couldn't speak.

Mellie went over to Alfie, knelt and gave him a hug. "You were so much help making the video," she said. "You've had quite a life already, haven't you, kiddo?"

He wiggled out of her arms, a theatrical expression of disgust on his face. "Can I go set up my new rock tumbler?" he asked.

"Yes, and then you can play two video games before bed."

He pumped his arm. "Yes!" he said, and ran toward the stairs.

"I told him he could play video games while you and I talked about some things."

Ryan nodded, eyes watering.

She handed him a box of tissues, and he blew his nose and wiped his eyes.

Mellie was doing the same thing. After a minute, though, she cleared her throat. "I hope this was okay," she said. "I knew it would be sad, but it's a tiny bit of what you missed that I can give back to you." She looked forlorn. "I'm so sorry, Ryan. I made a huge mistake. I stole his baby years from you."

He nodded, thinking, taking in what she hadn't said, what he could discern by reading between the pictures and videos.

She'd been the pillar holding everyone else up. Alfie, of course, but also her father and her two sisters. During the years Ryan been gone, her father had passed away and her sisters had left the island.

Georgie, according to the fishermen, hadn't been as protective or supportive as she deserved. Which was wrong, but maybe understandable. He was raising a child who wasn't his.

Mellie's life had never been easy, yet she never complained.

She had made mistakes. But none had been bad-hearted. Should she be held to the impossible standard of doing everything perfectly, at the same time that she supported and forgave everyone else?

For the first time, he put himself into her shoes. Pregnant, just having been rejected by the father of her child. A man who was known to have problems and issues of his own, issues that some, namely Wayne, thought rendered him unsuitable to be a father.

Should she be blamed for making the decision she'd made on the information she'd had? A decision that had given her an incredibly hard road to walk alone?

Oh, she had friends. Everyone loved Mellie. But who took care of her, the way she took care of everyone else?

Ryan looked into his own heart and found he wanted to be the person who did.

He reached out his arms, and she walked over, still sniffling. "You did the best you could at the time," he said. And then he pulled her into his lap and held her, and they cried together.

IT FELT SO, so good to be in Ryan's arms.

He was strong, his muscles hard, his chest broad. Yet he was comfortable enough with her and with himself to cry when the occasion warranted it.

Which this occasion definitely did.

Making the video with Alfie had been difficult, but a good thing to do. Watching it with Ryan… that had been excruciating, because it made her feel what he must feel, the pain and devastation of what he'd missed.

"You'd be within your rights to hate me forever," she said against his shirt.

He stroked her hair as if she were a child. "I can't hate you. You did the best you could." He paused. "And you're the mother of my son."

His words warmed her. She sat up and scooted to sit beside him on the couch. She blew her nose and wiped her eyes and took a few deep breaths. "You're not mad at me for making the video?"

He shook his head. "No. Watching it was hard, but it's a gift I'll always cherish. Thank you."

She looked into his eyes, got a little lost there because he was gazing into her eyes, too.

He reached out and thumbed a stray tear from her cheek, and then his hand tangled in her hair. His eyes flicked down to her lips, so quickly that she wasn't sure whether she'd seen or just imagined it.

Her breathing quickened. She wanted him to kiss her.

But that, in a strange way, would be a temporary solution. She wanted so much more, but she was scared to ask. Scared to break the mood and send him running.

She looked away from him, sat up straighter, and his hand fell away.

It felt like a loss. *Don't be silly*, she told herself, and scrambled to her feet. "I'd, uh, better clean up," she said, breathless.

She moved to the kitchen, feeling hazy and dreamy and scared. She started putting leftovers into dishes.

You have to ask him.

But he's going to say no.

At least try. For Alfie's sake if not for your own.

Behind her, she heard him come in, bringing plates and dishes to the counter.

She stole a glance at his face and recognized his thoughtful expression. He was trying to figure things out.

Once everything from the table was in, he leaned back against the counter and watched her load the dishwasher. "We need to talk about visitation," he said.

She pressed her lips together.

Now or never.

Wind rattled the windows. Upstairs, she could hear Alfie walking around.

The kitchen was warm. Almost too warm. "I don't want you to visit," she said finally.

His head jerked toward her. "What?"

She sucked in a breath. "I want you to stay."

He tilted his head a little, frowning. "To stay. Here?"

She nodded, watching him, trying to read his reactions. "Stay on the island with me and Alfie. Or live here most of the time, around your work responsibilities."

He studied her. "For Alfie?"

"For Alfie and Betty and…for me."

He opened his mouth as if he were going to speak and then closed it again.

He was going to say no.

She went for broke. "I know I have no right to ask, but I want to make up for lost time. Not just between you and Alfie, but between us, too."

His eyebrows drew together but he still didn't speak.

"And I know you say you can't get close to people, but…you can, Ryan. I've seen it."

"I do feel close to you, Mellie."

"I feel close to you, as well. And I want to be closer. I want to take a stab at being the couple we were for those few weeks, when we were teenagers. Only better." She pressed her lips together. She was talking too much, while he was saying almost nothing.

She closed the dishwasher door and rinsed her hands, dried them on the dish towel and tried to think. His nonreaction: Was it him trying to figure out how to say no, or was it him not sure of an answer?

She twisted the dish towel in her hands, sucked

in a breath and went for it. "The truth is, Ryan… I've fallen in love with you."

RYAN HELD HIS BREATH, staring at Mellie. Had she said what he thought she'd said?

The kitchen was bright and warm against the wind and cold outside. Upstairs, Alfie—his son, *their* son—pattered back and forth, the sound punctuated by bursts from the rock tumbler Ryan had gotten him.

Here and now, there was only Mellie. "You've fallen in love. With me."

She nodded.

"But I'm not… I can't…" He didn't know what he was trying to say. He only knew that it couldn't be true, because that would be too much joy.

Mellie knew, though. "You *are* capable of loving and being loved, Ryan. Don't believe the lies. You've overcome so much that it's probably hard to take in, but you *did* overcome it."

It was the same thing Betty and Luis and Cody had said.

He narrowed his eyes and took her hands, enfolded them in his own. They were small, but strong and capable, like Mellie herself. "When you say we should take a stab at being a couple…" He shook his head slowly.

Her face fell. "You don't want to?"

He let go of one of her hands and touched her chin, making her look up at him. "If we do that," he said, "I want all of you."

Her eyes widened and she studied his face. "Okay," she said, her voice a whisper.

He could tell she thought he meant something else. He shook his head. "I don't mean just physically, and I don't mean temporary. I mean permanent."

Had he really just said that? Was it true?

He looked around Mellie's kitchen, listened to Alfie upstairs and then let his eyes return to the lovely, strong woman in front of him. In his heart, joy and certainty settled.

"You mean, something permanent...for Alfie?" she asked.

He shook his head. "No. Well, yes. For him, but equally, for you. Mellie, you've added so much color to my life. You're so much smarter than me—"

She pulled her hands away, laughing a little. "No way."

"Yes way," he said. "You're so much smarter in so many important ways. You made a mistake, but..." He gestured toward the living room. "You fixed it. Beautifully."

Her smile widened. "I'm so glad. That was a big risk and it could have backfired."

"It didn't. You gave me something truly special." He had to do something physical, so he put his hands at her waist and lifted her onto the counter, then stood in front of her, holding her hands, lightly.

He couldn't resist dropping a kiss on her lips, and then he wanted to keep going with that, but he made himself back up. He had to go through with the conversation. "You know what? I never stopped being in love with you."

She sucked in a breath. Her eyes were huge.

Was that good or bad? He forged on. "You saved me as a teenager, but it's more than that. Being with you and Alfie, it would be more than I could ever have imagined having. To love you, and be loved back, to raise him together…" He was getting ahead of himself and he made himself pause.

She pressed her hand to her mouth and didn't speak.

Something inside him, bigger than he was, pushed him on. "So I don't want to play at it. If we get together, I want to go for it."

"Go for it how?" she asked, her voice unsteady.

The kitchen, the sound of Alfie upstairs, the smell of a candle she'd lit, all of it faded until there was only the woman he loved in front of him. "I want us to get married."

He didn't always know the right thing to do, socially, but he did now. He reached for her waist and eased her off the counter and then knelt in front of her. "If I stay," he said, "and if we make it work, and our feelings keep growing…will you marry me?"

MELLIE GASPED AS everything she'd ever wanted came into view before her. Right here, in her home, with this man she'd fallen in love with all over again…

One tiny doubt remained. "Are you asking me for practical reasons? So we can take care of Alfie together?"

He stood then and wrapped his arms around her. "Mellie, Mellie, Mellie. I'm asking because I love *you*. Because I want to be with you for the rest of my life, to get gray hair together, to dance to oldies and babysit our grandchildren." He hugged her tighter. "I'll spend the rest of my life helping you know that I mean that."

She lifted her face to his and saw the sincerity in his eyes, and the chains she'd wrapped around herself, the idea that she wasn't lovable, broke and fell and dissolved. "Yes, Ryan," she choked out. "Yes, I'll marry you."

His smile was huge, and he nuzzled her hair and then kissed her thoroughly.

Much later, footsteps tromped down the stairs and Alfie burst into the kitchen. She and Ryan pulled apart as he came to a sudden halt. "Hey, what are you guys doing? Ugh, Mom!"

She and Ryan both reached out an arm to him. "We're just emotional," she said, and pulled him into a three-way hug that he accepted for about five seconds before pulling away.

"Stop being emotional," he said, "and come see how this cool rock tumbler works." He tugged at both of their hands.

They looked at each other and shared a laugh. This was how it would be for them, and that was fine. Perfect, even. Because in their lives and their loves and their hearts, they were a family.

EPILOGUE

Six weeks later

"You STILL HAVEN'T given her a ring, man?" Ryan's brother Luis snatched the basketball Ryan was dribbling and lobbed it into the air for a perfect basket.

It was Christmas Eve, cold and blustery, but Mellie had sent "the boys"—him, Alfie and Luis—outside to burn off some energy.

"I have the ring." Ryan grabbed the ball and passed it to Alfie, who passed it right back, giggling. "I just haven't given it to her yet. Sometime today, I promise."

Alfie's smile was broad now. He was in on the secret. "Can I run down to the bay for a little while, Dad?" he asked.

Every time Alfie called him "Dad," warmth suffused Ryan's chest. "You can run down for ten or fifteen minutes, but come right back," he said. "We have to get dressed for church soon."

Church and a wedding, though most attendees didn't know it.

It was the way he and Mellie had wanted it. Cody and Luis had agreed to come for Christmas, and the rest of the town would be there at the Christmas Eve service. They'd do a short and sweet wedding ceremony and then share champagne with the crowd at the community Christmas Eve dinner afterward. No fancy clothes, no decorations to worry about, no gifts. One ring—a very pretty one—rather than both an engagement and a wedding ring. Simple, like life on the island was. Like *they* were.

The only problem was, Cody hadn't arrived yet. For reasons he hadn't been clear about, he'd been released from duty and was to stay on the island for the next few weeks at least. Ryan hoped he'd agree to help care for Alfie while he and Mellie went on their honeymoon the day after Christmas.

Ryan didn't have much of a family, but Cody and Luis were central. If Cody didn't make it, there would be a pall on his wedding. Ryan wanted his true family, what there was of it, there to celebrate with him.

"Hey!" There was a shout from the street, and Ryan turned to see his mentor, Charlie, arriving, dressed in a dark suit, carrying flowers. That would have given things away, if anyone was paying attention. Since Ryan couldn't choose between Cody and Luis, Charlie had agreed to serve as his best man.

The three of them, Ryan, Luis and Charlie, chatted for a few minutes, and then Luis went down to the docks to tell Alfie it was time to come back.

"How's Betty doing with all that's going on?" Charlie asked. Of course, they'd had to let Betty in on the secret so that she could help with Alfie.

"Great. Excited about her trip to Paris with Peg."

"Great, just great." Charlie looked rueful and Ryan briefly wondered what that was about. Charlie obviously had interest in Betty, but did he seriously expect to make something of that when Wayne hadn't even been gone a year?

The door from Mellie's house opened. "Ten minutes," she called. "Where's Alfie?"

"He'll be here."

She blew him a kiss and Ryan found himself smiling like a kid with his first crush.

Which Mellie was, in a way. His first and only. He still couldn't believe his good fortune that she'd agreed to be his wife.

"Got a little bit of news today," Charlie said as he and Ryan walked together toward Betty's house.

"Uh-oh." They hadn't heard yet about the grant, but Ryan was resigned to losing it. Which meant he'd have to teach more on the mainland, but he and Mellie would manage it.

"No, it's good. No news yet for the big grant," he said, holding up a hand. "But I shared your proposal with a friend of mine who's looking to set up a field lab, and he liked your ideas. They don't have the budget of the NSF, but it's a tidy sum and they're looking for a discrete project to invest in. He thinks we might be able to work out starting up a field lab right here on the island. He needs a principal investigator."

Ryan's jaw almost dropped.

"If you'd be interested. It doesn't have the status of the other, or even of a professorship, but it's doing what you want to do, working directly to help save the bay."

Ryan surprised both of them by wrapping Charlie in a bear hug. "That would be a dream come true."

"I'll put you in touch. Now, I'm going to make nice with the woman who's currently breaking my heart," he said, his voice gruff. "You deserve this, Ryan. You deserve every happiness." He patted Ryan's back, awkwardly, and then strode toward the house.

Ryan turned to check on Alfie, his heart soaring. To stay on the island full-time, or almost so...to work to save the bay, and with the one he loved...he looked heavenward and offered up a prayer of thanks.

AT THE TWILIGHT Christmas Eve service, Mellie sat between Ryan and Alfie and could barely hold back tears of joy. She had the family she'd always wanted, and soon they'd make that official.

Very soon.

Evergreen branches and a live Christmas tree, sparkling with ornaments and lights, mingled with candle wax to make the sanctuary fragrant. The choir belted out "Little Drummer Boy" with more enthusiasm than skill.

Ryan held her hand tightly, but he kept looking around and checking his phone, almost as fidgety as Alfie.

Mellie didn't blame him. She knew he was hoping to hear from Cody. "Any word?" she asked.

He shook his head. "No reception."

"If he doesn't make it, should we postpone?"

He dropped her hand and slid an arm around her shoulders, and when she looked up at him, his expression was hot and hungry, not at all appropriate for church. "I don't want to postpone," he said.

"Me, either." She couldn't wait for their wedding night, and it was obvious that Ryan felt the same way.

As they rose and lit candles for the last hymn, "Silent Night," the buzzing of a loud motor pierced the air. Soon, it overpowered any efforts of the organist.

"Merry Christmas, everyone," Pastor David called. "God bless us, every one. Go in peace."

The motor noise got louder, so rather than lingering inside to talk and exchange Christmas greetings, the entire congregation spilled out into the field beside the church.

As they stared up into the night sky, a collective shout went up.

Santa Claus was rappelling down a line that dangled from the helicopter, a giant bag harnessed to his back.

Kids called out and parents ushered them to a safe distance from the spot where the brightly clad Santa would land.

Beside her, Ryan barked out a laugh.

Luis came up beside them. "Let me guess. Cody?"

"Pretty sure it is," Ryan said. "I don't know too many department store Santas who can rappel like that."

The Santa dropped to the ground and waved. The line retracted back, and the helicopter disappeared into the night sky, the sound receding, but replaced by the excited talking of the little crowd.

"Ho-ho-ho," the Santa called. "Listen, I heard there were some good kids on the island. Who wants a present?"

All the kids, about twenty of them ranging in age from toddlers to teens, raced to where Cody knelt beside the bags. "Hey, Alfie. I need you to help me distribute these gifts."

The two of them started studying packages and passing them out. The gifts must have at least been chosen for age and gender, because as the kids ripped into them, they looked delighted rather than disappointed.

"I can't believe Cody came to the church this way," Mellie said.

Ryan and Luis looked at each other and laughed, deep and long. "We can," Ryan said when he saw her puzzled expression.

"Cody is a showman." Luis rolled his eyes. "Always has been."

"Show-off, more like," Taylor said from behind them, sounding disgusted. "Talk about making an entrance. He made church end early!"

Mellie turned toward her friend. "He's not just showing off, or if he is, it's a cover for something else, I think," she said quietly. "He's had some problems. I hear he's out of the service for good."

Taylor shook her head. "Sorry, sorry," she said. "I don't mean to be petty. I just…have a little history with Cody, that's all." When Mellie opened her mouth to ask her about it, she waved a hand. "No big deal. Tell you later."

Some people, Betty and Peg among them, were headed back into the church. "I'm going in, too," Taylor said as Cody strode toward them in his Santa suit. She hurried off.

Even with all that was going on, Mellie looked after her, thoughtful. Something about Cody, or this time of year, seemed to have gotten to her usually even-keeled friend.

Cody, Ryan and Luis were hugging and pounding each other's backs, all talking at once. From what Mellie could gather, it had been hit or miss whether Cody could get here in time, but he'd still managed to collect gifts for the kids from all the soldiers in his unit.

Extravagant ones, from the looks of things.

Alfie was now comparing gifts with Jimmy. It looked like they'd both gotten drones they'd been longing for. A couple of the little girls held the latest fancy dolls.

Linda the librarian walked around with her phone out, recording the scene.

What a fun addition to an already amazing day. Their wedding day wouldn't be fancy, but it would certainly be memorable to everyone in town.

Mellie leaned on a snowy bench and just watched.

Ryan came over after a few minutes. "Are we okay to go ahead and do this thing?"

"Of course." She smiled up at him. "It's fine. It's fun."

He kissed her, hard and fast, and then put his fingers to his lips and gave a piercing whistle. When everyone turned to him, he spoke out loud and clear. "Back in the church, people. There's one more thing to do before the community feast. We—" He reached for Mellie's hand and lifted it high. "We're getting married."

Gasps and hugs and congratulations followed, along with questions that Mellie and Ryan did their best to answer. No, they hadn't wanted a big wedding. No, they hadn't wanted to wait. No need for decorations. They hadn't wanted gifts or a big to-do.

"We just want to be married," Ryan said.

Mellie's grandmother pulled her aside. "You're sure you're okay with this? You and Georgie didn't have a big wedding, either."

"I'm good. I don't want to put people to a lot of trouble. And I'm completely thrilled to marry Ryan."

Mellie's grandmother nodded knowingly. "You two will be fine."

Over the past few weeks, they'd let it be known to a few people that Ryan was actually Alfie's father. There'd been a little gossip and some speculative expressions, but for the most part, the island people were accepting.

Things didn't always work out in a straight line; they knew that from living in this place. Sometimes you had to improvise. But with hard work and a good heart, you could build a happy life.

They walked into the church and Mellie stopped and stared. "What on earth?"

The sanctuary was decorated in flowers. So, so many colorful flowers. The side of every pew held a bright display, and poinsettias lined the front of the church. Someone thrust a big multicolored bouquet into Mellie's hands and pinned boutonnieres on Alfie and Ryan.

And everyone cheered, because there had apparently been a number of people involved to get the flower delivery smuggled into the church and to distribute and arrange everything so quickly. Even Cody's arrival had been predetermined by Betty and Luis to make sure that Mellie and Ryan were outside, so the decorating crew would have time to work.

Tears rolled down Mellie's face. "They did all this for us." And it was the one thing that could make a perfect day even more perfect, because flowers were Mellie's thing.

She adored them. They were gorgeous. Even more, she loved the fact that her friends had done this for them, had worked in secret to make her day special. She felt more loved than she ever had in her life, and that last remnant of worrying that people only liked her for what she could do for them faded away on the notes of the organ music.

"We are very glad to have you on this island," Hector said, speechifying as usual. "We hope you stay, and that you bring many children to be on our island, as well."

"We're staying," Ryan said, putting an arm around Alfie.

More children? Hmm. Mellie tucked that thought away in her heart.

Amid the shouts and congratulations, as people settled into the decorated pews and Mellie and Ryan walked to the front to say their vows, Mellie lifted her face to heaven with a prayer of thanks. Ryan pulled her close to his side, and she smiled up at him.

Dreams. Here on Teaberry Island, they definitely did come true.

* * * * *

Read on for a sneak peek at the next
Hometown Brothers book,
The Bluebird Bakery,
coming in January!

CHAPTER ONE

IT WAS FIVE A.M., and US Army Staff Sergeant Cody Cunningham—retired staff sergeant—couldn't sleep.

No surprise there. He hadn't really slept, not for more than a few hours at a time, since he'd been found wandering just outside of an enemy camp, naked and with no memory of what had happened to him. If he slept, the demons just outside his conscious mind might make their way in. Whatever part of his brain controlled sleeping didn't think he could tolerate that apparently.

At least here, on Teaberry Island in the Chesapeake Bay, he had a few friends, a few loved ones and a place to stay.

Temporarily.

He slipped out of his newlywed brother's home and walked the short distance to the island's Main Street. As he'd expected, it was deserted. Except...

There was a light on at the Bluebird Bakery.

He walked by, staying in the shadows out of habitual caution he couldn't seem to shake. When he saw the Help Wanted, Housing Included sign, though, he couldn't resist stopping to study it.

Sudden movement inside the bakery alerted him that his presence had been detected and he backed up.

"Who's there?" A woman flung open the door, saw him and stepped backward, shock warring with simple dislike on her face. "You scared me. What are *you* doing here?"

He blew out a sigh and scanned Taylor Harp, the instant assessment also habitual. She stood in the doorway of the bakery, a hand propped on either side as if she were a bouncer ready to physically block him from entry. Silvery moonlight washed over her hair, tied back in a practical bun. Her wide, happy smile had captivated him when she'd visited the island as a teen, but now those full lips had turned downward into a frown. "I couldn't sleep," he admitted.

"Some of us wish we could, but we have to work." Just like the last time he'd spoken with her, at the end of their high school acquaintance, she was as disapproving as an old-fashioned schoolmarm.

Prettier, though.

She started to close the door, from which wafted the smells of bread and cake baking. Familiar, good smells.

"Wait, Taylor."

"What?"

He gestured toward the sign. "That job, have you filled it yet?"

She snorted. "No. No one of legal age to work nights has applied. Doesn't help that I can't pay much, even though housing's…" She trailed off and studied him. "Why are you asking?"

He shook his head. "No reason. I'm looking for work, and a place to stay, but I know…" He paused. His therapist said he shouldn't automatically discount opportunities. "Is there any chance I could apply?"

"Are you *kidding* me?" She squinted at him like he was a two-headed rockfish. "You want to work night shift at a bakery?"

"Never thought about it before. But I was a cook in the army."

"Oh, my Lord, that's right. That chef show." She shook her head. "You were funny."

He'd definitely been more lighthearted. Quick with a joke or quip. The military channel show had gone viral, army chefs competing for silly prizes. It had eased the monotony of wartime and entertained the troops.

And then everything had blown up.

He hadn't cooked since then, aside from fixing breakfast for his nephew or heating up a can of soup.

"You're not seriously thinking—" Taylor broke off, still staring at him like he had a few screws loose.

Which, in fact, he did. "No. It could never work," he said.

"No," she agreed.

He breathed in the smell of baking bread and looked at her kind, pretty face. "Could it?" he asked.

"No," she said firmly, and shut the door.

TAYLOR SHUT THE DOOR and then leaned back against it, willing herself to settle down after the shock of seeing Cody Cunningham. How could he still be so handsome, with those eyes that seemed to see right into her soul? How had he gotten even *more* handsome than when she'd seen him, at a distance, on her friend Mellie's wedding day? She was half waiting for Cody to knock again or try to open it. That was what he'd have done when she'd known him as a teenager.

And Taylor, foolishly, would have opened the door and let him back in, because she'd have hoped against hope that he wanted *her*, wanted to be with her, cared about her.

When, of course, it was always about Savannah.

Cody didn't knock, and when she peeked out the window, she saw him disappearing down the street. She blew out a breath and headed back to the oven to check on twenty loaves of teaberry sweet bread.

The sight of Cody had brought her sister to the forefront of her mind, and now she was stuck there. Where was Savannah now, how was she doing? Why hadn't she been answering Taylor's calls?

Even though the island was distant from the everyday world in some ways, accessible only by boat, old-fashioned, they had the internet and cell phones and news, at least most of the time. There was no excuse for Savannah to be out of touch.

No excuse except that she was ashamed of the way she was living. Taylor, having spent her adolescence under Aunt Katy's influence, was the wholesome type: be strong, do your duty, go to church. Savannah had lived in a different, more glamorous world, with completely different values.

Taylor didn't judge her sister, or not too much. She prayed Savannah hadn't descended to the dark place they both feared after losing their mother to it. Surely, whatever had caused Savannah to pull away from Taylor, she'd land on her feet and get back in contact, just like the other times she'd run into some kind of trouble.

Taylor straightened and went to the window, looking out into the now-empty, moonlit street. She was half glad, half sorry that Cody was gone. What had the world come to, when a heroic and decorated veteran was seeking a job as a night-shift baker and wanted to live in an apartment above the shop? Cody should have come home to more fanfare.

She looked inside, tested her feelings the way you'd poke at an old scar. Did she still feel *that* way about him?

Slowly, she walked back to the kitchen and washed her hands. She'd been rolling out dough for cinnamon rolls, and now she touched the big sheet of it with one finger. It had gotten dry while she'd been talking to Cody, so she dipped a brush into the bin of melted butter and recoated the sheet. Today's customers would find the rolls a bit richer than usual, which wouldn't arouse any complaints. People didn't come to the Bluebird Bakery for diet fare.

She looked at the clock and started sprinkling the streusel she'd already prepared onto the dough. She added nuts to one half. Ideally, she'd have made two separate batches, one with nuts and one without. She'd probably sell out of these by 9:00 a.m. But she didn't have time to do it all. There were still scones and muffins to get ready before the bakery opened at six thirty.

Which was why she needed a night baker.

She yawned and stretched, rolling her shoulders. It was a good problem to have. She'd started the bakery on way too little capital and an intuition that it would go well, that it was what the island needed. She'd worked her fingers raw for the first two years, and it had paid off. Not only during the tourist season, but the rest of the year. She'd had a steadily growing customer base. She'd hired summer help—a high school and a college student—and she'd kept the high school student on to help on weekends and the occasional weeknight. A local young woman with special needs and a temperamental senior citizen worked for her in a random way, too.

But since she'd put out feelers about distributing teaberry baked goods more widely, she'd started getting off-island orders. More than she'd expected. Now, she *really* needed a night baker.

She was on her way to achieving her fondest goal. Not just owning her own bakery, not just scratching out a living, but making a huge success of it. Enough that what had happened to her and Savannah would never, ever happen again. Enough that she could take care of Savannah and maybe, one day, the kids she desperately hoped to have, without the constant dark cloud of financial and emotional disaster following her around.

She could do it, but she had to have help.

The fact that she'd had exactly one applicant, and it was the man who'd come close to breaking her heart…well. It was par for Taylor's course. She put it out of her mind and focused on her baking.

SAVANNAH HARP WISHED this party were over.

She smoothed down her sparkly dress and waved away the caterer's assistant who was circulating with a tray of champagne glasses. She was new enough to all of this to marvel that there was a caterer, in her own apartment.

Well, not her apartment, but Rupert's. She straightened her back and moved through the room, making sure people felt welcome. She'd spent enough time feeling unwelcome herself, after her mother had died. She was a natural at making sure that no one else felt that way on her watch, that no one was off in a corner by themselves, feeling shy.

Or feeling a desire to steal the silver, said her more skeptical side.

No one's going to steal the silver, these are your friends. Well, Rupert's friends. Whatever. The forty or so guests were all as well off as Rupert, with no need to put a knickknack or piece of silverware in their pockets.

She greeted Clint Fitzgerald and his wife, whom everyone called Cookie. Clint and Cookie were some of the nicer of Rupert's friends. They sometimes asked Savannah about herself and whether she missed the pageant world, which she definitely didn't.

It was what everyone knew about her: that she'd

been a beauty queen. First Runner-up in the Miss Maryland pageant four years ago. One of the oldest near-winners, at age twenty-four.

She hadn't quite made it. Just as she hadn't quite made it in the competitive world of professional modeling, not after a few promising gigs as a kid. She still had hopes, but not as many as she used to have.

Savannah was pretty sure Rupert had tried and failed to date Miss Maryland herself, but the woman was a medical student and on her own path. Whereas Savannah had had no path planned after pageants, aside from some vague idea that she'd get back into modeling. She was nothing like her sister, Taylor, who'd always had a dream and pursued it relentlessly.

That was just one reason Taylor held her in low esteem.

"Come here, sweetheart," Rupert said. His voice was soft, but nonetheless, it was a command. "I want you to meet someone."

She approached the two men. Rupert was still handsome, at fifty-three, a silver fox, fit from tennis and weight training at the gym. At the height of his powers professionally, too, doing whatever he did with hedge funds to make possible the swanky apartment and expensive parties. And her, she guessed, though she could have been swept away by a much less affluent man who'd offered her a home and a sense of direction.

"This is Alistair McVeigh," he said, and the man, whom she now saw was a little older than Rupert, smiled and gave her a not-too-subtle once-over. A network of broken blood vessels across his nose and bags under his eyes indicated some hard living.

She made small talk, something her beauty queen education had taught her to do, but Alistair wasn't interested in getting to know her nor in talking about himself, surprisingly. He looked expectantly at Rupert.

"Alistair has had a hard trip in from LA," Rupert told her. "Why don't you go back to his hotel with him and help him settle in?"

The clinks of glasses, the sparkling laughter around them, seemed to fade. So *that* was what Rupert wanted. He was doing it again. She glared at her so-called fiancé.

Alistair let his hand rest on her hip, then slide down to cup her butt.

She gestured for Rupert to look, telling him with her eyes that he needed to *stop his handsy friend right now*. But, big surprise, he didn't do a thing to help her. She moved away from the man, bumping into Rupert and causing him to spill a few drops of champagne.

"Watch it," he said, his voice cool. His eyes on her were steely, letting her know he meant more than the spilled champagne.

How had it evolved to this? He was supposed to make her a top model, maybe even send her to acting school. "I need to talk to you," she said.

For a minute, she thought he wouldn't go, but he nodded. "Excuse us a minute," he said to Alistair.

He guided her to a corner of the living room. Outside the window, the expanse of city lights suggested freedom, fun.

"What's the problem?" he asked as if she were a teenager who wouldn't do her homework.

"I told you I'm not doing that again." It was the third time he'd tried to set her up with one of his business acquaintances. The first time, she'd fended the guy off in horror and taken a cab home to a penitent Rupert, who said he hadn't known what the guy meant to do.

The second time, he'd made sure *she* had had enough to drink that she was in a pliant mood, and he'd orchestrated an encounter in one of their spare bedrooms while a party similar to this one, but a little drunker, took place outside. Things had gone far enough that she felt sick, not just physically but about herself, when she finally flung the guy off her. She'd rushed to the master bathroom and thrown up. That was when she'd laid down the law the next day. She wasn't a possession to be shared with his friends or brokered as part of a deal. And when were they going to talk about acting school? A wedding date?

Now, clarity so bright it nearly blinded her shone from the tasteful mood lighting and the single, gaudy chandelier.

Rupert wasn't going to marry her and he wasn't going to send her to acting school. And he wasn't going to stop offering her up to his friends. "I'm not doing it," she repeated.

He crowded her against the wall like he used to do when he wanted her. She'd liked it, liked that he knew what he was doing and she didn't have to make decisions. She liked that he was older, too, probably because she'd never had a father.

Now, Rupert's aggression had a different feel. "Look," he said. "You have nothing. You earn nothing." His words were a little slurred. "You do what I say."

Did she have a choice? If she made a scene, shouted out what was going on, one of the partygoers might take pity on her. They might call the police or give her a ride somewhere.

But where?

She looked around and spotted Clint and Cookie, whispering together while looking in their direction. Cookie's facial expression looked avid, curious, not compassionate.

No help there.

Despair and darkness rose up inside her, the kind she fought each day but a million times worse. Rupert was right. She did nothing, earned nothing, *was* nothing. Nothing but an ex-beauty-queen.

And now, it looked like, she was on the path to becoming a high-end hooker.

She thought of the sleeping pills in her medicine chest. There were plenty of them for her to end it, and knowing the danger, she kept three-quarters of them locked in a drawer, the key hidden in yet another room in the house. Her logic was that the time it took to hunt down the key and unlock the extras would stop her from doing the unthinkable.

Although it obviously wasn't unthinkable. She'd accumulated the pills, after all, and not for no reason.

If you ever feel like Mom felt, you come to me.

She'd remembered Taylor's words so many times, but never with so much of a notion that she might put them into effect.

Rupert waved a hand to someone behind them, and she felt that possessive hand on her rear end again. Not Rupert's. Alistair's. "She's ready to go."

The clinking cutlery and the laughter and the murmur of conversation went on. Cookie and Clint were out of sight. None of the guests were paying attention to the hosts' little drama off in the corner.

A caterer's assistant gave them a quick, curious glance, but when Savannah caught her eye, she looked away.

Savannah was on her own and three paths opened up before her. Least resistance: go with Alistair and playact her way through an encounter that, even thinking about it, made her sick.

Excuse herself and go swallow a handful of pills.

Or think of Taylor and be strong.

She was out of practice at that, but she channeled her sister and smacked Alistair's hand away. "I'm not going anywhere with you."

Alistair and Rupert exchanged glances. Alistair looked affronted and Rupert looked angry. Alistair turned and disappeared into the small crowd.

"If you don't go with him you're out on the street. Tonight."

"You can't do that to me." Savannah reeled back and stared at him. "I live here."

"You live here because of my generosity, which has just about reached its limits. You go with him or you leave. And don't come back."

He looked…smug. Like he knew she couldn't make it alone.

Taylor wouldn't put up with this. "Let me get my things."

His mouth dropped open.

She spun and went to their bedroom and looked around wildly, her heart hammering. Was she really going to leave him?

Maybe so. She unzipped her dress and stepped out of it, threw on a sweater and jeans. She fumbled around her underwear drawer, found the two one-hundred-dollar bills she kept for emergencies and slipped them into her shoe. Then she grabbed her purse and her coat.

She emerged from the bedroom to find Rupert standing outside, arms crossed. "You're not leaving."

"If the choice is being pimped by you or leaving, then yes, I am." Maybe he'd change his mind. Maybe he actually cared for her.

His jaw squared. "Then use the back door. And I'll take that." He tried to pull off her cross-body bag.

She clutched the strap and stepped back. "No way! That's mine."

"Everything you have is mine." His voice held a sneer.

"I need my ID." And her credit cards.

He seemed to read her mind. "I'll be canceling your cards within the next ten minutes, so don't even think about making a withdrawal."

She stared at him, pain and sorrow pushing their way through her anger. "Don't do this, Rupert," she whispered. "I want to marry you, you know that. I don't want to be with other men."

His mouth twisted into more of a sneer. "You're nothing. Beautiful, but nothing."

The words hammered at her and she thought again of the pills. She should have thrown them into her purse, but it was too late.

Tears blurred her eyes, but she brushed them away and spun and headed toward the back door. The servants' door. All she'd ever been to him apparently.

And then she was outside on a cold night with nothing, almost, and no place to go.

Except to Taylor. Somehow, she had to get to Taylor.

Don't miss
The Bluebird Bakery *by Lee Tobin McClain!*
And join Lee's newsletter to gain access to
a free prequel novella featuring
Pastor David and Tiffany from
The Forever Farmhouse.

FARMHOUSE DECORATING TIPS

#1: Neutral can be fabulous! Don't give in to the temptation to add a lot of color to your farmhouse decor. White or cream, as well as natural wood shades, are restful to the eye and fit the farmhouse feeling. Not good at painting? That's okay—a white-wash look is total farmhouse and is forgiving of brushstrokes and partial coverage.

#2: If you want a pop of color, go primary: red, yellow or blue. Shepherd check or gingham are wonderful ways to connect those colors to your basic white/cream shades.

#3: Bring the outdoors in. A simple mason jar full of dried reeds and grasses makes a wonderful centerpiece. Tie a ribbon around it and you're done.

#3: Baseboards, moldings and ceilings can all be the same neutral color. Easy on the eye and easy to paint!

#4: Breezy half-curtains frame the outdoors and block out any inconveniently urban aspects of your view, leaving you with rural-looking trees and sky.

#5: Mismatch! Try dark wood chairs with a lighter wood table, or various white or cream dishes from the thrift store.

#6: Simplify. After you've painted the walls in a new, neutral color, stop. Don't automatically fill the walls with decorations—even so-called farmhouse ones like a big wooden Eggs for Sale sign. Live with the blank walls for a week or two and you may find you need fewer pictures and wall hangings than you think. With farmhouse style, less is more.

ACKNOWLEDGMENTS

I would first like to thank my colleagues at Seton Hill University, Jamie Forsigliano and Diana Hoover, who helped me to understand the lifestyle of a young scientist as well as the process of applying for a scientific grant. I hope I've gotten it right, but all errors are my own.

Thanks, too, go to Anna J. Stewart, who helped me figure out my characters and their goals early on, and to Shana Asaro, who helped me strengthen the book in later drafts. I appreciate Susan Swinwood and her team for taking on another Chesapeake trilogy and for working through a million different titles until we figured out the one that works just right.

Bill, my travel companion of the heart, thank you for being willing to change directions—literally—when stormy weather nixed our plans to visit Tangier Island. Your flexibility and sense of fun make my books, and my life, so much better. And, Grace, thank you for letting me use bits and pieces of your childhood in my stories, and for all your support and love.

Finally, to my readers: thank you for your kind encouragement of my work. Your messages, emails and reviews give me more joy than you can know.

SPECIAL EXCERPT FROM

🍃

LOVE INSPIRED
INSPIRATIONAL ROMANCE

When a wounded veteran and his service dog seek work at the Bright Tomorrows school for troubled boys, can the principal—who happens to be the widow of his late brother—hire the man who knows the past secrets she'd rather forget?

Read on for a sneak peek at
The Veteran's Holiday Home
by Lee Tobin McClain!

Jason stared at the woman in the doorway of the principal's office. *"You're* A. Green?"

Just looking at her sent shock waves through him. What had happened to his late brother's wife?

She was still gorgeous, no doubt. But she was much thinner than she'd been when he'd last seen her, her strong cheekbones standing out above full lips, still pretty although now without benefit of lipstick. She wore a business suit, the blouse underneath buttoned up to her chin.

Her eyes still had that vulnerable look in them, though, the one that had sucked him into making a mistake, doing what he shouldn't have done. Making a phone call with disastrous results.

She recovered before he did. "Come in. You'll want to sit down," she said. "I'm sorry about Ricky running into you and your dog."

He followed her into her office.

He waited for her to sit behind her desk before easing himself into a chair. He wasn't supposed to lift anything above fifty pounds and he wasn't supposed to twist, and the way his back felt right now, after doing both, proved his orthopedic doctor was right.

Beside him, Titan whined and moved closer, and Jason put a hand on the big dog. "Lie down," he ordered, but gently. Titan had saved him from a bad fall.

"I didn't realize the two of you knew each other," the secretary said. "Can I get you both some coffee?"

"We're fine," Ashley said, and even though Jason had been about to decline the offer, he looked a question at her. Was she too hostile to even give a man a beverage?

The older woman backed out of the office. The door clicked shut.

Leaving Ashley and Jason alone.

"The website didn't have a picture—" he began.

"You always went by Jason in the family—" she said at the same time.

They both laughed awkwardly.

"You really didn't know it was me who'd be interviewing you?" she asked, her voice skeptical.

"No. Your website's kind of…limited."

If he'd known the job would involve working with his late half brother's wife, he'd never have applied. Too many bad memories, and while he'd been fortunate to come out of the combat zone with fewer mental health issues than some vets, he had to watch his frame of mind, take care about the kind of environment he lived in. That was one reason he'd liked the looks of this job, high in the Colorado Rocky Mountains. He needed to get out of the risky neighborhood where he was living.

Ashley presented a different kind of risk.

Being constantly reminded of his brilliant, successful younger brother, so much more suave and popular and talented than Jason was, at least on the outside…being reminded of the difficulties of his home life after his mom had married Christopher's dad…no. He'd escaped all that, and no way was he going back.

His own feelings for his brother's wife notwithstanding. He'd felt sorry for her, had tried to help, but she'd spurned his help and pushed him away.

Getting involved with her was a mistake he wouldn't make again.

Don't miss
The Veteran's Holiday Home *by Lee Tobin McClain,*
available October 2022
wherever Love Inspired books and ebooks are sold.

LoveInspired.com